BRAIN STREET

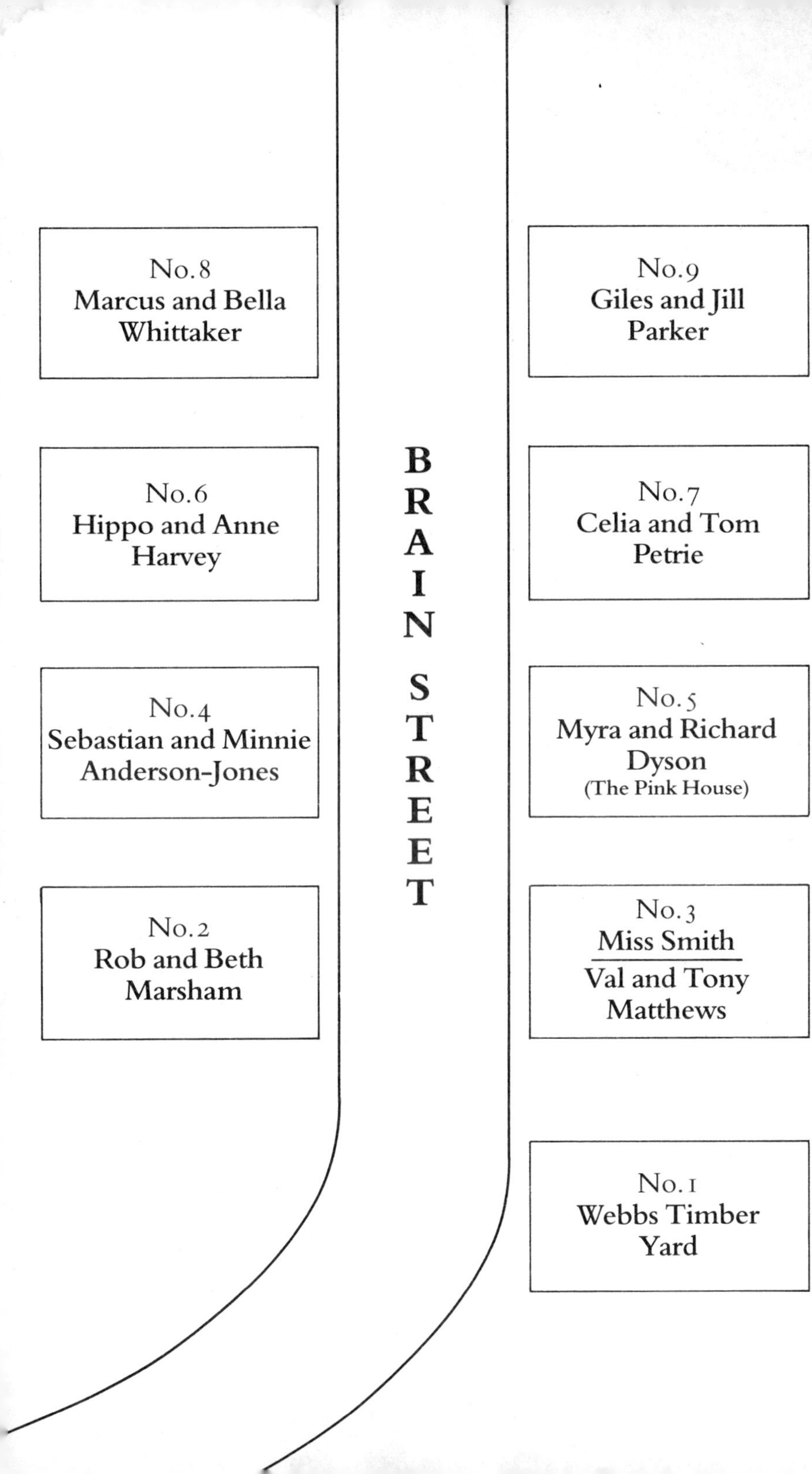
No.8
Marcus and Bella
Whittaker
No.9
Giles and Jill
Parker
BRAIN STREET
No.6
Hippo and Anne
Harvey
No.7
Celia and Tom
Petrie
No.4
Sebastian and Minnie
Anderson-Jones
No.5
Myra and Richard
Dyson
(The Pink House)
No.2
Rob and Beth
Marsham
No.3
Miss Smith
Val and Tony
Matthews
No.1
Webbs Timber
Yard

BRAIN STREET

Barbara Toner

Macdonald

A Macdonald book

First published in Great Britain in 1986
by Macdonald & Co (Publishers) Ltd
London & Sydney

All characters in this publication are fictitious and any resemblance to actual persons, living or dead, is entirely coincidental.

British Library Cataloguing in Publication Data
Toner, Barbara
Brain Street.
I. Title
823'.914[F] PR6070.04/

ISBN 0-356-12211-5

Photoset in Plantin by Tek-Art, 55 Stanhope Road, Croydon.
Printed in Great Britain by
Richard Clay (The Chaucer Press) Ltd,
Bungay, Suffolk

Macdonald & Co (Publishers) Ltd
Maxwell House
Greater London House,
Hampstead Road,
London NW1 7QX

A BPCC plc Company

Chapter One

In certain South London streets which are close to the river and largely Victorian, it is the easiest thing in the world to give offence without noticing. In Brain Street, a small tree-lined terrace in a prime position by Battersea Park, giving offence without noticing is almost as frequent as taking it without appearing to.

Brain Street has six loft extensions, four Volvos, a Mercedes and three sets of barred drawing-room windows which suggest incoming wealth to the local estate agents and burglars but recession grandeur to the market researchers. When recession is combined with grandeur in a terrace perhaps it is to be expected that stress will expose the finer feelings which can so easily and so often be injured by unthinking neighbours. What could never have been expected, even in Brain Street, however, was that anyone should take offence, conceal it and then go looking for revenge without the slightest regard for an old lady's heart.

Hippo Harvey certainly didn't expect it when he planted his honeysuckle, not even when it swarmed up the trellis of No. 6 and around the corner towards No. 4's frail robinia. Revenge was the last thing on his mind when, on a pink spring morning just after dawn, the honeysuckle flicked yet another tiny, lethal tendril out towards the robinia and threatened to squeeze the life from its graceful, slender body. Hippo was asleep and dreaming of comas.

The honeysuckle didn't wake him. Nor did the robinia screaming with rage and fear because the robinia is a tree. What woke him was the plaintive wail of a Volvo. Its cry echoed down the street and curled up around the loft extensions, through the double-glazed windows and interfaced curtains, and landed with a thud in the centre of his head. 'Brouark,' he eructed, puzzled.

He put out his hand to feel for his wife and he found her soft and crumpled, puffing little gusts of garlic at him across the pillow. He tugged at her shoulder. 'Wake up,' he said. 'Anna, wake up. I can hear a car.' Anna stretched languidly, then she kicked her husband's thigh with astonishing force and speed. 'Get off,' she said.

Hippo sighed. 'We're being robbed,' he thought. He opened his eyes and scratched his chest, then he closed his eyes again. The alarm stopped. His head ached. He thought, 'I have been clubbed to death.' There was no reason for him to imagine anything else because he had planted the honeysuckle in all innocence.

No. 6 Brain Street was distinguished by its very new loft extension which was the first to be built with family money. Hippo's cousin was a lord and his father had made a mint out of glue. The Harveys were the first family in Brain Street with close aristocratic connections, if you ignored the Dysons' which more or less everyone did.

Hippo wasn't the only person to be woken by the Volvo. At No. 8 where the loft extension was older and there was no honeysuckle, though a small weeping cherry dropped blossoms onto the salvaged york paving stones, Marcus Whittaker leapt out of bed and rushed to the window crying, 'My God, oh no, my God.'

He tore back the curtains and when he saw his Volvo where he had left it, over the road outside No. 5 which had no loft extension, no honeysuckle, no weeping cherry but a burglar alarm attached to the wall above the front door, he went back to bed. 'Must have been the Petries'.' he said to his wife Bella. 'Poor old Tom,' he added with satisfaction.

Marcus was not a spiteful man. He worked for a large bank in the City which had lent him the money to buy his house and build his loft extension on terms so favourable that he had nothing to be spiteful about. But he was thirty-two and ambitious and his ambition was matched only by his caution, so he was watchful. As a matter of fact he had his eye on Parliament. South of the river there are many cautious men with their eyes on seats in Parliament.

Bella said, 'I'm going to be sick. I can't stand it. *Pot-au-feu*. I'm going to be sick.' She put a pillow over her head. 'Help me,' she moaned. The smell of *pot-au-feu* wafted casually across from No. 9 and soared up her nostrils, which in pregnancy somehow opened to allow more in.

'I hope it is the Parkers', she cursed. Bella wasn't a spiteful woman either. On the contrary, she was kind and gentle and sweet, and in pregnancy bore a strong resemblance to the Princess of Wales. But *pot-au-feu* can curdle the best of pregnant natures, as the Princess of Wales may well have found herself.

The Parkers lived at No. 9 Brain Street. Their loft extension was well-established, rather like the decrepit roses by the front gate which were considered exotic. No. 9 didn't look very different from the other houses in the street but it smelt different because in its kitchen Jill Parker ran Brain Street's only cottage industry, Haute Food. She cooked sensible but sophisticated lunches and teas for rich, greedy people and less interesting meals for their employees. Bella was her partner, but as Jill had complained to her husband Giles, using a clever golfing analogy, she was more of a handicap, particularly around the first tea.

'You only ever drink coffee,' Giles had replied. He wrote thrillers. He was a small good-looking man who was pampered by his wife and allowed to believe that he was a genius, if only a tiny one. The Parkers considered themselves very well bred, even if they weren't as well off as they should have been. They had long ago spent the money from Giles' first and only success and now they survived on Haute Food and deaths in the family.

Jill heard the Volvo from her kitchen where she was buttering bread. She strolled to the front door, opened it, listened, decided it wasn't hers and strolled back again. She was buttering two hundred slices of bread for a boardroom lunch and she had a large *pot-au-feu* simmering on the Aga for tomorrow's Putney Ladies' Buffet for Africa. She sang as she worked because she couldn't have been happier.

Only five minutes before, rummaging through her pantry, and hers was the only pantry in Brain Street though she sometimes called it a larder, she had found two wonderfully mature black sausages tucked away behind the beetroot in sherry. She smiled at herself in the kitchen's large pine framed mirror, adjusted her Alice band and asked herself whether Bella would be sick before or after coffee that morning. Then she threw the sausages into the pot.

At No. 7, where fumes would have overwhelmed the Princess of Wales, the Petries smelt nothing through the smog of steam and Musk-with-Ginseng body-mist which swirled from their *en suite*. Celia Petrie, on hearing the alarm, climbed out of the newly installed Victorian roll top bath and pattered to the window to peep through the lilac Venetians.

The bleeping stopped. She could see three Volvos: theirs, the Harveys' and the Whittakers', parked neatly one in front of the other with a couple of Citroens before and aft like dear little book ends. 'What's happening?' her husband asked.

'Nothing,' she said.

'What are you looking at then?' he mumbled.

'I'm looking at nothing,' she laughed. Tom Petrie was an enquiring man, a large bleary-eyed media man. He liked to know what was going on, especially where his wife was concerned. Celia was a media woman and they both earnt large media salaries which they felt rendered them classless. Media people from modest backgrounds become classless as soon as they join a union, the NUJ or the ACTT. It's one of the perks.

While she laughed, Celia continued to stare through the blinds wearing only two thick white towels, one around her head and the other wrapped carelessly around her body. As she peered down onto the road she told herself she stood a good chance of being seen and she asked herself what on earth

Sebastian Anderson Jones was doing on the footpath when he not only didn't have a Volvo, his Citroen didn't even have a bleeper.

'The Harveys' honeysuckle is going mad,' she observed.

'The Harveys are mad already,' yawned her husband, making a grab for one of her towels.

The Petries' loft extension looked ugly, angular and unvictorian because there wasn't another to its right at No. 5. The Dysons, being extroverts, hadn't bothered to convert. At No. 5 the Dysons had slept through the car alarm because they had been up all night with Poppy, a sweet child who should never have been made to eat cheese.

The Parkers' nanny, Brigid, had made Poppy eat cheese for tea because cheese and broad beans were all that could be found in either fridge or pantry that was fit for a three-year-old child to eat, so Poppy had spent all night having terrible dreams about fat, red people called Brigid.

The Dysons didn't have a loft extension or a Volvo but they had a Mercedes and a burglar alarm which they needed because their drawing room shelves were lined with African *objects d'art* in gold. Myra Dyson was something royal, something blackish and royal. Both the Dysons were blackish. They were the only wholly blackish family for several streets, which had caused a small amount of heartburn among the estate agents but had intrigued the burglars, who liked the idea of the gold. The burglars never gave a second thought to No. 2 where the Marshams lived.

The Marshams had heared the car alarm and ignored it since they did not own a car, but it led them, at half past seven when they were sitting around their laden kitchen table eating yoghurt and bran, to ask themselves where they stood on the ethics of ownership. 'Nowhere,' Charlie Marsham grumbled. He had deep circles under his eyes because he had been experimenting with mascara. 'I wish we were rich.'

Beth Marsham said, 'Pass the bran.' She no longer knew where she stood on the ethics of ownership. They had put up Brain Street's first loft extension twelve years ago when Charlie was only two, in the days when south of the river was almost as worthless as the pound in your pocket. They had been proud to be pioneers. Now they were appalled at the way the working people had been forced from Battersea terraces which were theirs historically by the downwardly mobile upper classes. Or at least Rob Marsham was. Beth wasn't sure anymore. Ownership had stopped being a clear-cut issue.

She felt bad about thieving from the jumble she collected for Save The Children but then, she asked herself, was it really thieving? To be needy was relative, she told herself, and she was relatively needy. She needed Anna Harvey's dresses more than the starving children who couldn't eat jumble anyway. But she squirmed at the thought because the truth was she couldn't wear Anna Harvey's dresses down Brain Street any more than the starving children could. She said without prompting, 'Poor Minnie Anderson Jones.' This caused Rob Marsham and the children, Charlie, Johnny and Rose, to stare at her in astonishment. They couldn't imagine anything remotely poor about the Anderson Joneses.

Minnie was still asleep when Sebastian crept back from the pavement to their bedroom in No. 4, where the loft extension was only slightly older than the Harveys'. She was huddled like a tiny little animal under the goose-down duvet, like a little brown kitten, Sebastian thought, or a stoat. Minnie tried to sleep at least twelve hours a day in the belief that she could stockpile it for use after the birth of their baby which was due in four months. Not that she would need it. A nurse was coming to live with them until the baby was six months and after that there would be a nanny and any day now, a Volvo.

The Anderson Joneses were the youngest home-owners in Brain Street. Minnie was an adolescent twenty-two and though Sebastian was twenty-seven he looked twenty-one and was generally reckoned not to need a razor. They had been able to buy No. 4, not because both sets of parents were stinking, but because Sebastian was an estate agent and estate agents have access to property in up and coming areas in the same way that bankers like Marcus have access to money. This happens both sides of the river.

Sebastian decided as he looked at her not to wake his wife. He decided to creep back downstairs and to think about what he had done. He chuckled, then he frowned. He needed time to assure himself that what he had done was in everyone's best interests. He was pretty certain it was. He had given Harvey fair warning, he assured himself. But that was as far as he got, for even as he slid as quietly as he could in the cat food, dislocating his knee, he heard the tiny scratching noises of his wife stirring and preparing to quaver.

'Sebastian,' she warbled. 'Sebastian, where are you?'

'Right here, darling,' he called. 'Coming. Oh Christ!' The pain of his knee brought tears to his eyes. 'I must not scream,' he told himself. He longed for the days when men like him lived in detached houses where neighbours couldn't hear you scream and where their stinking honeysuckles could do what they liked.

Sometime between half past seven and eight o'clock, a paper boy wandered dopily down Brain Street from the river end, sticking *The Times*, the *Financial Times*, the *Guardian*, the *Mail* and the *Star* through random letter boxes. He ignored the Volvos, the Mercedes and the Citroens glinting prosperously in the early morning sun, but he stopped by Rob Marsham's Harley Davidson. He put his bag down to have a closer look and then he climbed onto it. This simple action summoned forth a ghastly screech from Miss Smith, upstairs at No. 3, who, in her anxiety to intervene had thrust half of her body through the window. 'Watchoo think you're doing?'

He looked up at her, untroubled, used to being challenged. 'Delivering papers,' he said.

'You watch it,' she squawked. 'I've got my eye on you.'

At No. 3 there was no loft extension, no burglar alarm, no honeysuckle, no weeping cherry, just a white picket fence and a whippet called Tango who lived in the flat downstairs. Tango had howled when the car had howled, waking Miss Smith who had banged on the floor with her crutch. 'Shut up! Shut up!' she had roared, with astonishing volume for a 91-year-old.

Having been woken by the whippet, Miss Smith had seen no point in trying to sleep again so she had hopped over to her chair by the window, with some tea from her Teasmaid, to wait for something to happen. She did this every morning and was rarely disappointed. Miss Smith was the only person in Brain Street to have watched every loft extension go up and she had become an expert on space conversion. Giles said she was the biggest bore outside the North Sea, which everyone said was really funny but awful actually, poor old thing, when she only had one leg.

Tony Matthews came out of the bottom flat at No. 3 while Miss Smith's head still hung from the top. He looked up at it and then at the paper boy. 'What are you up to?' he said.

Miss Smith yelled, 'He's mucking around with that bike, that's what. And you ought to get that dog put down. It's vicious. I've said before. Vicious.'

Tony didn't acknowledge Miss Smith. He said to the paper boy, 'That's all right then.' He didn't care what happened to the bike because he hated Rob Marsham. He hated the way Rob Marsham looked at his wife and he had fantasies about Tango tearing Rob Marsham's throat out. He had fantasies about his wife's fantasies and about Rob Marsham's fantasies, but his wife, Val, didn't have any fantasies. Even if she'd wanted to, she wouldn't have known where to start. Val Matthews was a practical woman whose life was devoted to balancing books. She only looked as if she had fantasies.

He waved cheerily to Giles Parker who had spotted the paper boy from his bedroom window and called out to him, 'Hang on. I want to talk to you.' Giles dragged a pair of tight white trousers over his pyjamas as he scrambled downstairs and he bawled as he came through the front door of No. 9, 'If you deliver the *Telegraph* to me one more time, I'll have your job.'

'You'd hate it,' the boy said, adding to Rob Marsham, 'Want your paper?' Rob Marsham and Marcus Whittaker appeared at their front doors at exactly the same time every morning and usually pretended not to see each other, which was easily done.

Marcus had to struggle with his bicycle and his clips and his trousers and his daughter who, even though she was seven, flew through the door each morning crying 'Kiss, kiss,' past his outstretched lips to his bike which she would embrace passionately and Rob Marsham had to fight his way into his large red helmet.

This morning, as they emerged, Richard Dyson opened his front door to bring in the semi-skimmed milk and the orange juice from his doorstep because Poppy had woken thirsty. And

Celia Petrie opened her front door to show out her teenage daughters who travelled across London to a school for clever children where they worried about job loss, nuclear waste and the holes in their noses where the safety pins had been. She called good morning to Richard Dyson.

Hearing the activity outside, Sebastian Anderson Jones limped painfully upstairs as fast as he could and hid behind the curtains in his loft extension to spy. He watched Natasha Petrie, followed by her sister Rainbow, slouch past her parents' dirty brown Volvo and step onto the road between it and the Harveys'. He saw her pause between the cars to arrange her shirt and her expression as she turned to stare at the paper boy, and he saw her stare fall short.

Her scream rose, as the Volvo's had done, high into the air and out towards the park. For someone had painted on the gleaming rear window of the Harveys' car in dripping letters of cardinal red, where white would have announced Just Married, the single word: 'Adulterers'! Natasha screamed again as Rainbow, in her amazement, trod hard on her heel.

Celia Petrie, wearing a lemon towelling dressing gown with scarcely a thought for the way it exposed her banana breasts, ran to her daughter's side. Rob Marsham, Tony Matthews, Marcus Whittaker, Richard Dyson and Giles Parker all followed suit, Giles to sneak another glimpse at the breasts and everyone else from genuine curiosity. Only the paper boy stayed where he was. He had already seen the breasts and the Volvo and he liked the bike better.

A small silent circle gathered around the car, silent but for the gentle giggles of the Petrie girls for whom life had, until then that morning, seemed mostly bleak. Someone had to say something, eventually, and in the end it was Rob Marsham who spoke. 'Do you think they are?' he said.

Chapter Two

As a matter of fact they were. In their loft extension. Hippo Harvey sold old books which he kept on shelves in his loft extension. Anna Harvey made love to his partner behind the books on the shelves in the loft extension and when Anna was out, having her legs waxed, her hair done, her body tanned, her clothes fitted, or just being a marriage guidance counsellor, Hippo made love to the nanny behind the books on the shelves in the loft extension. Hippo, Anna, the partner and the nanny didn't believe anyone else knew just how handy those books were, but practically everyone did because Brain Street is a very small street.

The nanny, whose name was Sarah, had told Minnie Anderson Jones and the partner, whose name was Rupert Fox, had told Marcus Whittaker, but as well as that, Mrs Butt who cleaned for the Harveys, the Whittakers, the Dysons, the Petries, the Parkers and the Anderson Joneses had told them all. She hadn't told the Marshams because Beth Marsham didn't believe in cleaners, but Minnie Anderson Jones had confided in Beth because she told Beth everything. Beth hadn't told Bob because she told him nothing. So Rob Marsham, apart from the Matthewses, was the only person who didn't know that it had been a talking point for months, off and on.

'The mistake Anna made . . . ,' Jill Parker called to Bella Whittaker later that morning. 'Can you hear me, Bella?' Bella was sitting on the downstairs loo with small amounts of toilet tissue stuck up each nostril to block out the smell of stewing black sausage. 'Bella?'

'Gumming,' Bella muttered.

'I'm just saying, the mistake Anna made was to take on a nanny who could have been her own sister. An accent isn't everything, is it? Who cares if the children say toilet and pardon for the first five years of their lives?' She was shelling prawns and throwing their startled heads (with military precision) into the *pot-au-feu*.

'Absolutely,' said Bella, who, when she emerged, took to scattering clumps of watercress about the boardroom sandwiches.

'It's not even as if she's any good with Flora. I mean, the child can barely speak. Amanda said to me, "Mummy Flora can't talk properly, can she? She can't even say lasagne." I've told Amanda she has to be kind but you can't stop them noticing, can you? And Flora's a good month older than Amanda.'

'Don't,' said Bella agreeably. She wanted to point out that her own child, Poppy, could say escargots when she was two but she was reluctant to open her mouth for more than two syllables at a time.

To mention Poppy in any case would only lead to the inevitable, 'Poppy? Oh, your Poppy. I thought for a minute you were talking about Poppy Dyson,' which always caused Jill to hoot with laughter. Poppy Dyson had been named after her Poppy and Bella had naturally been flattered and delighted, though very slightly delighted, because as she had said to Marcus at the time, it would cause confusion and embarrassment, and it had. It had nothing to do with the Dysons being blackish. Blackish people were as entitled to whitish names as anyone else. Stacks of white men were called Richard. It was just the confusion. So she kept quiet about Poppy's skill with the word escargots at such a tender age.

'Oh heavens,' cried Jill, 'you've used all the watercress. The watercress is for Thursday's soup.' She scooped it off the sandwiches irritably and the bits that fell to the floor she rescued and slung into the pot on the Aga.

'Sorry,' said Bella. 'I thought we always put watercress on the sandwiches.'

'Not for this lot. Not for what they are paying.' Jill gave Bella a gentle shove and she strode into the pantry from where she called, 'Anna's never home anyway. I don't know what she expected. You wouldn't catch me leaving Giles alone in the house all day with a nanny. I don't mean Brigid of course.' She screamed with glee and Bella, watching her scrabbling through her shelves like Mrs Tiggywinkle, wondered if she could slit her up the back with a cheese knife.

'Poor Brigid,' she said.

'I know,' said Jill. 'Now if you'll just drop these prunes into some tomato paste and roll them in sesame seeds I can feel I've done my bit by Minnie.' Bella paled and casting about for something to divert her, landed on the Marshams.

'Minnie says the Marshams don't have a sex life,' she said. 'Did I tell you?'

'Doesn't surprise me,' said Jill. They don't have a nanny, either. Frankly . . .' she turned to face Bella in order to be more completely frank and stared at her in disbelief. 'What on earth have you got up your nose?' she said.

She asked this at half past ten, by which time most of the Citroens in Brain Street had changed places and some of the Volvos had disappeared altogether. The Harveys' car, however, was still parked outside the Petries with its rude information untouched.

In the tiny space they called Hippo's dressing room to which they had retreated after Celia Petrie's alarming phone call, the Harveys were grappling with the best ways to confront their neighbours and deal with each other. Whose mistake had caused the adultery was the least of their worries, or perhaps the Marshams' sex life was. They weren't even especially concerned about whose adultery was alluded to because they both believed it to be their own and were determined to admit nothing.

Aloud they considered how to rid themselves of the

accusation before it went much further than the rear window of their car. Silently they wondered, with regard to each other, whether attack was seriously the best form of defence. Since they both wondered this at the same time they found themselves unexpectedly becalmed, with neither able to jib or tack in any way that could give them the advantage in case it led to an unlucky admission.

Hippo earnestly wished it was the night before when he had been a happy and carefree man, among friends, eating heartily, with a beautiful wife across the table and a pretty mistress at home, tucked safely in her bed beneath the loft extension. He lay on the *chaise-longue*, prostrate with nervous dyspepsia, a martyr to his oesophagus, and he tried to fathom how much Anna suspected or guessed, but there was no way of knowing. As she sat on the floor beside him her face revealed nothing.

This required some effort. It wasn't easy to look neutral yet Anna believed neutral was a reasonable thing for an injured but bewildered party to be. She rubbed cream into her feet with a lack of interest the feet had never before experienced.

'I don't suppose you want the police brought in,' she said flatly. Flat was neutral but hurt.

'God no,' moaned Hippo, clutching his stomach. 'The police would make it looked as if we cared.'

'I do care,' sighed Anna. Only a guilty person wouldn't care.

'Of course we care,' Hippo sighed back. 'But we can't appear to. We must laugh it off. Whoever did it is mad so we must laugh it off.'

'It's no laughing matter,' Anna pointed out sorrowfully. An innocent woman wouldn't be laughing.

'I know it's not a laughing matter but if we don't take it in good part everyone will think we are taking it seriously.'

'Vandalism is serious.'

'Adultery is serious.' This dangerous observation swung wildly about their bunker and caused panic to seep from the seams of their self control. Hippo cursed himself for going too far. Anna braced herself against the outburst she was certain would now come. But in the silence it quietly slunk away. 'We'll have to get it off,' Hippo said eventually.

'Of course we'll have to get it off,' said Anna. 'The point is, where?' She couldn't take her eyes off her toenails. Hippo breathed deeply. He didn't know what she meant. In all the years they had been married, seven, he thought, or ten, he had never been a practical man. He didn't know what she meant—where? It was obvious—where—but Anna was never obvious.

'Where it says "adulterers", where do you think?' he said finally. He wished he could take the edge from his voice and the fear. But then, he told himself, a cheated husband had a right to sound edgy.

Anna stopped rubbing cream into her feet and raised her eyes at last. Communication had never been their strong point. It had been lack of it that had driven her into Rupert's arms, that, vague desire and easy access to the loft. 'Are you trying to be funny?' she asked, 'Because you're not succeeding if you are. I for one am not going to stand out in the street scratching paint off a car that says "adulterers" with everyone watching. And I'm not going to drive it anywhere, either.'

'Nor am I,' said Hippo. 'God, no.' As he thought about it wind surged through his diaphragm. He wished he had never set eyes or anything else on Sarah. 'Sarah can do it,' he declared suddenly. 'That's what she is paid for.' He smiled for the first time that morning.

In betraying the poor nanny he was confident he had found the perfect cover. But the fact was, he had had no real need.

Anna didn't suspect Sarah. She didn't really suspect Hippo. And while Hippo might have suspected Rupert, he would not for a minute have coupled him with his wife. This had nothing to do with anyone's mastery of deception. The Harveys simply never gave each other's spare time a minute's thought.

'You can tell her,' said Anna. 'I am going back to bed.'

'We still have to go to Minnie's, you know. We can't get out of that. We have to face everyone.'

'I know,' said Anna. 'Of course.' A woman with a clear conscience would not have flinched so Anna didn't flinch. Not on the outside. Inside, everything recoiled at the prospect. A marriage guidance counsellor with the crux of the sixth commandment emblazoned across her car could be nothing less than a laughing stock. She said to herself, 'I will wear black,' and she felt comforted.

Nothing could comfort Beth Marsham, however, as she drove her Hoover relentlessly around the bedrooms in her loft extension. The assault on the Harvey's Volvo could have been an assault on her.

It is impossible to comfort a woman who, to avoid being bored to death, falls in love with her neighbour's husband just as her neighbours' neighbours are jointly accused of adultery.

She hadn't wanted to fall in love with Sebastian Anderson Jones. She hadn't wanted to fall in love with anyone, not when she had three children and a part-time job teaching slow learners at the local primary. But she had, via Minnie, who had rained on her head intimate details of her husband's many short-comings and a few saving graces. Beth had fallen for the details which met her requirements completely. Halfway through her life she longed to be held in the arms of a man who would never dream of uttering the words "empirically sound" or "socio-political dimension" and there was positively no chance that Sebastian ever would.

Chapter Three

When Minnie emerged from her hide at midday to telephone Sebastian, it wasn't to talk about the Harveys' car or what he had done to it because she didn't know about the Harveys' car. Sleeping for large parts of the day tends to cut a person off from the outside world. She phoned him to discuss her fatigue. But he wasn't there. He was sitting in St. Stephen's Casualty waiting to have his leg examined and his telephone at the estate agent's in Sloane Square was answered by Fiona at the next desk.

'I'll wait,' Minnie said to Fiona.

'I shouldn't,' said Fiona. 'It's going to be a very long meeting and I know he's due somewhere at one.' Sebastian had left clear instructions that Minnie was not to be told where he was in case she worried.

'If I want to wait, Fiona,' said Minnie, 'then I'll wait.'

Fiona put her hand across the mouthpiece and said, 'Cretin.' Then she said into the receiver, 'Fine, Minnie, wait.' But Minnie had already rung off in tears. She had been sensitive all her life and marriage had made her more sensitive. In marrying Sebastian Anderson Jones she appeared to have made the most appalling mistake. Instead of marrying her father, which is what she had hoped to do, she had apparently married a damp version of her younger sister.

Sebastian was not only weedy, in Minnie's opinion. He could be positively effeminate. What, for instance, had he done about confronting the Harveys over the honeysuckle? All he had had to say was, 'I would like you to prune the honeysuckle before it kills Minnie's robinia.' But he hadn't. He couldn't. What he had said was, 'By God that honeysuckle's healthy, Hippo.' And, 'If that honeysuckle keeps going the way it is, it will take over the whole street. Ha. ha.' Her father would have pulled the honeysuckle up by its roots and wrapped it around Hippo's throat, like they'd done with the natives out in Egypt or wherever it was. She yawned. She hoped Jill would remember her nibbles.

She sat at her white wrought-iron kitchen table, sipping boiled water with a slice of lemon in it, and she gazed out onto the terrace where that evening, weather permitting, she would be entertaining the Webbs sub-committee of the Brain Street Residents' Association. The committee consisted of practically everyone in the association except for the Matthewses and Miss Smith because membership was by invitation only and Myra Dyson, who chaired the sub-committee, had done the inviting. Myra couldn't stand the Matthewses. She didn't speak to them on account of the Matthewses perfectly hideous clothes line which overlooked No. 5 and Tango who fouled the Dysons' pavement.

Minnie shuddered, then she yawned again. She considered crying again but decided she couldn't be bothered. Had she known about the Harveys' car she would have had something to think about, but she didn't so she thought about the afternoon ahead. She would go to the hairdresser's, the florist's and to Justin de Blank for the cold food she had promised to serve the Harveys, the Parkers and the Petries when the meeting was over. She supposed she should have asked the Whittakers to stay as well but the idea of sitting down to eat with another pregnant woman disgusted her. She couldn't help being easily disgusted.

The reason why she had booked into the Lindo wing at St. Mary's to have the baby as privately as possible had nothing to do with snobbery. She simply couldn't stand the smell of queues and there, she had supposed, they were greatly experienced in avoiding them.

She leapt to her feet at the sound of a key in the front door and made a run for the stairs but Mrs Butt was in before she was anywhere near them. 'Just up?' asked Mrs Butt, pointedly. She bustled in on her very high heels with her Peter Jones bag and Fiorucci jacket. 'There's going to be trouble now, wouldn't you say?'

'I've been up for ages,' Minnie protested, pulling her paisley kimono about her for protection. 'Just not dressed.' Mrs Butt smiled at her in disbelief.

'You don't know, then,' she said. She slung her jacket over the sofa and climbed out of her shoes and into her slippers which she fished out of the bag, smiling all the while to herself.

'What?' said Minnie. Mrs Butt was infuriating, dressing in designer clothes bought at sales, with her maddening face which was always smug and knowing.

'The things that go on in this street!' she said. 'You ought to look out of your window.' But before Minnie could decide whether she should, the phone rang. Mrs Butt lingered, as if it might be for her.

'Minnie,' whispered Sarah. 'Thank God you're awake. What am I going to do? Someone's told Anna. They've painted it all over the car and Hippo wants me to get it off. What am I going to do?' Her voice disappeared into a squeak of panic and despair. Minnie caught Mrs Butt's eye and looked away.

'Hang on,' she said to Sarah. 'I'll take it upstairs, Mrs Butt, so you can get on.'

Minnie wasn't exactly comfortable being the friend and confidante of next door's nanny when she would have liked to have been the friend and confidante of her employer, but Anna was not her confidante and only distantly her friend, what's more Sarah had been at school with her younger sister so she could hardly ignore her. She felt she should listen to all Sarah's gossip. She had warned her about getting too involved with

Hippo. 'You are mad,' she had said. 'God, what a scream.'

'Who could have done it?' Sarah wept down the phone. 'Who could have done it?'

'Shshsh,' Minnie soothed her, in case Mrs Butt was listening. Mrs Butt could hear through walls thicker than anything China could produce. 'It doesn't matter who. It's done now and it's not your problem, it's theirs.' But Sarah wasn't to be soothed. She wanted to go home to Wiltshire immediately. She wanted to run as far and as fast as she could away from the scandal and the recriminations. 'Don't be silly,' Minnie said. 'It will all blow over.' And she hung up, promising to be on hand should the crisis deepen even though she would almost certainly be at the hairdresser's.

Sarah refused point blank to clean the car in spite of all Hippo's wheedling. She said she wouldn't know where to start and anyway, she was paid to mind the children. Hippo said, 'Please, please, Sarah. You only have Olly in the holidays and Flora sleeps all afternoon. Please do it. For me.'

Sarah was unmoved although she was only nineteen. Hippo who only yesterday had been so devastatingly attractive seemed suddenly pop-eyed and balding. 'I've done the last thing I am ever going to do for you,' she said coldly. 'I'm resigning.' Even as she watched, the facade of cool sophistication and wicked experience crumbled before her.

Hippo groaned. 'Don't resign. Please don't. There's no need. If you resign it will look terrible. Everyone will think there was something between us and that the car was right. It's the first thing they will think.'

'There was something between us,' Sarah reminded him sulkily. 'And someone thinks so already.' Her sweet creamy face glowered in the sun pouring past the shelves in the loft extension.

'I know,' said Hippo wincing and attempting to stroke her arm. 'I know. But the smartest thing we can do is pretend we don't know and that whoever does is mad and should be in the bin. We will brazen it out. That's what Anna says.'

'Huh,' scoffed Sarah. 'She would.'

'That's enough, Sarah,' said Hippo quietly. It was one thing to make love to a nanny, even to be a little in love with her, but it was quite another thing to have a nanny slander a wife. He had never allowed Sarah to speak ill of Anna. If he had, things might have been different. As it was, he knew as much about his wife's extra-marital interests as the Matthewses did, and the Matthewses knew nothing. They kept themselves to themselves on the whole, though not necessarily from choice.

While Hippo was trying to exert whatever charm he still had for Sarah to persuade her to clean the car, Tony and Val Matthews were chatting over their dinner, which they both came home to eat at lunchtime.

'It's a terrible thing,' Tony remarked.

'I don't know,' said Val. 'They mightn't be too bothered.'

'They'll be bothered,' said Tony. He chewed for a while in silence, wondering what it was his wife had cooked. 'I am going to try and help them.'

'Don't be daft,' said Val. 'They don't need helping.'

'Everyone needs helping from time to time,' her husband replied. 'What the bloody hell is this?'

Val shrugged. 'Meat,' she said. The Matthewses were simple, decent people.

On his way back to work Tony knocked at the door of No. 6. 'Er Hippo,' he said. 'I know it's not a good time for you at this exact moment but I think perhaps I can be of some use.'

'Come in,' said Hippo. 'Come in.' Tony Matthews wasn't the first person in the world he wanted to see, but then he wasn't the last either. 'Want a drink?' Tony held up his hand.

'Not for me, thank you, Hippo. It's a little early in the day.' He followed Hippo into the drawing room which opened onto the dining room which lead through its French windows out onto the mature, east-facing garden with its clematis, climbing rose and pyracantha. 'It's a bad show—the car business.'

'Rotten,' said Hippo. 'Well, funny, in its own way, but rotten. I hate vandalism.'

'So do I, Hippo. I couldn't agree with you more which is why I have popped by. I think I can help you on two counts. First I can tell you how to get the stuff off and second I believe I know who did it.'

By the time he left ten minutes later Hippo was quite a lot better off but really none the wiser. He had never heard of cellulose thinner and nor had he heard of Darrin.

It was Tony Matthews' opinion that cellulose thinner would remove the paint and that Darrin, the paper boy, had put it there. Hippo had greeted both bits of information blankly. The first seemed plausible, the second was the stupidest thing he had ever heard.

How would the paper boy know about his affair with Sarah? He doubted that he had ever seen the paper boy let alone that the paper boy had ever seen him. But Tony had seen him that very morning, and as Tony had said, 'Kids these days seem to get up to all sorts of mischief.'

Where Hippo was infinitely better off was in Tony's coupling of one with the other. He had recommended that since Darrin had put the paint there, Darrin should remove it, with the cellulose thinner. 'He'd never do it,' Hippo had said.

'Oh yes he will,' Tony had insisted. Tony was going to make him. Tony knew his father. Once Tony had persuaded the father that this was the easiest way for justice to be seen to be done, faces could be saved all round. Except Darrin's.

And so, that evening, as the Dysons, the Harveys, the Whittakers, the Petries and the Marshams drifted into the Anderson Joneses, the paper boy was to be seen, with his cellulose thinner and very soft cloth, rubbing gently away at the cardinal red.

Tony Matthews was standing over him with Tango at his side. As Rob Marsham appeared at the gate, Tango began to bark and growl and strain at his lead. 'Down Tango,' murmured Tony. 'Sit boy, sit will you. If you can.' But Tango couldn't.

'Evening,' called Rob uneasily.

'I know,' snarled Tony Matthews. Rob flinched. It wasn't the dog that rattled him or even guilt about Val Matthews whom he admired only as another human being. It was his inclusion on a committee which excluded the Matthewses. He felt like a scab.

Beth Marsham, bumping into Hippo in the shade of the robinia, blushed deeply and whimpered a little. She heard Tony Matthews say proudly to Marcus, 'Cellulose thinner,' and she wished, oh how she wished, that she could use it in her life to remove its blemishes. Then she followed her husband into No. 4 banging him in the groin with her clutch bag as she did.

Chapter Four

Webbs was the reason Brain Street could never rise as rapidly or as high in the world as Mary or Protheroe Streets, which ran parallel on either side. It nestled snugly on the corner of Brain Street and Dishwater Terrace, with its entrance in Dishwater Terrace, and although it was only a tiny timber merchant's, it was undeniably a timber merchant's. It had timber in it and everyone knows there is a class of Englishman simply not prepared to countenance lumps of wood for neighbours. This understanding accounted for the Webbs sub-committee of the Brain Street Residents' Association.

Not that many of its members said aloud that they wanted to attract any particular class of Englishman to their part of London, but it stood to reason that Webbs did nothing for property prices and the fact remained it was a pollutant in a residential area. Brain Street parents were concerned for their children.

"They have enough lead in their systems already without adding wood shavings," Jill Parker had declared at the last meeting of the BSRA, when the idea of a sub-committee had come up. It was the pollutant aspect of the problem which had enabled Rob Marsham to join the sub-committee with only a slightly muddied conscience. The prospect of job loss was troubling but he was a staunch friend of anything to do with the earth.

'There's the matter of the trees. Trees must be protected,' he had said to Beth on at least three occasions. But it was Rob's conscience which left the Marshams teetering on the edge of Brain Street society, or at any rate, the way he paraded it. They were by no means the only people in Brain Street ever to have voted Labour but they were the only ones who looked as if they voted Ecology or Communist.

The Petries, being media people, voted anything except Conservative as a point of principle, but they made up for it by sending their children to a private school. Bella Whittaker indicated a socialist tendency by having her baby on the National Health and sending her daughter to the local primary and everyone admired her compassion and the happy way she blended idealism with economy. Poppy, however, was soon to change schools. She could still say escargot but her parents knew she stood no chance of recognizing it on a menu. 'I don't want to be rude,' Rob had said quietly to Bella, when informed of the imminent desertion, 'but I don't think money changing hands will improve her reading.'

What Beth loathed most about their position was the teetering. Either you were part of something or you were not, but to hover on the edge was humiliating, and Brain Street society was well enough defined to have an edge. It billowed out from the Residents' Association and the school runs and it flowed through its kitchens, drawing rooms, gardens and occasionally to the very heart of its dining rooms.

Brain Street wasn't mad about friends mixing too freely with neighbours so it only extended to full-blown dinner parties when the circumstances were exceptional. When Tom Petrie, for instance, needed to prove his influence in the world of fine arts to an ancient potter he hoped to film, he invited the Harveys to dinner because Anna's mother painted water-colours. And when Bella Whittaker needed someone from television to make up an eight with some stockbrokers she asked the Petries who refused. But no one ever felt the need to ask the Marshams. Rob Marsham's worthiness, it was generally agreed, was practically criminal.

This state of affairs was something Beth was beginning to suspect. Rob, on the other hand suspected nothing. As he accepted a gin and tonic from Sebastian Anderson Jones his sole suspicions concerned the behaviour of his wife. He wondered whether she had intended to whack him in the groin. He wanted to rub it but couldn't. He wanted to ask her if anything was the matter but couldn't, since something plainly was and this wasn't the place to discuss it. He wished he knew where that place might be. Times and places for him and Beth to be together were growing fewer and fewer by the day.

When everyone had a drink in their hand and had finished admiring the fulsomely flowering tubs on the terrace, Celia, the sub-committee secretary, called, 'Can everyone come inside now, please? Don't worry about the chairs, Minnie. Honestly, you must look after yourself.' She thought Minnie looked truly unusual with her bright pink cheeks, bright pink hair ribbon, pink shadowed eyes and glittery pink clown suit and she said as much to Myra Dyson who crooned, 'I adore Minnie.'

Everyone obediently trooped in and up the stairs, because the Anderson Joneses had sacrificed a large bedroom for a proper dining-room. Their dining-room took up the space on the ground floor that most people gave to their drawing-room cum dining-room and their drawing-room was where everyone else's master bedroom was. Their bedroom was in the rear addition, which in Battersea houses is so sadly prone to subsidence, but what it lacked in space, Minnie had made up for in lace and velvet.

Although it was upstairs, the Anderson Joneses' drawing-room was similar in every way to the other drawing-rooms in Brain Street. So as Minnie handed around the prunes in sesame seeds and her neighbours took their seats, everyone felt very at home. They were comfortable with the polished floors, rag rolled walls, heavy, floral curtains, and with the large mirror in its gilt frame over the renovated fire place, the two sofas, laquered coffee table and the profusion of oriental rugs. It was a pretty room, delicately lit with a variety of lamps, and everyone admired it.

'Delicious,' said Beth Marsham, taking a prune. She didn't have a drawing-room, and her living-room was quite different.

She tried to picture Sebastian in it but couldn't.

'Not for me, thank you, Minnie,' whispered Anna. She had taken the tiny chair by the door well away from the sofas. No one had breathed a word about the Volvo because everything anyone had wanted to say had been said earlier on the school runs, over coffee and tea and during phone conversations. She wished she knew what had been said. She wished she knew who knew about Rupert and whether anyone suspected Hippo who had hiccoughed as he combed his hair, 'I hope we don't have to talk about it.' She drew a deep breath and brushed her left shoulder.

'I suppose everyone's seen our car,' she said casually, as the group, trying to swallow prunes, found itself unpleasantly tongue-tied. Hippo cast her a sharp, warning look, not trusting himself to speak and so not trusting her. She ignored it. She was opting for a quiet but innocent dignity. She didn't know what he was opting for and she didn't care.

'Car?' gurgled Myra. 'What's wrong with it?' Several people blushed for her. Her opinion on the car was as well known as everyone else's. She thought they had had it coming.

'You saw it, Myra. We were talking about it,' said Bella who, like Anna, had managed to resist the prunes. 'Someone's scrawled all over the back windscreen.'

'Oh yes,' said Myra, offering Bella a smile of dazzling fury. '"Adulterers"! That's right. You pointed it out to me. Why would anyone want to do a thing like that?' Anna thrust her hands deep into her pockets because they were growing clammy. She had abandoned the idea of black, as being too close to adultery for comfort, and was wearing electric blue trousers nipped in at the waist and a large white shirt which flattered the colour she maintained all year round.

'Tony Matthews saw the paper boy doing it, little sod,' she said. 'I mean, honestly. What have we ever done to him? I'm sure we tipped him at Christmas.'

'We didn't,' Hippo said, having removed some prune from his palate with great difficulty. 'I hope everyone else did.' He grinned at them charmingly. He could be extemely charming. Celia, although she was classless, had once told Tom that Hippo's charm came from his breeding but Tom had been contemptuous. 'Pigs' tits,' he had said.

Sebastian, staring out of the window, struggled with a terrible urge to smirk at the paper boy's dreadful predicament. He dared not turn round in case he did smirk when no one else was smirking. 'Well, he's got it off now,' he reported and laughed desperately, hoping no one would hear guilt in a laugh of relief on the Harveys' behalf.

'You wonder where they learn the language,' said Minnie and everyone roared with merriment and tension. 'Oh Minnie,' they said. 'Really!'

Myra called the meeting to order and invited opinions on what best could be done to have Webbs closed down. Celia took notes:

1) Ring council about bye-laws (me)
2) Investigate Webb (Richard)
3) Consult Clapham lot who did similar (Myra)
4) Something's burning (Jill).

This seemed to be as much as as anyone could manage and it was only achieved with difficulty since every suggestion was met with an argument which caused a discussion which led them in circles. Myra said, 'All right, another meeting in three weeks when we can all report back.' There was a lot of rummaging in bags for diaries then everyone discovered they couldn't make it on the same night as anyone else which always happened.

'Isn't something burning?' Marcus said, sniffing the air. Everyone sniffed.

Giles chuckled. 'No, it's Jilly's *pot-au-feu*. She has to cook it for thirty-six hours.'

'Wonderful,' murmured Anna.

'You look lovely, Anna,' Jill said. Anna smiled and relaxed. She was relieved the subject had been brought out and put away with no obvious ill-effects. She even began to feel pleased that Minnie had asked them to stay for supper where she would be able to gauge the mood more carefully and possibly even influence it. But still, her heart trembled as she thought of it. Someone was bound to remember and she was a marriage guidance counsellor.

'Just one more thing,' called Myra. 'I know Richard wants

to say something. It's not about Webbs but it does seem timely.' She began piling up her papers and Richard, being a barrister, arranged himself to address the drawing room.

'Only a thought, everyone,' he said. He had a rich, deep voice and a slow delivery that gripped everyone except his wife, whom it sent to sleep. 'As you know, we all have quite large cars and this is a very small street . . .'

'Get a move on,' said Myra.

'No, just a minute Myra,' Minnie interrupted. 'Actually we don't, Richard, not all. The Marshams don't have any car, small or large.'

'Nor does Miss Smith,' Rob Marsham said, clearing his throat. 'And the Matthewses' Escort isn't big. I'd like to say at this point that we have a tendency at our meetings to forget both Miss Smith and the Matthewses. Now may not be the time to raise it, but does anyone know why the Matthewses weren't invited here this evening?'

Myra rolled her royal eyes and said, 'No, it isn't the time to discuss it. Get on with it, Richard.'

'Certainly,' he said calmly. 'This is a small street . . .'

'Why weren't the Matthewses asked?' Hippo enquired. He sensed an obligation to champion Tony Matthews, a good chap if ever there was one. Myra's sigh might have filled a parachute but she smiled at the end of it because she was charmed by Hippo the same as everyone else. Women fell for the bags under his eyes in droves. They liked the suggestion of dissipation.

'I didn't ask them because I didn't think they would be interested,' she explained. 'They aren't owner occupiers.'

'Fair enough,' said Giles. He hated Tango. 'I think that's fair enough, Hippo.'

Rob Marsham cleared his throat again, this time urgently. 'I'm not sure I do, as a matter of fact,' he said. 'The Matthewses have to put up with the pollution as much as we do, more, because they live next door to Webbs. I think they should have been asked. They may not have children but they do have lungs and they might feel very strongly about trees.' A couple of people stared at him as if he had said 'Cancer is fun' and the rest of them prepared to move. It was getting silly as Brain

Street meetings often did.

'Just a minute,' Myra shouted impressively. She had been a Queen's Guide. 'Richard, for heaven's sake say your bit and get it over with.'

'Very well,' Richard said. 'All I want to suggest is that we rationalize our parking arrangements, especially in view of what happened last night.' Although all eyes itched to look at the Harveys no one did. It would have been terribly rude. Every nerve in the room, with a couple of minor exceptions, tightened in anticipation, however, because here was a chance to get to the nitty gritty.

'We have more cars than houses,' Richard continued, 'but there must be a fair way of arranging it so that we can all have at least one parked outside its owner's house in the interests of convenience and security.'

'Absolutely,' said Giles and Marcus.

'This means,' said Richard, now well into his stride and intoning quite beautifully, 'that we must make an effort not to park in front of each other's houses. Last night, for instance, I came home at nine o'clock and Marcus, with the greatest respect, there was your car bang outside my place while there was a bloody great space outside the Marshams' near the bike.' Everyone had resumed their places because of the scandal which lurked so close to the surface and the possibility that someone might actually raise it. Also, everyone resented it when they came home and found someone else's car where theirs should have been.

'You've parked outside my place often enough,' Marcus said irritably. 'It's inevitable unless a couple of us sell a car.'

'Quite,' said Richard. 'Which is why I am suggesting that the only fair solution is that those of us who own two cars park only one of them in Brain Street.' There was a small uproar of protest because no one like to park around the corner in Dishwater Terrace where anyone and everyone went along nicking hubcaps.

'It won't work because we need the small cars for school runs and they have to be parked near the houses,' Jill said. 'For safety's sake.'

'Then leave the Volvos around the corner,' said Rob

Marsham, being practical. The Petries, the Harveys, the Whittakers and the Parkers all frowned at him.

'That's lunacy,' said Marcus.

'I don't imagine,' murmured Sebastian, 'that what happened last night will happen again.' He had the room's undivided attention and felt himself blush. 'The paper boy would never be so stupid.'

'That's right,' said Hippo.

'And no one else has aff . . .' Minnie began before registering the room's astonishment. 'Can we stop now?' she said. 'I'm utterly whacked.'

So they stopped, with Marcus, who was chairman of the BSRA, yelling at them all to give the matter some thought. Then he took Bella home, noticing as he went that many of the others had been invited to stay, and it occurred to him that Sebastian Anderson Jones always had been the most unbelievable twerp. 'Must get Bella into bed,' he called loudly. 'Pardon my French,' which was the sort of remark those over the meagre supper put a great deal of thought into avoiding, because it is curious how often bed, sex, marriage and nannies can crop up in a general conversation when adultery is the very thing you don't want to talk about.

In the end they found it safer to backbite. Everyone in Brain Street knew everyone else's business or had a theory about it. And Minnie stopped feeling guilty about not asking Bella because they talked about her so much she clearly wouldn't have enjoyed it.

The party broke up early when Minnie grew tearful for want of sleep just before eleven, and the Parkers were anxious to get home anyway to eat a square meal before retiring. As they crossed the road Giles said to Jill, 'Look. There's a space outside our place. I'm going to move the car. Richard's right. You can't be too careful.' And Jill said, 'It's easier to be faithful.'

They would have laughed at that but they were far too hungry and all they could think of was porridge.

Chapter Five

Over his second helping ten minutes later Giles said to Jill, 'It's a laugh about the paper boy. He wouldn't know how to spell "sex", let alone "adulterers".' Jill stopped slurping and wiped her mouth.

'You're right, you know,' she said. 'I wonder who did do it.'

Giles shrugged. 'Could have been anyone. But I'm working on it.'

Perhaps he was working on it behind the wheel of his Volvo as he reversed it into the space by his gate. Perhaps it was the lack of concentration. No one will ever know. But there was a terrible squeal and a ghastly squelch and, without even realising it wasn't the kerb his wheels had mounted, Giles crushed poor Tango, who lay half in and half out of the gutter.

Tony Matthews had allowed his idiot dog to run on ahead because it was approaching midnight, and Tango had, for reasons bcst known to himself, decided to investigate in an intimate manner the moving Volvo's big end. There is no accounting for taste. Tony heard and sensed rather than saw what happened, and a cry rose in his throat too late to be of use to anyone.

'You fool. You bloody fool. You must have seen him,' he

roared as he sped down the road and Giles clambered from his car.

'Of course I didn't see him,' Giles muttered, hurrying around to the wretched animal. He felt like heaving. He didn't like animals and sick animals were the last straw. He dreaded the thought that it might have haemorrhaged on his tyres but it hadn't. It was panting rapidly and moaning gently to itself.

Tony dropped to his knees. 'There, there,' he said. 'There, there, boy.' He checked a sob and yelled furiously, 'You stay here. I'm ringing for an ambulance.'

Giles said, 'All right, then. Actually Tony, I don't think they'll come for a dog.' But Tony ignored him and sprinted home. Jill, who had been stirring the *pot-au-feu* and idly looking around the kitchen, tossed in the leftover rolled oats and came to the door.

'You haven't killed the dog, have you?' she said, breaking into a trot halfway down the tiny path of No. 9.

'Oh shut up,' Giles yelped. She hurried back inside and returned with newspapers and an old jacket, then she gently lifted the dog onto the newspapers and covered it with the jacket. 'That's mine,' gasped Giles. 'Get it off. He'll die on it and ruin it.'

'Don't be ridiculous,' said Jill. She had always wanted a dog but Giles had said she would have to settle for children. He could be difficult, but he was an artist; that's what she told herself.

He stood looking down at the dog, not wanting to touch it. 'I don't think it's going to last,' he said. 'I pretty well squashed it.'

'Poor chap,' said Jill. 'You'll have to offer to pay.'

'What for?' Giles asked indignantly. 'I don't want to buy a dead dog. What would I do with a dead dog?' Jill's thoughts dashed to the kitchen and the *pot-au-feu* but she said nothing.

'Don't be facetious at a time like this,' she said. 'Tony will be very upset. If this one dies he will want another.'

The ambulance wouldn't come as Giles had suspected, but the Whittakers, who like the Harveys and the Dysons owned a King Charles spaniel, knew of an all-night vet in Belgravia. Tango was taken there with his head on his master's lap in the back of the Parkers' Volvo, and he was put on a life-support machine where he proceeded to linger while Brain Street waited with bated breath. The street wouldn't be the same without Tango. It would be quieter and cleaner.

Tony waited anxiously in his lounge, having been dragged away from the surgery by Giles, who had cursed as he drove over Chelsea Bridge, 'I bet I've lost my parking place.' He sat bolt upright in his Italian-style chair with rage growing solid and heavy somewhere above his naval.

'Come to bed,' Val kept calling him. 'Sitting out there won't keep him alive.' But he wouldn't. He couldn't. Not even the thought of her wildest fantasy tempted him that night.

Giles managed to bate his breath until his head hit the pillow, then he could control it no longer. By the time Jill had said, 'Does third party cover dogs?' he was sound asleep and snoring.

The Petries, next door, not being dog owners, had stayed in bed during the crisis and noted the Parkers' comings and goings without interest. They lay in their four-poster with its shot silk canopy and they fast-forwarded their way through all the television programmes they had missed while they had been at the Anderson Joneses'.

'What is that hideous pong?' Tom asked, as sleeping Giles began REM next door and a nightmare about Lady Macbeth's dog, Spot.

'Jill's *pot-au-feu*,' said Celia.

'It smells like the Anderson Joneses' cat tray,' Tom observed.

'She's probably added a spoonful or two,' agreed his wife. They didn't have much else to say to each other. Tom was running a kissing sequence to and fro in his machine with the glazed expression of a man who has seen most of what life has to offer on television. And Celia was allowing her imagination to run away with her. It had found fruitful ground in the damage to the Harveys' car. And the damage its discovery might have done to the psyches of her two nubile daughters. She had researched adolescent trauma more than once for programmes on delinquency and she knew what shocks like that could do to the fragile pubescent id. Symptoms could appear years later—breast lumps, among others. She had researched breast lumps more times than she cared to remember.

'How do you think Rainbow took it?' she asked Tom.

'Took what?' he asked.

'Oh really!' snapped Celia. 'This morning. Do you think she was shocked?'

'She laughed her head off,' said Tom.

'Doesn't mean a thing. She might have been hysterical.'

'Rubbish. They see worse things than that on the tube. She thought it was a scream and so did Natasha. You saw them.'

'I saw them,' Celia acknowledged. 'But I didn't X-ray them. I didn't see what happened underneath. One day you will discover to your cost that children are far more complicated than they look. Or maybe you won't. Maybe you will die never knowing there is life beneath the surface.'

'If there is life beneath the surface,' Tom chortled, 'make sure I'm buried. Hear that?' But Celia wouldn't smile. She meant it and she wanted him to take her seriously. Because it was more than his sanity was worth not to give his wife what she wanted, Tom said, 'They are sensible girls. They took it for what it was, a joke. What can you do about it anyway? Take them to a shrink? Sue? There's no one to sue. Is there?'

'If there is, it certainly isn't the paper boy,' Celia declared. 'You can always find someone to sue.' She had researched American litigation three times.

'Who do you blame?' Tom asked. 'Do you know who did it?' He asked because Celia knew things no one else knew. It was what made her the tiniest bit dangerous.

'I haven't the foggiest,' she lied, because naturally she had.

Celia Petrie was like a squirrel with secrets. When she came across pieces of information or insights which she suspected were hers alone she kept them to herself and stored them, not necessarily with the intention of using them but on the off-chance that she might one day want to. This gave an attractive glint to her wide green eyes which was often described as cunning.

Minnie Anderson Jones wasn't at all sure about Celia Petrie. She didn't trust her and she was rattled by her self-confidence, rattled by the way she could insinuate her body between any two men who happened to be about, urging it into the space between them, leading with her breasts, which were small, Minnie had often said to herself, but leading. She considered Celia's sexuality common. It was common, she felt, to dress like a twenty-two-year-old when Minnie could give her a good fifteen years.

Minnie was easily offended by women like Celia but she didn't lose any sleep over them. She didn't know what caused her to wake in the night, which she did all the time now she was pregnant. All she knew was that she would wake up, suddenly, and once awake she couldn't get back to sleep. No one understood how wretched it made her feel.

It was why she paid so much attention to catching up on her rest during the day and why she had given up her job as soon as the pregnancy had been diagnosed. It had only been a little job anyway, in an art gallery. Nothing to cling to. What she earnt had barely covered the cost of petrol and parking tickets. The loss of the job was nothing to cry about and certainly not the reason she was crying in bed while Tango's life was supported by the wonders of twentieth-century technology.

She was crying about the honeysuckle, she supposed. She couldn't be sure. 'Sebastian,' she said loudly to her sleeping husband, 'you will have to do something about the robinia.'

Sebastian was instantly alert. He sat up. 'What is it?' he yelled. 'What's wrong? Is your bag ready?'

'The honeysuckle is wrong,' sobbed Minnie. 'You'll have to do something. It's going to kill my poor little tree. I planted that tree. The honeysuckle is going to kill my baby.'

Sebastian lay down again. 'Oh Minnie,' he murmured, 'if only you knew. Stop crying. It's in hand. Don't upset yourself.'

'What do you mean, in hand?' she bawled. 'How can it be in hand. All you have to do is tell Hippo to prune it, or prune it yourself.'

'Minnie,' he sighed. 'Be calm. I will take care of the robinia.' He paused. 'When I am better.'

His wife snorted suspiciously. 'What do you mean, better?'

Sebastian rolled over and stroked her brow. 'I wasn't going to tell you but now I suppose I will have to. This morning while you were asleep I crept downstairs and I . . . fell. I hurt my knee so badly that at the moment it's all I can do to control the pain. I spent all morning at the hospital.' He wasn't a weak man but he was a mild man and like many mild men Sebastian had hoped to escape from the knowledge that he wasn't succeeding in a surgical ward.

He didn't tell Minnie that the hospital had been unable to find any significant injury to his knee and that he had been told to go home and forget about it. He saw no point in burdening her with that. But she asked anyway.

'What did the hospital say?'

'Never mind what they said. We've got enough to worry about with you and the baby,' he said softly. 'All you need know is that I am in a fair amount of pain and I will see to the honeysuckle when I am not.' Minnie tugged at the bed covers with more malice than was necessary. Either you had a bad leg and were given crutches or you didn't have a bad leg. You certainly didn't get a bad leg falling over unless you were skiing or chasing a robber. She guessed Sebastian had fallen in a ridiculous way in something silly.

'How did it happen?' she asked. Sebastian heard the lack of respect in her voice. It was the very thing he so badly wanted to escape and it was why he could see no point in confiding to her that the guerrilla tactic on the Volvo had been his. He knew she would shriek with laughter and distress and ask what it had done for the robinia, when it had been plain to him the minute he had thrown away the can that the answer was not much.

'I slipped in the kitchen,' he said. In the face of his grand deceit he couldn't be bothered with a petty one.

'In the cat food?' she asked, giggling.

'Yes,' he said.

'Oh Sebastian,' cried Minnie and she started to weep again, not for the catfood or for Sebastian's knee but for herself, tied to the father of her child-to-be who was really no man at all.

Minnie might have cried for Tango had she known about him, but probably not. She didn't like Tango any more than Giles or Myra Dyson did. But it was not until much later in the day, after several hours of uninterrupted sleep and a very long bath, that she heard it rumoured that the whippet was brain dead. She heard it from Bella who had heard it from the horse's mouth.

The Matthewses had told the Parkers in front of Bella, who had been hovering uselessly with a handkerchief over her face while the *pot-au-feu* was lifted carefully from the Aga and carried through No. 9 to the Volvo. Tony Matthews had taken the day off work to wait for news and the news wasn't good, he had informed the Parkers. He wouldn't lift a finger to help with the steaming pot and nor would he have the life-support machine turned off because he preferred even a cabbage to a dead dog.

Bella had thought at the time that the Putney Ladies would probably agree with him, but it had been a gruelling scene nonetheless. It had been made no easier, she reported to Minnie, by Jill's fury at her own refusal to travel with the festering stew across Wandsworth. Jill had been forced to put her nanny in the back of the Volvo with the pot, and she had insisted that Bella's au pair collect the children at lunchtime if Brigid wasn't back.

'I couldn't have gone,' Bella told Minnie as she loaded the rest of the Putney buffet into her own car. 'I just couldn't. The smell was agonizing.'

'I know,' Minnie sympathized. 'I don't mind food smells myself, but I simply can't take the smell of people. Isn't that funny?' Bella looked startled and hoped she was not emitting anything nauseating with the strain of lifting but Minnie looked reassuringly untroubled.

'I don't know how I'll cope at Putney,' she called to her. 'I hope to heaven there are lots of windows. I've put stacks of garlic on the garlic bread. I can cope with garlic.'

'But not on the breath,' Minnie answered.

'Don't,' Bella said. She slammed the door and climbed into the driver's seat anxious to get away. Minnie was a major pain as far as she was concerned and she had only stopped to talk to her because Jill's anger had made her uneasy, and there Minnie had been, watering her window boxes quite clearly ignorant as to the fate of Tango.

Minnie, Bella mused, as she drove along Battersea Park Road

and into the fumes of the brewery, always felt sorry for herself when, from two doors along, her life seemed spectacularly charmed. Look at the way Sebastian fell over himself to oblige her every smallest whim.

She considered Minnie from her own rather jaundiced position, three months into a second pregnancy and eight years into a marriage with a man whose meanness was legendary, not just among family and neighbours but as far afield as Clapham. It was to Clapham Market that he drove her each Saturday lunchtime to haggle with the traders over meat, veg and kitchen rolls with more spirit than decency permitted.

It wasn't even as if they were poor, though Marcus insisted they would be if he wasn't as he was. What he was was a man who included among the ideals of equality, liberty and fraternity, parsimony.

It was why she had an au pair called Griselda from Italy instead of a nanny called Marlene from Australia. It was why she was Jill's partner in Haute Food. 'You like cooking, you like Jill. Capitalize on it,' Marcus had insisted. She would much rather have been back in the City if she had to work, but she would infinitely have preferred not to work at all. As for liking Jill, she couldn't imagine a day when she would ever think fondly of her again.

She would never in the whole of her life rid herself of a view of Jill from the back, large and big bottomed, in an expensive skirt with an expensive top never quite fitting, so pompous and patronizing and offensive about her art. What art? Bella asked herself. I mean, really, what art?

She turned into the Putney Ladies' gravel driveway and saw Jill milling about the hall with a couple of flower arrangers. Who on earth would pay £20 to eat Jill's *pot-au-feu* and trifle and listen to a talk on African compost and grain?

'Hurry up,' screeched Jill through a window. 'Can you smell the *pot-au-feu*? Isn't it comforting?'

Chapter Six

Miss Smith noticed the absence of Tango more than anyone apart from the Matthewses because she hated that dog as much as they loved it. When Giles Parker had crushed the whippet with his Volvo she had given a small cry of exultation. Not that she wished the animal pain, she wished no living thing pain, but she did wish it dead, as she wished many living things. Death, as far as Miss Smith could see, was a simple solution, though not one she was anxious to hurry into on her own account.

What she had been unable to decipher from her upstairs window, although she had listened and watched for clues from dawn, was whether Tango actually had eaten his last meal. She badly wanted to know. There was no way she would stoop to pressing a glass to the floor on the off chance that the Matthewses might be grieving in the room below, because if she stooped she would never get up again.

Being an amputee at ninety-one had decided disadvantages. Not only was grovelling about the floor uncomfortable, so was sliding down the stairs on your bottom which is what she had to do if she wanted to leave the house on her own. When you've already lost one leg there is no sense at all in risking the other. But there were advantages. On the whole, people felt sorry for you and, provided you kept yourself clean, they always stopped for a chat. It made them feel kind. Occasionally, if they felt they were being observed, they even asked you in for a cup of tea.

As she saw Minnie and Bella talking together outside the Anderson Joneses', Miss Smith prepared for an immediate excursion, and she prepared with a light heart. Today as she bounced passed the Matthewses', the whippet would not be there to howl and throw himself against their door in his desperation to break out and eat her.

Miss Smith didn't always slide down the stairs. Twice a week she was helped down by an ambulanceman or two, who came to take her to the day centre where she ate lunch, played bingo and mingled, in a manner of speaking, with people of her own age, give or take thirty years. On days she went to the centre she found herself thinking of Brain Street and on her return she hurried straight back to her window to find out what she had missed. Brain Street was better than *The Archers* or *Crown Court* and it was on her own doorstep. By watching and listening it wasn't hard to follow its many and varied plots.

The stars of Brain Street in Miss Smith's book were the Harveys, because they were the most glamorous and the most deceitful. Miss Smith had known well before anyone else, including Minnie, about the goings on in the Harveys' loft extension, even though they occurred well above her eye-level. She had only to watch the curtains. On days when Anna headed off in her little yellow car she would hear Sarah call Flora in from the garden for her afternoon sleep and then she would watch the loft. Sure enough, within seconds, Hippo's face would appear briefly and the curtains would be drawn before she had time to adjust the focus on her binoculars. Or, if she had seen Hippo leave with his brief case and Sarah take Flora to the park, she only had to wait minutes for Rupert Fox to hove into view as they disappeared from it. Slam would go the curtains again. She could put money on it.

She also knew better than anyone how many hours Minnie Anderson Jones slept, even though Minnie slept at the back of her house. This was because Minnie always looked out of her dining-room window the minute she came downstairs to inspect her robinia. What Miss Smith couldn't fathom was why she spent so long gazing at the tree. It was just a tree. Miss Smith knew too that Sebastian was a deeply troubled man. She watched his face as he hurried out in the mornings and dawdled back at night and she banged her crutch on the floor when she saw him, crying, 'Life isn't all beer and skittles.'

She spent a long time watching people's faces through her binoculars and trying to decide what went on behind them. Very often, she concluded, it wasn't much. Sometimes not much happened in Brain Street, apart from the postman's round which she always woke up for, or a Peter Jones delivery, which had her on the edge of her chair, or a Webbs' truck, which bored her. So attuned was she to the street's rhythms that she automatically stirred for periods of peak activity or if anything untoward happened.

Her day began at a quarter to eight when she sat in her usual spot with a cup of tea to watch the daily charade of No. 8 on his push bike and No. 2 on his motor bike trying not to notice each other. She liked a bit of comedy to start with and sometimes a bit of audience participation. 'Cooeee,' she occasionally called to them. 'Cooeee. Lovely morning isn't it? Why don't you have a race to the end of the street. I'll be judge.' Then she would howl with laughter because the thought terrified them. She liked to see the Petrie girls too, but some mornings they scooted off around the far corner before she could get her head out of the window. She especially liked it when one of them forgot something and had to run home, while the other stood in the road yelling. 'Just as well her head's screwed on,' she would cry.

The Matthewses always left on the dot of half past eight. They called good-bye to the man-eater, then she would hear the clicketty-clack of Valerie's high-heeled shoes on the lino in the hall before they appeared at the gate. She liked to torment Tony Matthews who, to her mind, was an extension of his dog; another bit of dog at the wrong end of the lead. 'Yoo hoo,' she often called down to them. 'Bring me back a loaf at dinner time, would you?' and he would scowl like his dog and look hungrily at her flesh.

'All right, Miss Smith,' Valerie would call up, without ever looking at her. To look at her would mean she liked doing it, which Miss Smith knew she didn't. No one did. No one liked to be asked a favour by a person who could never return it.

Shortly after the Matthewses chugged around the corner in their Ford Escort, the Marshams and the Whittakers would appear with the next lot of school children. Miss Smith had watched the state of affairs between the Marshams and the Whittakers degenerate badly over the past few months. She put it down to morning sickness, though she knew it couldn't possibly account for Beth Marsham's crabbiness. She didn't mind what caused it. She enjoyed the new tension and the interplay of human emotions, as they tossed on an undercurrent of deep-seated social conflict.

The arrangement between Beth and Bella had lasted ever since Poppy Whittaker and Rose Marsham started school together at the local primary. Three mornings a week, Miss Smith knew, Mrs No. 2 went off with the little ones to help slow readers and, on those mornings, she took the children. On the other two days, the foreign help at No. 8 took them. It was a simple arrangement but the simplicity was deceptive. Miss Smith thrilled to the angry exchanges between Beth and her big boy on their doorstep, as she tried to get him to leave with the little girls. And she hugged herself if Bella spoke crossly to Griselda, or if Bella had to turn out herself because Griselda had decided she was sick.

Days when Poppy Whittaker was sick were a joy, because it meant that Beth had to rush inside and get dressed to take Rose to school herself. She didn't trust her sons to get Rose there safely. 'What's wrong with 'em?' Miss Smith had once yelled down. 'They're big enough and ugly enough.'

A taxi always called for Richard Dyson at exactly nine, which was interesting but uneventful. The highlight of the morning came at quarter past nine when the Dysons, the Harveys and the Parkers tried to organize a school run for five children which, had it been made even on their very small feet, would have taken no more than ten minutes.

She had seen more variations on their rota than she had seen pigeons on the roof at No. 9. To begin with, the Harvey nanny had taken it week about to do both delivery and collections with the Parker nanny and Myra Dyson. This turned out to be inconvenient, so for a short while one collected one week, another delivered the same week, then everyone changed for the next and the next. But no one could keep track of whose turn it was. They decided the fairest thing was for everyone to make one journey a day because there were three journeys in all. There were two collections because Flora Harvey, Toby Dyson and Amanda Parker came home at lunch time but Benjy Parker and Poppy Dyson ate lunch at school.

It wasn't long before the Harvey nanny said this wasn't fair and everyone agreed, not for her sake, but because no one wanted to collect when their charge was sick or invited out for the afternoon. The latest plan, as far as Miss Smith could make out, was to allocate a journey a day to the Dysons and the Parkers and two journeys every three days to the Harveys, regardless of whether their charge was involved or not and, as far as Miss Smith could make out, this was working as badly as all the other schemes, if not worse, because there was more bad grace involved.

At a quarter past nine the family making the collections would appear at its front gate and with any luck the other families would too. But more often than not they wouldn't, because those who weren't doing the driving that day didn't seem to be quite so concerned that coats were found and hair brushed in good time. At least one gate or car door was slammed crossly every morning and Miss Smith adored it.

Sometimes there would be a long run featuring a clinging child who had to be wrenched from its mother, and Miss Smith would call out to it, 'Never mind. The bomb hasn't dropped,' which usually made the child cry louder, because it didn't know what she meant and she looked so old.

Between half past nine and ten there was a flurry of late starters. The senior Petries and Sebastian Anderson Jones would take off and Bella would hurry across the road to No. 9.

Sometimes she went earlier, sometimes later. It depended on what smells were coming from the kitchen. Occasionally Giles Parker would go for a run around the block, but not very often. He was frightened of dogs. Then finally, everyone was settled, and Miss Smith would hop to the bathroom and into the kitchen for some light refreshment.

As Miss Smith watched Bella talking to Minnie she decided to time her appearance on Brain Street to coincide with the arrival of the very small children home for their lunch at a quarter past twelve. She dragged herself away from the window and into the bathroom, where she scrubbed her face and hands and sprayed herself with lavender water. She knew how the young liked the old to smell of lavender. Then she hunted about for a nice old crocheted shawl and a pretty brooch which would give them a talking point. What she found most painful about the young was not that they yelled at her as if she was deaf or mentally deficient, but that they found so little to say to her. She liked to give them a starting point, like the brooch or the shawl, and then she moved on as fast as she could to scandal.

Bella was driving towards Putney by the time Miss Smith threw her crutch down the stairs ahead of her and steadied herself for her descent. She was turning into the gravel driveway by the time Miss Smith made the front door. Minnie, having watered and talked to her flower boxes and soothed her robinia, caught sight of her too late. 'Yoo hoo,' Miss Smith called. 'Stay there, Mrs How's-ya-father, I'm coming across.'

Miss Smith had never seen any reason to remember her neighbours' names although she had so few of them. She vaguely knew the Marshams and she occasionally remembered the Parkers but after that she gave up and called them anything that came into her head. She knew they liked Mr and Mrs, because they dreaded passers-by mistaking her for a relative, so she called them Mr and Mrs unless they were being especially evasive then she called them 'You' or 'Mary', anything to annoy them really and to show them that she didn't need them.

A normal neighbour would have sworn silently at the sight of Miss Smith swinging across the street but Minnie had decided at the age of fourteen that to curse was unladylike. She waited for Miss Smith, smiling, because the school run was due back any minute and she composed herself to sound kindly and concerned but not in the least bit patronizing.

'Lovely day, Miss Smith,' she said. 'And don't you look pretty.' She took a handkerchief from her pocket and lifted it to her face in case Miss Smith's odour was as old as she was.

Miss Smith grinned at her. 'Handsome is as handsome does. What's happened to that dog?'

'Do you mean the Matthewses'?' Minnie asked.

'I don't mean the Queen's,' Miss Smith replied.

'He's as well as can be expected,' Minnie said gently. 'He's in the best possible care, at a vet's in Belgravia.

'Where?' Miss Smith asked crossly.

'Belgravia,' Minnie repeated. 'You may not know it. Near Victoria.'

'What's he doing there?' Miss Smith snapped.

'He's on a very complicated machine to keep him alive,' Minnie said loudly and slowly. 'Unfortunately an important bit of him is already dead.'

Miss Smith who had been glaring angrily at her foot looked up sharply. 'What are you talking about? Which bit's dead? He's either dead or he isn't.'

'They think his brain is dead,' Minnie said. She was getting sick of this. If the school run didn't come back soon she was going to say, 'Go away, if you don't mind.'

'That animal never had a brain,' Miss Smith declared. 'When's the rest of him going to die? You can't live if your head's dead, can you?'

Minnie looked puzzled. 'No,' she agreed, adding, 'I don't know.' She could smell something pungent apparently drifting from Miss Smith's clothes.

'And what about the paper boy? What are they doing about him?' Miss Smith enquired.

'I don't know,' mumbled Minnie, backing away. 'What paper boy?'

'The one that wants to steal the bike. Our paper boy. You had him cleaning next door's car up. You know the one.'

'Oh him,' said Minnie. 'Nothing. They told him not to do it again.' Miss Smith chuckled, then turned away before the school run arrived, to hop down to the corner.

By the Harveys' trellis she turned and bawled back to Minnie, 'You spend too much time in bed. Just like everyone else in this street.' Then she cackled to herself, and Minnie hurried inside to sniff her baby clothes and sob until lunchtime.

Chapter Seven

Two days later a Putney lady died for Africa of food poisoning. Which particular item of food killed her wasn't easy to decide since not everyone who ate the *pot-au-feu* fell ill and not all the ladies who had been to drinks with Mrs Henderson Smyth prior to the buffet and had enjoyed the prawn and guacamole dip waned that evening, though some certainly remembered feeling faint.

Naturally enough, the Putney ladies had no wish to point the finger at any of their own, so they declared loudly that the *pot-au-feu* had stunk the hall out, and if they had eaten it with gusto it had only been all that talk of grain. This was the thrust of the telephone call which Jill took from Mrs Henderson Smyth in the presence of six defrosting chickens on a morning when the last thing she wanted was more on her plate.

Mrs Henderson Smyth trumpeted down the phone that Jill was being held responsible. Jill replied with equal brass that that notion could be used as stuffing because her standards of hygiene and cuisine could not be faulted. She advised Mrs Henderson Smyth to investigate her own kitchen and the kitchen of the hall in which the food had been served.

'What's more,' she said stoutly, 'I would never add prawns to guacamole. Were they frozen?' And without waiting for a reply declared, 'You must be aware that food poisoning is almost impossible to prove.'

'Are you denying that you are responsible for Hermione's death?' Mrs Henderson Smyth enquired.

The baldness of the question knocked Jill sideways. It all but laid her out, but she recovered herself sufficiently to say, 'I would like that accusation in a letter which will be placed immediately in the hands of a lawyer. I have nothing more to say to you, good-bye.' Then she collapsed onto the kitchen sofa to perspire profusely and to anguish alone. She breathed deeply and said to herself, 'It is nothing I can't handle,' but even as she spoke, she wondered if it might not be.

She didn't weep, as Minnie would have wept, or throw up, as Bella would have thrown up, or fall into the arms of the nearest available male, as Anna would have fallen, because there were no arms handy and none even remotely fond of her which could have handled her weight. Jill Parker was a big woman, a solid woman, a woman built to absorb worries and cares, and that was why she was married to a short and struggling, but fine-featured, thriller writer.

She picked up her hacking blade and tore into the frozen chickens in a bloodless but watery frenzy and when she had finished she opened a bottle of Muscadet and proceeded to drink herself into oblivion. At least, she aimed for oblivion but the closer she got to it the more clearly she began to comprehend her plight, so she turned on the television and sat there, waiting for the letter.

During a commercial break she asked herself where everyone was when she needed them, but she knew. They were out, all out. Bella was over at Hill House, a prep school famous for its pupils' knickerbockers. She was trying to persuade the headmaster to take Poppy even though she couldn't read, because Poppy wanted to go to a school where she could wear trousers like Johnny Marsham, though Johnny Marsham's trousers were decidedly comprehensive and Hill House's most certainly were not.

She sipped at her wine and looked at the chickens dispassionately. She wished one of them was Mrs Henderson Smyth or the stupid whippet. She didn't need Mrs Henderson Smyth or a brain damaged whippet when she already had a husband with a block. Giles was stuck on chapter two of *Hunk Billet's Son*, despite her best efforts to inspire him. 'Didn't Hunk have a daughter?' she had cried only the day before.

She went over and over again what had gone into the *pot-au-feu*, and it was hard because so much had gone in. She was positive, however, that nothing had been lethal and that, even if it had, there couldn't be a single organism deadly enough to withstand thirty-six hours on the Aga. She asked herself if she was certain the stew had been thoroughly heated before she had served it. 'It was, I know it was,' she informed the chickens.

'Oh God,' she prayed. 'Oh God.' She didn't know how much more strain she could take. She might be built for it, but would there never ever be anyone to stand behind her with a piton or guy rope or something? Would she always have to live under the weight of Giles' creativity? She looked into her free-offer wine glass, from a full tank of petrol, and thought she could see an abyss, but she couldn't. It was only the blueness of her Jaeger skirt stretched across her lap.

'Pull yourself together,' she said, adding to the chicken pieces, 'Not you.' It was no use expecting Giles to be something he was not. It didn't matter that he was a creator and not a piece of scaffolding. She loved being married to a writer. She understood him, being a cook, because of the parallels he could never see.

She fiddled with her Alice band and wondered why she was feeling so lonely when she was used to not relying on anyone. She could always telephone Mummy, she thought, but what would Mummy say about a poisoning? Everyone said she was like her mother, a brick. But her mother wasn't much of a brick, more a rock which rolled on top of you and squashed you flat just as you thought you were making progress.

She was reminded of Tango, squashed, but lying in specialist comfort on a heated pad without even having to make the effort of breathing for himself, at their expense. The vet had told

Tony he quite understood why he wasn't anxious to turn the machine off. He had said that Tango might recover spontaneously but then again, he might not. He had recommended that the Matthewses come to terms with their grief before doing anything as drastic as launching the dog on the final step of his journey from living pet, via living vegetable, to dead animal, vegetable and, eventually, mineral. Jill wondered if Hermione had been put on a life-support system before pegging out.

It occurred to her slowly as her thoughts lumbered along this morbid track that she knew very little about the circumstances of Hermione's death. Then it seemed to her suddenly, as she drained her glass and dropped her Alice band on to the floor, that there might be hope after all.

Hermione might yet have died at the wheel of her car or in her bath, and the Putney Ladies, because they had all had a nasty bout of gastric flu, might only have assumed they had been poisoned and that Hermione, being greediest, had been most poisoned. She heard Bella ring at the door just as a fantastic surge of confidence restored her to most of her former substantial self.

'Let me in, let me in,' Bella squealed. 'The Dysons are putting up scaffolding.'

'No,' cried Jill. 'Surely not a loft extension at last.'

'You won't believe it,' Bella gasped, staggering into the kitchen with a load of provisions from the supermarket for the chicken pies. 'They're painting their house.'

Jill stared at the provisions. 'The woodwork?' she asked.

'Not the woodwork, the house, the bricks. They are going to change the colour of the bricks.' Jill gasped and took another bottle of wine from the fridge, causing Bella to gape a little. It was pretty astonishing news but it wouldn't have driven her to drink, not before the afternoon school run.

'Do we know what colour?' Jill asked, no longer tormented by the image of Hermione's poisoned carcass.

'Guess!' Jill's eyes glistened with pleasure which Bella knew was about to give way to joyous outrage.

'I can't. White.'

'Pink.'

'You're not serious.'

'I am serious.'

'Pink!'

'Pink.'

'They will have to be stopped.'

'Absolutely,' said Bella. 'Don't.' She cast her eyes around the kitchen and saw the hacked chickens, the blaring television, the wine bottle in the sink and the Alice band on the floor. 'Brigid taken the children to the park?' she asked, starting to unpack.

'To lunch with Flora and Sarah. I think they were going to the park this afternoon. You can never tell. Nannies are a law unto themselves.' Bella knew perfectly well this wasn't so, since Brigid was ruled to within a second of her last waking minute, but the point wasn't worth raising. She had enough trouble with Griselda and regretted again the economy of trading a nanny for an au pair. 'Just as well,' Jill was saying. 'It's been a truly awful morning.'

'What?' Bella enquired, thinking it must have been, in view of the state of the kitchen.

'One of the Putney Ladies died of food poisoning.' Bella stopped unpacking and sat down.

'Don't,' she screamed. 'Jill, she didn't! Which one?' Then she began to laugh. She laughed and laughed until she thought she might miscarry and Jill, sipping wine with her hair flopping all over her pale round face also giggled until she suddenly began to moan, a horrible lowing noise which put an end to all merriment near the Aga.

'It's terrible,' she moaned. 'It's terrible. I could go to jail.'

'Don't be daft,' said Bella, not entirely sure of the procedure for comforting Jill, uncertain as to whether it required bodily contact. She decided it didn't. But her tone was gentle and she strove to sound confident. 'It's almost impossible to prove food poisoning. Anyway, we're insured. Remember? Marcus fixed up the policy. It's in the book, £60 a year and we're covered for a million or a quarter of a million. Something, anyway.'

'I know, I know.' Jill sniffed, wiping her nose on her sleeve so that Bella had to look away. 'But we'll have to have the Environmental Health Officer in and there'll be an inquest and I could be charged with manslaughter; we could be charged with manslaughter.

Bella's stomach made the short rapid journey to her enlarged womb and began to bounce. 'I didn't do a thing to the *pot-au-feu*,' she protested.

'You did the garlic bread,' Jill said, sipping again to console herself and fortify her accusation.

'You can't die of garlic bread,' Bella said. 'Be sensible, Jill. I think you are panicking.'

Jill stood up. 'I have never panicked in my life. I do not intend to start now. What I am saying, Bella, is that although I do the lion's share of the cooking in our catering business, it is our catering business and we will be held jointly responsible.'

Bella stared at Jill and noticed how astonishingly plain and old she looked. Perhaps this was the face of a murderer. But she steadied herself. Whatever she wanted to believe about herself, she, Bella, knew that Jill was panicking. 'Were many of them carted off to hospital?' she asked coldly. Jill sat down again.

'I don't know,' she said. 'I didn't ask.'

'What do you know?' Bella enquired.

'Nothing. Only that someone called Hermione has died of food poisoning and we are being accused.'

'Let them prove it,' Bella said. 'I am going home. And if you don't mind my saying so, I think you should have a sleep. I'm sure Brigid can hold the fort for the rest of the day. Is Giles in his study?'

Jill shook her head. 'Gone to lunch with his agent. He's been out all day.'

'Then go to bed,' Bella repeated. 'Take the bottle with you if it helps.'

'I might,' said Jill. She stared at Bella and shivered. She wanted to hack Bella. She wanted to hack Bella to kingdom come, for having seen her as less than a rock. She wished she hadn't broken down. She wished she hadn't sounded mean and vicious, though if anyone was entitled to she was. Why should she be the only woman in Brain Street not to give vent to her frustrations, when every single other woman did all the time, whenever they wanted to, except Beth Marsham, who was too bloody perfect for words. Any wonder she didn't have a sex life. She hated Bella now. Knowledge is power, she said, as Bella crept out. Knowledge is power and now Bella knows about me and the Putney lady she has power over me. At this she burst into tears and, taking the wine, lurched up to bed.

That night, shortly after Giles discovered the empty bottle under the bed and his wife asleep with nothing for supper, Tony Matthews took the most painful decision of his life and told the vet to pull the plugs on Tango, who promptly died. He walked home to Battersea leaving the body to be disposed of by the vet and when he finally made it to the comfort of his small orange settee he said to his wife, 'Tango signed off without a squeak.'

Val said, 'Never mind, love,' and put an arm around him. But he did mind. He not only minded, he wanted justice, justice for the death of his poor inoffensive whippet who had no more than half a dozen enemies in the world. He was going to sue. He said this without even knowing if you could, without knowing the basis of the claim, without being very certain how to go about it.

He sat stony-faced through the early evening programmes and the ten o'clock news, then, without thinking, he got up, put on his anorak and made for the door and his nightly walk. In a daze he looked about for something he knew was missing and realized it was Tango who was missing, cut down in his prime. 'Don't worry boy,' he said softly to himself. 'Don't worry. We'll get 'em.'

He walked sadly around the block, and down by the park, over one bridge, along the embankment, back over another bridge, around the block, and back into Brain Street. 'Uh, hello,' Rob Marsham called across the road as he reached the gate of No. 3. 'Saw you passing. Thought I'd pop out and ask after your dog.'

Tony glared at Rob Marsham with a mixture of fury and wonderment. Why would he of all people care? Didn't he know

Tango had been trained to go for his neck? Tony didn't have even the slightest inkling of class solidarity or the dignity of the working man.

'He's dead,' he said. 'They killed him.' Then he turned his back on the hand of comradeship Rob so innocently extended and went inside. To Rob, the death of Tango seemed somehow to represent the death of a martyr in Brain Street's struggle against progress. 'Right,' he said to himself. 'Right.'

Chapter Eight

Myra Dyson had devoted a lot of time to deciding what to do to her house in order to distinguish it from everyone else's. She had considered a wrought-iron balcony for the first floor and shutters. Through her house Myra hoped to distinguish herself, because being blackish and royalish was not enough. As a matter of fact she rarely ever gave a thought to being either. In the end she had plumped for pink brick-work, or, more precisely, off-fuschia, because she had seen it used to wondrous effect in Hampshire, where a gloriously off-fuschia farmhouse had dazzled surrounding fields for miles and miles. She intended to dazzle Brain Street.

'It will amaze them,' she informed her husband, who was himself already fairly amazed. She announced that she would paint the whole house pink from top to bottom, back and front and the woodwork.

'I don't think the woodwork,' Richard had advised melodically. 'The woodwork might be overdoing it.' He was tactful with his wife and generally agreeable. Since he spent all day disagreeing he found it a relief to come home and acquiesce, no matter how peculiar the proposition.

'What about the door?' Myra had said. Like most of the

houses in Brain Street theirs had a reinforced door.

'Nor the door,' he had replied. 'Paint the door and the woodwork white for emphasis.' He wondered what the consequences would be. He wondered if, in the end, they might have to move.

The reason they were not living in SW1, 3 or 7 when they could easily have afforded to, lay in Myra's overwhelming need to be part of a community, not, she had insisted, for her own sake, but for the sake of the children. 'They should grow up with a sandpit and children next door. I never had it so I know what I'm talking about.'

She believed they had found it in Battersea where she had dragged him in pursuit of a carefully-worded advertisement in the *Sunday Times*. 'Exquisite three bedroom terrace in gloriously tree-lined street by stunning park.' The minute she had stepped into it she had recognized the sort of closely-knit neighbourhood in which children and family life could thrive and where there was a common good she could work for. She had tried to explain it to Giles Parker when they had first moved in. She had been drawn by the warm family-based spirit she said, to which he had replied tartly, 'spirit-based families more like.' Giles, she now knew, was a facile drunk, but no neighbourhood was perfect. Once ensconced, she had made it her business to coordinate activities which strengthened it still further.

Brain Street had welcomed this favour with clenched fists. Life would have been simpler, so far as its residents were concerned, had she undertaken the career in germ warfare that she had contemplated in the sixth form. In the absence of anything better to do Myra devoted her time to causes, which she rammed past her neighbours' protesting mouths and down their choking throats without even a passing thought for Civil Liberties.

She would torment them with pictures of earthquake victims, threatened monuments, dying children and paralysed vagrants and cry, 'Come on, cough up.' If a newspaper launched an appeal she became the Brain Street coordinator and rushed from door to door demanding they hand over their filthy lucre, leaving them no option. She placed them in the impossible position of having to admire her even though they wished she could be somehow struck down and confined to bed or to a nice cosy grave somewhere. And she kept suggesting they have a street party, a concept odious to any respecter of recession grandeur.

She remained unaware of the irritation she caused. She didn't hear Jill observe loudly to Bella, 'It's tribal, you know. It's her roots,' or Bella's embarrassed reply that Myra's roots were somewhere in Knightsbridge.

Richard, who knew his wife moderately well, was intrigued by her need to paint their house. He found it curious that while she so badly wanted to involve herself in a community on the one hand, she also wanted to make her mark by shocking it on the other. It struck him as being potentially certifiable, although this would depend on which psychiatrist you consulted. He didn't actually want his wife put away but it was an interesting hypothesis, and he couldn't help wondering.

Myra saw nothing odd in what she was doing. She saw it only as the act of an artistic radical. Brain Street would find it odd, she knew, but where were the other artistic radicals in Brain Street? She hoped she would make the neighbourhood sit up and notice her and ask themselves what they wanted out of life. She would try to explain it to them in those terms though she wasn't confident they would understand. Brain Street was light on intellectuals, but then so, she was sure, were SW3, 7 and 1.

So up went the scaffolding and by the time Tango had hung up his dancing shoes the painters were ready to move in. Naturally the scaffolding on its own had drawn comments. Bella, returning from Hill House via Sainsbury's, had said in amazement, 'Not a loft extension.'

'Sorry,' she had laughed. 'Just a paint job.'

'Couldn't they have managed without the scaffolding?' Bella had enquired. 'It seems a bit excessive.'

'We're doing the whole house,' Myra had explained. 'Pink actually.'

'You're not,' Bella had said.

'We are,' she had replied. 'Have to dash. If I don't do something with Poppy today she will forget that she has a mother.' She had thought she had heard Bella's jaw dropping as she hurried away and she had allowed herself the smallest chuckle of satisfaction. Myra wasn't really a laughing woman.

In many respects she was like Rob Marsham, sharing with him the belief that life has a serious motive which would one day be clear and in the meantime it was nothing to joke about. Had Rob Marsham been less concerned about the jobs of the men at Webbs he would whole-heartedly have endorsed the spirit of commitment with which she pursued the anti-Webbs campaign.

The day the painters started on the undercoat, she set out, of her own accord, without further reference to the rest of the sub-committee, to canvass adjacent streets for support. She wanted several hundred signatures for a petition protesting that the timber yard was a health hazard. She loved canvassing and knew that a dull but worthy pitch worked wonders because most people sign anything rather than listen to a case for or against.

That very evening Rob Marsham also set out of his own accord to strike a blow for Tony Matthews. He too strode out with a sense of commitment though he had far less confidence. Unlike Myra, he had agonized over the rights and wrongs of his action. He had tormented himself over the ends and the means and whether the one justified the other and how best to affect one to achieve the other. He had tried asking Beth for her opinion but all that had accomplished was the leaden understanding that she couldn't appreciate his problem because she seemed to have stopped appreciating him.

'Beth?' he had said as they were washing up and Myra was knocking at the door of No. 3 Dishwater Terrace. 'I think something should be done for the Matthewses.'

'The Matthewses,' she had repeated, scrubbing at a pan lined with overdone homemade wholemeal tagliatelli.

'I'm not saying Giles did it deliberately,' he had said, 'but I think he was expressing an unconscious wish to be rid of the last vestiges of the working class from our street.'

'The dog ran under his wheels,' Beth had pointed out and he had recognized at once the wall that now appeared between them. He could press a button and, without knowing how, where or why it was, suddenly there was a wall.

'I know he ran under the wheels,' he had said. 'But Giles reversed back onto him. It was as if the dog was drawn to his own destruction and Giles was happy to provide it.' This sort of analysis might have delighted Beth in the past. She might have taken time to consider it, argue with it, resist it and finally agree with it, but no more. She had said, 'Rubbish. Look at the fuss it's caused. They're paying a fortune in vet's bills.'

'I am very sorry for the Matthewses,' Rob had said. 'That's all. Everyone wanted that dog dead. It must be horrible for them.'

'Mm,' Beth had said. 'I didn't like Tango either.'

At this, he had thrown his tea towel onto the kitchen table and said, 'I'm off for a jog around the block. It will do me good.' He didn't know what he could achieve on a jog, except perhaps an increased pulse rate and a diversion from his distress, but he set out with an open mind.

The Parkers' Volvo, he noticed, was parked outside the Harveys' and the Dysons' Mercedes was outside the Parkers'. No one's car as far as he could tell, and he couldn't tell the Citroens apart, was outside the home of its owner. Clearly no one intended parking around the corner if a space was available in the street, even if it wasn't theirs. Richard Dyson didn't understand human nature. That was plain.

'Oh hullo, Myra,' he said as he crashed into her outside No. 27 Dishwater Terrace. 'I was just saying to myself that Richard's plan doesn't seem to be working very well.'

'Were you?' said Myra. She didn't want to stop because she didn't want to explain to Rob why she was acting independently of the sub-committee, but he was bobbing up and down in front of her, holding her up. 'How's Beth?' she asked impatiently.

'Fine, fine. Washing up, actually.' The Marshams were the only family apart from those at No. 3 who didn't have a dishwasher. This was because they couldn't afford one, but Myra had a feeling, as she often had with Rob, that he was pointing out the humble peasant activity unnecessarily. The truth was he didn't know what else to say. A truly terrible plan had invaded the front part of his brain with such force that he suspected she might even be able to see it.

He looked at the clipboard which she was clutching to her chest. 'Getting signatures for Webbs?' he panted, speeding up and preparing to launch himself down the street. 'Good work. Great job. Save our trees,' and he was off.

Myra gritted her teeth as she stared after him. 'Creep,' she hissed, which was a shame really because they should have been able to get on, and he certainly had nothing against her.

All the way round the block and into the park and around the running track then back to Brain Street he examined his scheme which he no longer doubted could be justified. It was glorious in its simplicity and all he needed to rely on was the element so badly underestimated by Richard Dyson.

As he turned into Brain Street, he was overjoyed to see Jill Parker climbing out of her Volvo outside his own house, nudging his bike because no one cared whether they hit his bike or not.

'Haven't hit your bike, have I?' she called nervously as she spotted him. 'Isn't it a gorgeous night?'

'No,' he said. 'I think it's OK.' He continued jogging and she stood there waiting. 'What's she waiting for?' he asked himself. She was waiting for him to speak. She wanted to know if he knew about the death of the Putney Lady which surely he would mention if he did. She smiled and waited and he jogged.

'I've just seen Myra,' he gasped. 'In Dishwater Terrace. She's collecting . . .' he panted and he should have said signatures but Jill butted in before he could.

'She's not! I'd better warn everyone. Thank God you saw her.' And she dashed across to alert the Whittakers, who turned off all their lights, and the Anderson Joneses, who turned their television up full blast so they could ignore the knock when it came with a clear conscience. The Harveys were out but Minnie told Sarah, and Jill also told the Petries who were extremely grateful.

Within five minutes the whole of Brain Street was in hiding except for No. 3 and No. 5. No one liked to intrude on the Matthewses' grief, it was presumed Miss Smith was asleep, and Richard, it was felt, needed no warning because he knew what his wife was like.

Rob Marsham, taking this extraordinary accomplishment as an omen, moved swiftly and discreetly. He had only to hope that the Harveys would not return, that Myra wouldn't bowl around the corner, and that he could rely on Richard not to look out of the window. No one else would look out of theirs, of that he was confident. There wasn't a soul in their right mind prepared to be at home to Myra on a collecting binge.

He didn't devote much thought to the amount of hope involved in his success. He just got on with it, with the slim cover of his tool box and his upended Harley Davidson. It only took five minutes and luck was with him. There was no angry shout from along the street or furious cry from a loft extension. The car alarm didn't even bleep, because Jill had failed to turn it on, so distracted was she by the sight of him when she had assaulted his bike.

By the time Myra came back into Brain Street with thirty-five signatures and two doors slammed in her face, it was all done and no one was any the wiser. So preoccupied was Myra by the slammed doors and the rather shoddy work on the undercoat that she failed to notice the street's unearthly hush, and she certainly didn't spot the vengeance that had been wreaked on the rear windscreen of the Parkers' Volvo.

It waited there, unobserved, until Tony Matthews walked Tango's ghost around the block shortly after eleven. Then it leapt out at him and froze his throat and his heart. It was horrible. Horrible! 'Killer' the car said in letters of ghastly dripping red. 'Killer, exclamation mark.' He was tempted to run. He wanted to cry out but he knew it was only his nerves playing him up. 'My God,' he whispered. He stood there mesmerized and was still there when the Harveys turned the corner and pulled up outside the Petries'.

'Look at this,' he said hoarsely, as they staggered uncertainly from their car. 'Look what someone has done.' Anna wobbled over to where he was standing.

'What is it?' she asked sweetly. When she focused on the writing she roared.

'I don't believe it,' she yelled. 'Look, Hippo. Come and see. The paper boy strikes again.' She fell against Tony who was obliged to lean sideways with the weight of her mirth.

'Killer,' read Hippo carefully. 'Killer!' He too began to chortle.

'How awful,' she laughed. 'It's a much deadlier sin than ours. How shocking.' He winced as he laughed because of his indigestion. Tony smiled as well, relieved that someone else was in the street and that it was only a bit of aerosol paint.

'I don't think Darrin would have done it,' he said. 'He doesn't even know about Tango.' The Harveys looked at him blankly, then they looked at each other and Anna started to laugh again, loudly and rather vulgarly, Tony thought.

'He's done it, Hippo. Look at his face, you can tell. You've done it, haven't you. You wicked man.'

'At least you know how to get the blessed stuff off,' Hippo chuckled. Tony moved away from Anna.

'You're wrong there,' he said. 'I didn't do it even if he was my dog. I told you the other day, I don't hold with vandalism. I want justice but I'll get it through the courts, in the proper manner. I will sue.'

'You're suing the Parkers?' Hippo asked. 'Over the dog?'

'I'm taking advice,' Tony admitted. He wanted to go home. He wasn't over his grief yet. All this made him sick. He wanted to get away from it.

Marcus Whittaker, hearing Anna's laugh in the street, decided to put out the milk bottles although he was in his dressing gown. Catching sight of him Anna called, 'Quick, Marcus, get a load of this. Someone has done the Parkers.'

'Hang on,' he said. He dashed back into the drawing-room to check his hair in the mirror, then hurried into the street. 'Oh no,' he cried when he saw the car. 'Oh no. This is terrible. Someone knows about Putney. It'll be all over the place by now.'

'Tango,' Hippo corrected him. 'The dog was called Tango. I don't think it was called Putney, was it Tony? I may be wrong. Was it Tony, Tango or Putney?'

'Mango chutney,' Anna said. She was pretty well gone. She hadn't expected to run into any sober people on the way home and so had enjoyed three final brandies.

'I'm going to bed,' Tony said. 'Someone should tell the Parkers.'

'I'll tell them,' said Anna. She longed to see someone else at the wrong end of a can of spray paint. But she caught sight of her reflection in the windscreen and changed her mind.

It was Marcus who finally broke the news. He said to them, 'Something pretty ghastly has happened to your car.'

On the whole they took it fairly well, the blow being eased, more than likely, by the two bottles of claret they had drunk over supper and while they had been hiding from Myra.

'Can we get it off before morning?' Jill asked.

'With what?' Marcus and Giles said. They were not handy men and no one liked to ask Tony Matthews what had been used on the Harveys' car.

'I've got some rabbit stock with herbs on the stove,' Jill suggested. But it didn't do the trick and nail varnish remover only took off the exclamation mark. After that they were simply too tired to continue.

'Honestly,' said Giles, 'no one's going to take it seriously. No one cared that much about the Harveys. And it's only a dog.'

'You're right,' said Jill in order not to frighten him. 'Let's leave it.' So they went back to bed where she lay rigid with fear. If the accusation was directed at her then she was lost. The reputation of Haute Food was down the drain forever, along with the remains of the *pot-au-feu* which she had brought back from Putney to freeze.

Chapter Nine

All a black sheep has to do to win massive public support is become an underdog, which Tango did by dying. A scant twenty-four hours after his death Brain Street was beginning to think he hadn't been such a bad animal, and a mere twenty-four hours after that, the accident was being described as a tragedy and Giles as a man with a drink problem. His neighbours agreed that he ought not to have got away scot free with slaughtering a defenceless dog. Whoever had written 'Killer' on the car was only stating what everyone else felt, though no one else, they told themselves, would have stooped to graffiti.

Anna Harvey, however, found a kind word for Giles in her bosom as she languished in the loft extension, to which she had adjourned with Rupert Fox to look over some catalogues. 'You're mad if you don't have at least one stiff drink before you go to the Anderson Joneses',' she demurred.

'I know,' Rupert agreed lazily. 'But a dog is a dog. It's rotten to kill one. How would you feel if a drunk ran over your little Pansy?'

'Devastated,' Anna admitted. 'But a King Charles Spaniel isn't a whippet. I can't imagine carrying a whippet around Peter Jones.'

They were perfectly alone. Hippo was on his way to Norfolk to examine a collection of Victorian first editions, Sarah was at the hairdresser's on her morning off, Flora was at her nursery, and poor little Olly was away at school although he was barely seven. Rupert was stretched full length on the futon, a Japanese sofa which unravelled into a bed, the very thing, Hippo had declared, for looking at books on the floor, a notion which everyone had admired with what must have been indecent haste.

Anna, who had been wondering about the shelves, dropped lightly down beside him and gazed thoughtfully into his deep brown eyes. 'I would rather commit adultery than kill a dog,' she murmured. Rupert slid his arm about her and pulled her to him. He kissed her curvy pink lips and removed her crisp blue shirt which she was wearing half-open for easy access. He didn't care what Brain Street thought about his affair with her. He didn't need to, since he neither lived in it nor owned a Volvo.

It was less than a week since attention had been drawn to the Harveys' adultery and since then, Anna had tried very hard to end it with Rupert, once and for all. But Rupert was tantalized by the resistance she offered and so an arrangement which might have petered out amiably, had it been left to its own devices, was suddenly restored to the full vigour of its youth.

Even as they grappled on the futon with the word whippet on their lips, Anna pushed her lover away modestly and returned herself to her shirt. 'We are supposed to be looking at catalogues,' she cried.

'Anna,' he laughed. 'You hate catalogues.'

'But we must stop. Someone is watching us.'

'I know,' he said. 'Who do you think it is? Do you think it's Hippo and that he has crept back from Norfolk?' He threw back his head and roared at the thought.

'Of course he hasn't,' Anna said. 'He trusts me. Oh, stop it, Rupert. It's not funny. I can't bear the thought that we are being spied upon.'

They huddled together and looked towards the window through which sun streamed and the world and his dog could have looked had they been on the roof of No. 3 because Rupert had failed to close the curtains. She wouldn't have allowed him to close the curtains. It would have made resistance impossible.

'It couldn't be that old lady over the road, could it?' he chuckled. 'She often waves at me when we're up here.'

'She doesn't,' Anna cried in alarm. 'She does not, Rupert. You are making it up.'

'I'm not,' he insisted. 'I've always liked the idea of her sitting there, wondering what on earth we were up to.'

'For God's sake, Rupert,' Anna said. 'She's a neighbour of mine. How could you?'

'Like this,' he said, getting up from the floor, walking over to the window, and raising his hand in a gesture of recognition.

'Oh no,' Anna gasped. 'Come away, Rupert. Please come away.'

'No,' he said, waving and smiling. 'You come and wave too.'

'I can't.'

'But you must. She won't know what to make of it.'

So Anna did. She joined Rupert and smiled and waved to Miss Smith, murmuring, 'She could never have done it. She's only got one leg.' Then Rupert closed the curtains and fell upon his mistress because Miss Smith's presence magnified his excitement beyond endurance.

Hippo didn't have Miss Smith on his list of suspects for the very reason Anna had so instantly dismissed her. No one could stand on one leg to spray a Volvo in the middle of the night and hop up two flights of stairs without being noticed. As a matter of fact he didn't have anyone on his list because he had crossed everyone off, one by one. He couldn't imagine anyone with grounds for wishing him ill because he was a soft-hearted man and not one to wish anyone ill himself.

The public denunciation had had a drastic effect on him. To be discovered in adultery, even via a notice on the back window of your car, was humiliating in the extreme. He had taken immediate steps to put it as far behind him as possible and these led him away from Sarah. He no longer made love to her because his conscience was made of sterner stuff than his wife's. Having thanked his lucky stars for the narrow escape he determined not to embark on anything so foolhardy ever again.

This caused him surprisingly little pain. Sarah, though

peachy, was barely out of school and charming though this undoubtedly is to begin with, it is decidedly less so somewhere towards the middle. By the end Hippo had been finding her girlish little speeches less than entrancing, even putrid, and to be rid of them caused him a joy he would never have anticipated.

In the vacancy this created, and only now did he appreciate just how vacant Sarah had been, Hippo applied himself to the mystery of his foe. He wasn't sure that he wanted to confront him, because that would only prolong the unpleasantness, but he needed to know whom he should be avoiding. Listing everyone who might have been aware of his relationship with his nanny and everyone who might have begrudged him turned out to be useless. Top of the list was Anna but there was no way he could raise the matter with her and not incriminate himself totally. Beyond her, it could have been anyone but no one he could think of.

The Parkers' misadventure was a huge weight off his mind. It made the attack on him less personal. And whoever it was clearly had his work cut out if he intended scrutinizing Giles' behaviour as well as his own, should he intend to strike again. As he drove to Norfolk he considered this new dimension to his problem and he struggled with a ton of pastry en croute which, as far as he could remember, was what he had eaten the night before. Did last night's assault on the Parkers' Volvo mean that he and Giles had a joint enemy? Would Alka Selzer do the trick?

He wondered what the Parkers were doing and he remembered with awful discomfort the morning their own car had been found disfigured. The night before he had eaten a trifle which had fought back horribly. It occurred to him that the Parkers might be feeling very lonely and puzzled and that they might have no one to turn to, as he had had no one to turn to until Tony Matthews had appeared on his doorstep with the perfect solution. On a sudden generous impulse, he turned his car around and headed back down the A11, arriving in Brain Street at more or less the very minute Rupert ripped into Anna's thin silk and breathed fire between her immaculately tanned breasts.

Luckily for them and the course of true lust, he went straight to No. 9, so keen was he to help and so plain was it to him that the Parkers needed it. Their car stood in ghastly isolation outside the Marshams' with 'Kille' and half an 'r' leaping from the rear window. Jill had had a small success on half the 'r' with some of the beetroot in sherry.

The Parkers' nanny, Brigid, opened the door. 'Hullo Hippo,' she said. 'No one's in.' But Jill appeared at the top of the stairs as Hippo was on the brink of going home to catch his wife and partner, and she saved the day by crying, 'It's all right, Brigid, come in Hippo.' She skipped heavily down the stairs and into the hall. 'School run time, I think, Brigid,' she burbled.

'No it isn't,' Brigid said. 'Myra's doing it today.' She stood her ground in the hall.

'Then I think you should clear out Benjy's drawers,' Jill said primly.

'I did them yesterday,' Brigid replied.

'What about Amanda's?' Jill's hand was on the drawing-room door and she wanted to shut it but Brigid was standing like an enormous draught excluder in the middle of the doorway.

'The day before,' she said, smiling.

'Well I'm sure there's plenty for you to do upstairs.' Jill's mouth folded into a furious tight line as she tried to make an impression on the girl.

'I've done everything,' Brigid said.

'You've done all the washing, ironing, scrubbing, cleaning and tidying?' Jill asked in disbelief, coming back into the hall, shoving Brigid before her.

'I've done the lot,' Brigid agreed triumphantly.

'Then for God's sake go out and do some weeding or something.'

'I've done it,' Brigid protested. 'All of it.'

'Look, Brigid, I want to talk to Mr Harvey in private. You know very well that today has been a very trying day and that we are in a state of crisis that has absolutely nothing to do with you. Will you please excuse me now and go away. I don't care what you do.' She closed the door and bounced into the room sighing, 'Nannies, honestly. They are more trouble than they are worth.' Then she blushed hotly. She didn't know why Hippo made her forget herself but he always did.

She was delighted to see him. Not only had she always found him fascinatingly rich and attractive, but she sensed, as she offered him the sofa, that he was a kindred spirit in the way people are who have vandalized Volvos in common. Of all the men she might have been able to turn to, he was the only one who lived down the road. In fact, he was the only one, she realized as she clapped eyes on him.

Jill knew she could do with his advice. She needed to hear what someone thought of her plan to salvage her reputation by ruining Bella's because it hadn't crossed her mind to assume, as everyone else was assuming, that it was Giles who was being accused. It only goes to show how short-sighted a large woman can be when she is in the habit of shielding a very small husband.

She intended to stand up and say, 'All right, so Hermione died of food poisoning,' and then to offload the blame onto Bella. She would imply that it was her morning sickness which had contaminated the *pot-au-feu* and her panic which had caused her to accuse Jill. It didn't dawn on her that the street believed the vandal was a celibate dog owner with a high moral tone, which ruled out any of them and the paper boy. She chose not to accept, for the sake of her husband, that no one in Brain Street had the foggiest idea that anyone called Hermione had lived, let alone died, in Putney or that the Parkers had been involved in any death apart from the dog's. As Hippo had done before, she wanted to put as much space as she could between herself and the whole nasty business.

'I hope it's not a bad time,' Hippo said, ignoring the sofa and crossing the room to the French windows. He gazed out onto the artistic mass of shrub, herb, tree and weed and said, 'I thought you might like some help. Getting it off and that sort of thing.'

'Getting it . . . oh, the car, you mean?' Jill laughed, flushing again. 'No, no, it's fine honestly. It's only a bit of spray paint. Just Bella's joke. Stupid, I know, but there you are. I suppose she got the idea from the paper boy.'

Hippo turned from the window and studied Jill carefully. He wondered if she might be a little mad. She often looked a little bit mad and certainly the house often smelt mad. Sometimes he was attacked by the most formidable heartburn just walking past the gate. 'Bella?' he repeated.

Jill giggled. 'I know,' she agreed. 'Silly, isn't it. I daresay it will wash away eventually.'

'Are you saying that Bella wrote "Killer" on your car?' Hippo said.

Jill took off one of her shoes to examine the heel. It wasn't going to be quite as easy as she had hoped, judging by the disbelief on Hippo's face. 'Well I can't be sure, naturally. It just struck me that it might be.'

'But why?' Hippo said. 'I'm certain Bella would never do such a thing, no matter how distressed she was over the dog.' As Jill carefully considered how best to introduce the Putney death Hippo declared, 'If it was anyone in the street it was Tony Matthews.' It was a spontaneous and ill-considered declaration but Hippo was devoted to the Princess of Wales and extremely fond of Bella. 'We practically caught him red-handed.'

Jill giggled again. She spun out the giggle for as long as she could as she tried to decide whether or not to accept the idea. 'It would be, wouldn't it,' she twittered. 'Red.' She put her shoe on again and looked up at Hippo who was frowning at her. 'Red-handed,' she explained.

'Seriously,' he said. 'We came home at about eleven and there he was, standing by your car. I've never seen a man so shaken. Then Marcus came out and he was as astonished as we were. It couldn't have been Bella, Jill, Marcus didn't even know the dog's name. He thought it was Chutney. I'd stake my life on it.' He would have, too, almost. And he would have taken the same odds on it not being Tony Matthews whom he had nominated only out of desperation. He was convinced it wasn't Bella because he couldn't imagine Bella writing 'Adulterers' on anyone's car, not when she was three months pregnant.

'But why would he?' Jill said. 'I mean, the vet bills and everything.'

'Grief, I suppose,' Hippo said. 'If you want my advice I'd wipe the stupid word off and not give it another thought.' He might have had even wiser things to say had he not been interrupted by the sound of crashing crockery and a saucepan being hurled through the kitchen window. Brigid was having a nervous collapse. She had picked up one too many toys, scrubbed one too many floors, collected one too many a miserly cheque and worked one too many a twenty-hour day, and now she had had it. 'What on earth was that?' he said instead.

Jill remained in her chair. 'Brigid?' she roared. 'What's going on?' There was no reply. Jill lurched to her feet. 'I'd better go and see. Blast! I thought she was over her clumsiness.'

Hippo smiled sympathetically. 'Listen,' he said. 'I'll call by later with the stuff you need.'

'Oh, Brigid,' Jill shouted. 'What have you done?' Brigid was standing in the middle of the kitchen surrounded by shattered earthenware and splintered glass, smiling sweetly. 'I've had an accident. I fell and the saucepan knocked the vase off the ledge and flew though the window.'

'Honestly!' screamed Jill. 'That's all I need. It really is.' She wanted to run at Brigid and ram her against the wall but Hippo had appeared at the door.

'Gosh,' he remarked. 'What a mess. Where's the broom?' And being the gentleman he was, he found the broom, gave it to Brigid and took off, telling Jill to keep her chin up.

'I don't think I can go on much longer,' Brigid sobbed when he had gone. 'I'm so tired. I'm so, so tired. I want to go home. Let me go home. I'm tired.' Jill watched her briefly with her arms folded, astonished by the behaviour. Then she sat her in a chair.

'We are all tired,' she said. 'But we have to carry on. This is the way life is. Of course things have been a bit hectic lately, but I really do need you here. I pay you to be here. You can't go home yet. I'll tell you what. Why don't you go and lie down for a while and I'll clear up this mess for you.'

Brigid went to bed and stayed there for several weeks despite the guilt Jill piled on to her. She couldn't go home because Jill wouldn't let her, believing that once she set foot outside the door she would never come back.

In her absence, Jill turned to Bella. Bella was the only person whose good opinion she didn't value. She decided not to denounce her but to let everyone believe, as Hippo believed, that it was Tony Matthews and to demonstrate her generosity by forgiving him. It was a neat solution. It meant no one outside Putney need ever get to hear of the poisoning and Bella could continue to come and do the dogsbody work.

It would have worked splendidly except that Marcus bumped into Rupert Fox and mentioned, after a wine or two, quite in passing, that Haute Food was in a state of crisis what with a death in Putney and the writing on the car which looked decidedly like the first move in a blackmail attempt. Rupert, in passing, mentioned the food poisoning to Anna, who told Sarah who told Minnie who told Beth, all in passing, and somehow Celia Petrie and the Dysons got to hear of it as well. Everyone's first thought was, 'Oh no. Those prunes,' and everyone admitted they hadn't felt well since, including Anna who had forgotten she hadn't eaten any. Minnie, as a precaution, rushed off to have a scan to make sure the baby had not been affected.

Chapter Ten

Had it not been for Myra's off-fuschia, the Parkers might well have had to move. But what to do about the colour of the Dysons' house turned out to be as fortunate a diversion for them as the death of Tango had been for the Harveys.

Anna Harvey became obsessed by it. Neighbours who might have felt inclined to tell all their friends and relations about the poisonous nature of Haute Food found themselves beginning conversations about Anna and the colour of the house and failing to get to the poisoning at all because when they had covered the house, the friend or relation wanted to hear more of the adultery and by the time that had been discussed again, a child would be threatening to pee on the floor or the washing machine man would be at the door. So Jill's reputation lived to simmer a little longer and nothing in anyone's manner suggested to her that the whole street knew about Hermione but had something better on its mind.

One morning, when the honeysuckle's embrace all but suffocated a lower branch of the robinia, Anna said to Minnie, 'I wouldn't mind if I didn't have to wake up to it. I can't tell you how desperate it makes me feel, first thing in the morning, to wake up and find myself confronted by something so vile. It's too gruesome and I'm not going to stand for it.'

Mrs Butt, hoovering carpets at the other end of the sleek Harvey drawing room, told herself that Hippo might be a little on the sloppy side, a bit fleshy maybe, but he wasn't vile, not really. Minnie, staring glumly out into the vicious semi-evergreen wanted to say, 'You think you have problems?' but there was no stopping Anna in full flight. She was giving Minnie five minutes of her precious time and making the most of it.

Minnie was on the verge of tears, having been cruelly rebuffed even though the honeysuckle was killing her tree. She had called to ask if Anna wanted to go with her to an exhibition at the Hayward where a friend of her mother's had seen the Duchess of Westminster, or Devonshire, but Anna had said, 'Heavens, Minnie, I don't think I have a single free hour between now and Christmas.' She wriggled uncomfortably in the deep Harvey armchair. She had sunk so deep into it that the bump on her stomach seemed to have risen to the level of her nose.

'I know,' she said of the off-fuschia. 'I've told Sebastian we must do something but action isn't his strong point, I'm afraid. And really, Anna, what can anyone do? It's their house. Are those new shelves?' She eyed the carpentry on either side of the fireplace with a well practised eye. She could value other people's property to the last penny and always did because it was a way of knowing where you stood, or sat.

She tried to put her feet up under her but failed. She no longer seemed to have enough thigh. And she reflected, as she weighed up the shelves, that she might just as well have asked Beth Marsham to the exhibition because Beth would have loved to have been asked. The only reason she hadn't was that, quite honestly, Beth wasn't the sort of woman Minnie liked to be seen out with. She suspected that was exactly how Anna felt about her. 'Did you use the Petries' carpenter?' she asked, biting her top lip manfully. 'Celia is a very peculiar woman don't you think?'

'What?' said Anna. 'Oh, the shelves. No. We had them made by a sweet man who works for Hippo's mother. The point is that it's very hard to say exactly what you think because they are black. Do you know what I mean?'

Minnie looked from the shelves to Anna and back to the shelves again. 'Pale black,' she agreed, because the shelves were nothing if they weren't varnished wood.

'Pale doesn't make any difference, does it?' Anna said. 'The Dysons are a charming couple but the fact is that their taste is not the same as ours and I think it is grossly unfair of them to inflict theirs on us. Really, isn't it? As a matter of fact, Minnie, I would never have expected it of either of them. They are both intelligent people. Didn't Myra go to Roedean? You'd think they would know that we simply don't paint our houses that pink, not in town, not in the country either if we can help it. We're going to have to persuade them to remove it. For heaven's sake, Mrs Butt, this room has never been cleaner. Can't you do some hoovering upstairs now?'

'But it's too late,' said Minnie, as Mrs Butt without a word or change of expression unplugged the cleaner and heaved it out into the hall. 'The damage is done. They could never get all that paint off even if they wanted to.'

'Paint is paint,' Anna said. 'Anyone can get rid of unwanted paint in an emergency.' Minnie twittered, despite herself, and Anna smiled, pleased that she had made such a successful and relaxed joke about cellulose thinner. It was easy to laugh about the Volvo now that the Parkers were worse off. She had never felt as fond of Jill as she had since the attack on her car.

As far as her standing in the immediate neighbourhood went, Jill was probably lucky that Brigid had gone barmy when she had. To be left nanniless in so dramatic a manner and at such short notice won almost everyone's sympathy, though Beth Marsham's was paltry. She had never cared for the way Jill ordered her children to play in front of their own house and she would rather have liked to hear more of the Putney death, but, like everyone else, she was given little chance. Anna buttonholed her at the greengrocer's shortly after abandoning Minnie.

'I don't know how you feel about it but the Anderson Joneses are appalled and I must say I think it's frightful. Bright pink, for God's sake.'

Beth smiled at Anna and then stared gloomily at the ranks

of strawberries by which they were queuing. She truthfully didn't care much for the pink herself but she was uncomfortable with an alliance which looked decidedly like a conspiracy against a racial minority. 'I know,' she said, 'but honestly, it is their house. I suppose they're entitled to do what they like with it. Colour is a matter of choice, isn't it,' she said.

'Or an accident of birth,' Anna replied tartly.

'Lovely strawberries,' Beth said, tidying the display in embarrassment. She loathed tension.

'Foreign,' said Anna. 'I think they should have consulted us, I really do. They don't have to look at it. Living inside a horrible colour is not the same as having it assail you in your dressing gown.'

It was extremely awkward. Supporter though she was of action in the face of injustice, Beth, in all conscience, couldn't side with the Harveys against the Dysons, no matter how bored she was by her marriage. 'They probably like it,' she murmured.

'That goes without saying,' Anna drawled loudly. 'I'm going to ask Sebastian what to do. An estate agent is bound to know.' Beth moaned quietly. Just thinking of him caused her heart to thud and she felt her left breast throb. She moved away from the strawberries in case her bosom thudded onto the display and dislodged it. Would Sebastian know about pink houses, she wondered. She hoped Anna wouldn't make too taxing a demand of him. She could see his dear troubled features now, spread into that expression of mystification she had come to cherish. 'Do you think that's wise?' she asked. 'I mean it could embarrass him terribly.'

'What?' cried Anna. 'Rubbish. Look at the time. I must fly. But I'll keep you posted because we may all have to tackle the Dysons together.' She swept off to the Volvo which she had left on a yellow line with a lack of concern for fines and the flow of traffic that Beth could only gape at. As she gaped she took an absent-minded step backwards, into a woman who raised her bag to save herself and the strawberries went flying.

Anna's obsession with the Dysons' house diverted everyone from Jill's poisoning because Anna was easily that much grander and that much better looking and glamour or high birth brings so much to the quality of gossip. Everyone found it difficult to match her horror at the pinkness but no one discouraged it because no one wanted to see it extinguished. It was fanned into life at a very small opportunity.

Of course there were other things to talk about like property prices, dyslexia and boredom and there were occasional incidents which put it to the back of everyone's minds for minutes on end. One night, for instance, the street flew *en masse* to its drawing-room windows when the Petries' car howled shrilly for its owners. Tom, conscious of the enormity of the moment and the number of eyes upon him, strolled through his front door smiling in anticipation of an insult. But there was none. The alarm had simply been attention-seeking and, since this is a common fault, no one talked about it at all. They remarked on Tom's extraordinary reading glasses which he had failed to remove and which indicated a lie behind the smile, then they went back to the colour of No. 5.

'It really is so incredibly pink,' Bella volunteered from the doorstep of No. 8. 'Why don't you come in for a minute, Anna? It's cold out here.' This was a tactical error. Anna never failed to give the impression that requests for her company were so persistent and frequent that she never really had time to be anywhere. No one doubted her popularity. She was ravishing, despite the small suggestion of a shadow on her upper lip, she was clever, she was well-connected and she laughed beautifully and often even when nothing much was funny.

She was the sort of woman on whose side everyone wanted to be and in order to be on it and stay on it, friends and acquaintances went to extraordinary lengths. They had done so all of her life, so she had come to expect that her slightest displeasure, once expressed, would be dealt with by whichever dear person would take it upon themself to swat and grind into oblivion the source of her irritation. Anna's sister said Anna was a spoilt brat, but then Anna's sister was plain.

The curious thing about being so popular is that eventually you get up people's noses, a fact which Anna, over twenty-nine years, had entirely failed to grasp. You cannot go through life, or even up and down a small tree-lined terrace, cutting people off in mid-sentence, with the implication that there is an infinitely more fascinating place you should be, without upsetting them. Inevitably, when Anna said, 'Honestly, I'd love to, but I'm three hours late already and I still haven't had a shower,' Bella lost interest in aiding her little cause. Even when she added, 'Pink may be gorgeous in Africa but it's hideous in Battersea,' Bella could only offer a watery grin.

'I'm sorry, Bella, but it lowers the tone,' Anna persisted, unaware of the bruise she had inflicted on Bella's pride. 'I love Myra and Richard, we all do, they are enchanting, but to paint a house any colour when so many of us have gone to the trouble of having our brickwork restored to the colour God intended it to be . . . it's terribly, terribly unfair. Gosh, now you mustn't keep me a minute longer. Hippo will kill me. Bye.'

So while Bella and the rest of the street were enchanted by her outrage and only too happy to offer vocal support, after a while no one on this occasion felt too desperately inclined to help her. The Dysons' house, it was agreed, did look pretty frankly bilious, but there was nothing anyone could do since none of the houses were obliged to conform to standards laid down by a higher authority. Hippo had the nerve to suggest this to his wife who cried, 'Taste, Hippo. That is the higher authority,' to which Hippo had replied sensibly, 'I know.'

Hippo loved his wife. She was beautiful, clean, from a background almost as refined as his own even if she did have a cousin who was in leather goods, she was pleasant company, an efficient organizer and a concerned mother to Olly and Flora. She also understood him. But he didn't want to take on the Dysons because their house was none of his business and Richard was a barrister.

So Anna buzzed around rallying support in every doorway and waited for Myra to appear, chastened, with a few gallons of Tony Matthews' paint remover to clean the pink away. She waited in vain. The sole effect of her campaigning was to fuel talk, and everyone talked not only among themselves but also to Myra. Everyone took it upon themselves to explain the situation to Myra and everyone devoted a lot of time to it when really, they should have been concerning themselves with the celibate dog-lover who could not have been either Tony Matthews or Darrin the paper boy.

They told Myra they didn't mind the pink themselves but poor old Anna was distraught. 'I don't think she has ever been to Africa, either,' Minnie remarked. 'But you know how she is.'

Had Beth realized that Anna was in truth the oppressed minority and not Myra she might have acted differently but she said to Myra, 'You have to understand people like Anna. She is used to having everything exactly as she wants and that includes the taste of her neighbours. In a way, she is the unhappy victim of our class system.'

'I can handle middle-class conventionalism,' Myra had said loudly by the park entrance because she said most things loudly.

'Not middle-class, upper-class. I'm sure Anna would call herself upper-class,' Beth corrected her.

'I'm sure she would,' Myra agreed, and she smiled as only a royal woman can smile when confronted by middle-class conventionalism.

On the day the painters reached the first floor of No. 5 with their brilliant top coat, Jill collided with Myra in the nanny-and-mother's queue at the school door. They laughed shrilly together as mothers do when they have cocked up the run. 'I was sure it was our turn,' Jill squealed.

'No, it was definitely me,' Myra said, 'because if Sarah does it in the morning twice running, I know I have to do the following morning, the next day's late and the next day's lunchtime. Anyway,' she added, 'I've just done hospital visiting and it's always my turn after hospital visiting.' They stared at each other in irritation. 'It's a shame,' Myra said. 'You'll have to do four running now.'

'Oh, it doesn't matter,' Jill sighed. 'It's quite nice to get out. I can't stand the sound of Brigid's breathing upstairs. It's driving me insane. Garden House,' she chipped into a neighbouring conversation. 'And Eaton House.'

Myra said she knew precisely what Jill meant about the

breathing and then for a little while they joined the usual queue conversation about which schools everyone intended sending their children to once they left the Montessori and everyone said how ghastly it was for Susie whose son was going to Dulwich Prep but whose daughter had been refused a place at James Allen and Streatham High but now looked as if she had a place at Putney High which was miles away. The travelling would kill her and there would be no one to share. Then everyone asked each other whether or not they wouldn't be a whole lot better off in the country. The school queue was always threatening to move to the country and bits of it did when the tiny children failed to get into any decent London schools at all.

It was the same conversation every day and anyone could join in at any time perfectly confident of the route it had already taken and was going to take from there on. It was a comforting conversation, proof that everyone's child was brilliant if not a genius and that heads of schools could be asinine in their assessment of children at three-and-a-half or four.

Suddenly Jill said, 'How is the house coming on?' And while one or two tuned out of the school debate to listen, it continued to rage because it was an ever running thing without an end.

Myra moaned. 'You can see for yourself. Slowly. I complained this morning and they said pink was a hard colour to paint. They said they had to stop every few minutes because of the glare.'

Jill laughed. 'They really are the limit.' She took off her Alice Band and twirled it about. 'Seen anything of Anna?' Myra adjusted the silk sweater which was slung across her shoulders.

'I gather she isn't very happy at the moment.'

Jill shrieked. 'Not to put too fine a point on it. She said to me, you know how she is, that pink is fine for Africa but not for SW11. She's funny, she really is. Of course she is fabulous looking but I think she could be even more neurotic than Minnie, whom I adore. Pink is pink, isn't it. Not my favourite colour, admittedly, but it's nothing to make a song and dance about. It makes you wonder what she says to the couples whose marriages she is supposed to save.'

'Commit adultery, probably,' Myra said. They laughed

heartily together, not because they disliked Anna but because there they were, together, in the queue, and there is nothing more binding than a queue. They reached the head of it together and asked for their children. Benjy Parker, spotting his mother, burst into floods of tears and when she held out her arms to him he kicked at them. 'Sarah said I was going home with Myra. Not you. You go away. I'm going home with Myra, Sarah said,' He bellowed. Jill smiled at him and grabbed him firmly by his tiny squashy bicep and it seemed to her as she marched him to her Volvo that life could not get much more grim.

Chapter Eleven

Here she was wrong. Life's capacity for grimness is infinite no matter which side of the river you are on. By the time Myra's painters had packed up and cleared off, leaving a trail of pink paint across the footpath outside No. 5 and a small unpainted patch by its front door, Jill was on the verge of despair. The reputation which seemed to have survived by a narrow squeak, squeaked no more. Putney had talked and Haute Food's business had fallen drastically and dramatically away. One day there had been a steady flow of work, the next day there was none.

'Peacock and Futt have cancelled,' she reported icily to Bella as they poured over the Haute Food paperwork at the kitchen table in No. 9. 'The creature in Chelsea doesn't want her cocktail bits anymore and when I rang Bunyons for Friday's order they said there wasn't one. So there you are. There's nothing. We're finished. We might as well shut up shop and shoot ourselves.'

Bella swallowed to control her nausea. A hideous offal stock on the Aga had clutched at her adenoids and was melting them. She could feel her adenoids melting and the prospect of them running down her nostrils caused her to cling to the table. What she wished more than anything as she gazed past Jill's tormented face, was that Haute Food would melt away. If she shot herself, she mused, it would only be to avoid a lifetime in Jill's kitchen.

'Don't be silly,' she said, 'Why did they say they were cancelling? Did you ask them why?' She could feel herself swooning.

Jill gritted her teeth impatiently. She hated physical weakness and Bella was always so patently feeble. 'I didn't need to ask them. I knew why,' she snapped. 'What I want to know is how they found out.' She looked at Bella suspiciously. 'You haven't told anyone, have you?' Bella rubbed at her ankle distractedly. If you concentrate all your energies onto an untroubled part of the body, you can divert attention from the troubled part and not throw up.

'What do you mean, told anyone? Everyone knows,' she said. Jill slammed her fist angrily onto the table.

'No,' she roared. 'I don't believe it. How do they know? We agreed not to tell anyone, not to discuss it. Are you out of your mind? How could you have told anyone when you knew that our reputation depended on no one knowing. How could you? Oh it's all right for you, I suppose. You've got Marcus with a padlock on his wallet. I need the money.' Her face had reddened remarkably. Bella wondered if she was going to combust, spontaneously. She thought it would be amusing if she did. She sighed when it was clear she wouldn't.

'Calm down, Jill.' she said. 'We are all in the same boat. Who isn't hard up, nowadays? Why do you think we have Griselda? I haven't told anyone. It was Minnie who mentioned it. All she said was it was bad luck about the salmonella. It was perfectly friendly.'

'Friendly?' Jill screeched. 'Minnie is as friendly as a peach stone. She doesn't understand friendly.'

'You are getting it out of proportion,' Bella said. 'She wouldn't do anything malicious. I'm sure she hasn't told anyone else . . . oh, except Beth. I know she told Beth because I was there when she did.'

'Oh Bella,' groaned Jill, collapsing on to the table and sending wads of papers flying. 'All anyone has to do is tell one other person in confidence and everyone knows.' The colour was now draining from her face like sand in an upturned egg-timer. Bella considered peeping to see if her legs were now purple but she was suddenly overtaken by an enormous wave of concern. 'Poor Jill,' she thought. 'I couldn't stand being married to anyone as skinny as Giles, even if he does have wonderful eyes.'

'Look,' she said, taking deep breaths to soothe her adenoids, 'let's tackle this sensibly. No one has accused us officially of having killed Hermione with the *pot-au-feu*, have they, because anyone accusing us officially is breaking the law if they don't have proof. So you must ring everyone back and ask them why they have cancelled and tell them that if it is because of the Putney mishap they might as well know that court proceedings are underway, that we are in no way responsible for it and that anyone who dares suggest we are will be hearing from our solicitors.'

Jill stared at Bella with her pale bulbous eyes, and slowly hope crawled back into her irises. 'That's right,' she agreed. 'You are right. I haven't had a letter from anyone so I must have frightened them all off.' She jumped from her chair and gave the offal a triumphant stir which caused Bella to flee from the room, choking.

As she gasped for fresh air by the front door, Brigid appeared white and trembling at the top of the stairs, deep blue circles scooping chunks from her once rose-coloured cheeks. 'The school run,' she cried wildly. 'The school run. It's our turn for the school run.'

'Go back to bed, Brigid,' Jill called jovially. 'Last time you sent me off I doubled with Myra. Say hello to Bella and pop back to bed. You're looking very much better. Have you finished the mending I gave you?'

'Hello Bella,' Brigid said before turning and retreating obediently to her room.

'You haven't given her work to do, have you?' Bella asked, grinning to prove that she was in charge of her stomach.

'Honestly, Jill!'

Jill smiled sheepishly. 'Not work. Just some mending to keep her occupied. Well, she can't just lie there forever doing nothing, can she?'

Bella was still faintly aghast when she met Anna on her way home a few minutes later. 'Jill is the limit,' she observed in wonderment. 'Brigid should be in the bin, if you ask me. Or in a home for worn-out nannies.' Brain Street's unconscious mind couldn't help slipping in a Freudian manner over nannies when talking to the Harveys but Anna, unaware of her own nanny's treachery, took it all blithely.

'What's happening about that dead woman in Putney?' she asked without interest. 'Jill's not going to be arrested, is she?' Her gaze was fixed on No. 5 as she spoke. Nothing could really distract her from its colour. 'It makes me feel faint,' she declared weakly. 'It must be horrible for you, being pregnant.'

But Bella couldn't be persuaded to conspire. 'Heavens no. They only arrest you after an investigation. It'll probably fade, Anna. I think you're going to have to live with it.'

'I'd rather die,' Anna said.

'Poor Jill,' Bella persevered. 'Word's got out and everyone's cancelling their orders. There's no work lined up at all and she's in a terrible state because they're strapped for cash. Haute Food is all they have and a few miserly legacies.'

'No one's well off these days,' Anna said sourly. 'But she ought to pull herself together. We had to. Look how everyone's forgotten about our car.'

'I know,' Bella lied. 'I haven't thought about it in ages.'

'No one has,' Anna said. 'Except Hippo. Hippo thinks we should find out who is doing it because he says whoever it is should be stopped.'

'The paper boy, do you mean?' Bella asked.

'Of course not the paper boy. I don't know how he came to be involved in the first place. It was a mad idea. Hippo is going to see Giles to see what can be done. Has Jill gone to collect the children?' she asked suddenly. 'It's her turn.'

It was several hours before the three distraught little children who should have come home for lunch were returned to the bosoms of their families. A stray mother from Wandsworth, having obligingly said she would accept responsibility for them when they seemed to have been abandoned at school, had delivered them at the end of her run which had taken in Kensington, Chelsea, Tooting and, someone thought, Bognor. By this time Hippo was palpitating uncomfortably on the old church pew in Giles' study, shocked by the disappearance of his child but perfectly certain that life must go on.

'Their organisation is beyond me,' Giles declared to Hippo when news of their safe arrival drifted up to the loft extension. 'It's quite extraordinary.'

'I keep well out of it,' agreed Hippo. 'They end up with children all over the bloody place. More than once I've looked hard at the child in our garden and thought, "Hullo, that's not Flora." But they seem to work it out in the end.' Giles roared the deep, mellow laughter of a very small man whose trousers have been worn a size too tight all of his life. He loved Hippo and he couldn't find it in his heart to think fondly of many men. They were too successful and too damn young for his liking.

They sipped whisky and stared out from the loft extension across to the Whittakers' where Griselda was rubbing gel into her short black hair. 'Good looking girl, that,' Giles said. 'But vain. She spends hours on her face, scraping at it and what not. I've seen her start on it at ten and still be at it at lunch time.'

'Really?' said Hippo. He no longer had a great deal to say on the subject of youthful females who lived in to help care for the children and Giles, sensing his discomfort, because he could sense things like that being a thriller writer, clapped his hands together efficiently. 'Right then Hippo, let's get on with it. What can I do for you?'

'Yes, right,' Hippo agreed. 'Well it's not so much what you can do for me as what we can do for each other. I don't know if you intended doing anything about this car business but my very strong inclination is that someone should do . . . ah . . . something.'

Giles stared at Hippo with interest, suddenly fascinated by the idea that his books might one day be antiquarian gems and Hippo might be the very man to know, when that time came.

'It seems to me,' Hippo continued, pleased to have Giles' rapt attention, 'that someone has got it in for us and that they are doing their level best to cause us trouble; embarrassment at the very least. But what I've been asking myself is who? I suggested to Jill, she probably told you, that it was Tony Matthews in your case but of course I can't be certain, and as for my case I actually haven't the foggiest idea. I'm pretty sure it wasn't the paper boy, you only have to look at him, not that I'd say so outside these four walls.'

Giles banged his thigh with his hand which landed half on his chair and hurt like mad since his thigh was so astonishingly slim. 'I knew it,' he cried. 'I knew it. One gets a nose for this sort of thing in my business. Christ that hurt!' Tears sprang into his gorgeous green eyes.

Hippo took a sip of whisky. 'Really,' he said. 'I'm sorry. How did you know? I thought the street by and large accepted that it was the paper boy.'

'Oh I think the street did, by and large,' Giles replied, flapping his hand about to ease the sting. 'But the street by and large as you and I know only too well are not likely to think beyond what they are told, are they? They don't have the training.'

'I don't know,' Hippo said doubtfully. 'Tom's a pretty clever chap. And Celia. I'd say Celia was one of the sharpest women I'd ever met.'

'And those breasts,' Giles agreed. 'I've never seen breasts like hers.'

'Not so often, anyway,' said Hippo. He wondered what it was about Giles that caused conversations to stray so wildly away from the point. What it was was the very thing that caused his thrillers not to have a point – simple-mindedness – but Hippo wasn't to know this and as far as he was concerned whatever it was was no reason not to have a good man on your side, especially when he was the only man on your side.

'Quite,' Giles said. 'So what do you want to do about it?'

'What?' said Hippo.

'The car business.'

'Exactly. That's what I am saying. If it wasn't the paper boy, who was it? Who would want to scrawl anything as frankly dangerous on my car and as blatantly provocative as the word "Killers" on yours. I mean it's all very well to say it's the paper boy or Tony Matthews but that's just brushing it under the carpet and whoever this loony is must be stopped before he strikes again.'

Giles narrowed his eyes and took a deep drag on his Disque Bleu. 'So you're coming to me for advice,' he rasped. He couldn't pretend he wasn't chuffed. Not many men his own age rated him as anyone worth consulting, probably, he guessed, because so much time had passed since *Hunk Billet* had sold 100,000 copies. 'You think that between us we might be able to solve the mystery. You have to appreciate, Hippo, that fact is stranger than fiction and that my expertise is fiction. I use my creative faculties to enhance life, if you follow, to colour logic, to dramatize painstaking method, but I have an interest, I'll admit, in challenges of this sort. They appeal to the mathematician in me.'

'And it was your car that was done,' Hippo agreed. 'I thought it made sense for us to pool our information as the two victims. I don't mind telling you about my set-up if you don't mind telling me about yours. It's not something we want the whole of Battersea to be blathering about but if we keep the matter between ourselves and get on with investigating it as discreetly and as intelligently as we can, we could put an end to it all.'

'Great idea, Hippo,' coughed Giles. 'Great idea.' Small tingles of excitement crawled up the flesh inside his pleasantly green striped shirt. He had nothing to lose. Everyone knew he had flattened the whippet but to hear Hippo admit adultery, that would be something. And it might sharpen his wits for *Hunk Billet's Foster Child* which was going so badly. 'You start,' he said.

Hippo leaned across to the small rickety table in the corner of the room and placed his glass on it firmly and squarely. Griselda was examining her armpits intently in the mirror and had apparently found something of astonishing interest in them. 'I know this will go no further,' he sighed. 'The truth is that I was having an affair, a silly business because I am devoted to Anna and the last thing in the world I want is to hurt her, but these things happen. Of course when you are in the thick of it you never imagine you'll get caught. You tell yourself that what they don't know won't hurt them. But there are no guarantees against discovery and I was discovered. It's unnerving not knowing by whom. In fact it's bloody awful, Giles, I don't mind telling you. I must say Anna's being frightfully good about it, bless her, not asking awkward questions or throwing tantrums.'

Giles inhaled and coughed and felt extremely sorry for Hippo. He didn't deserve to suffer so much on Anna's account when the whole street knew that Anna suffered not a jot on his. The difficulty, as far as Giles could perceive a difficulty, was in putting Hippo out of his misery. You didn't put a man out of his misery by telling him that the wife he was so utterly devoted to was no more faithful to their marriage than he was. That was obvious. But Giles prided himself on a degree of subtlety.

'What puzzles me, though, Hippo,' he said casually, 'and it must have puzzled you, is why whoever wrote on your car wrote "Adulterers". "Adulterer –s", meaning more than one.'

'Yes, I know,' said Hippo, flushing gently and flicking imaginary ash from his lap. 'It was Sarah, you see, our nanny. It was Sarah I was having the affair with.'

'Very pretty girl, Sarah,' Giles said. 'I can't say I blame you. She's gorgeous.'

'You think so?' asked Hippo. 'Well she is, of course she is, and a jolly nice girl too but not a patch on Anna.' His tea took this opportunity to explode between his ribs which he clutched in agony. He had eaten the fish fingers prepared for Flora which had been left sadly on the kitchen table while she was trapped on the school run. He had eaten them to quell his concern that she was missing and now he was paying for it.

'I have never been tempted by a nanny,' Giles observed. 'Well, we've only ever had Brigid.'

'How is Brigid?' Hippo enquired, pleased with the side issue while he suppressed an air bubble which was struggling to surface. 'She looked very peculiar when I last saw her.'

'She has always looked peculiar,' Giles assured him. 'Actually I'm not sure how she is. She is behaving very oddly, even for someone confined to bed, but Jill says she will be right as rain in a few days and there's no point in letting her go because it's such a bore finding a replacement.'

'That's exactly what Anna says,' Hippo said. 'It's terribly difficult. Sarah was all for leaving when the car thing blew up and she told Anna she wanted to go home because she was homesick but Anna persuaded her to stay. Flora is attached to her and we haven't had our money's worth for all the driving lessons we paid for. She had over thirty you know.'

'And they're not cheap,' Giles sympathised. 'Right. Let's look at what we have. Someone knows you and Sarah are having an affair and wants to embarrass you by plastering the information all over your Volvo. The same person knows I polished off the whippet and wants to embarrass me by implying, on my Volvo, that I did it deliberately. What does that lead you to think?'

He refuelled his glass from the bottle on the desk and then shoved it towards Hippo who, topping up his own glass, imagined the fish fingers disintegrating in the alcohol and felt comforted. 'What does it lead me to think?' he repeated. 'What do I think? Well, nothing really. What about you?' Giles smiled at him.

'It leads me to think that someone has it in for both of us. What we must each do is write a list of our enemies and see who appears on both lists.' He grabbed for pens and paper. 'Right. Go. People who hate you.' They both sat, poised over the desk. It was hard. Hippo struggled to remember. Enemy. He looked vacantly around the room. Help . . . enemy!

'You know, I don't think I have any. I don't remember falling out with anyone in years,' he said finally.

'Oh come on,' cried Giles who had been scribbling busily. 'What about the cut and thrust of commerce. Surely you've conned a couple of people in your time, given them raw deals, insulted their intelligence.' He drank excitedly. This was wonderful.

'There was an old lady in Chipping Sudbury once. I gave her

next to nothing for a poor Tristram Shandy . . .'

'What was her name?'

'Ah . . . er . . . Brown? No, something like Brown.'

'Green? Grey? Smith?'

'Johnson, I think. That was it, Plott-Johnson. But she died.'

'Then it wasn't her,' Giles said drily.

'Of course not. I can't even begin to think who it might have been. What about you? Who's on your list?' Giles laughed and crumpled his paper before throwing it into his bin. He stubbed out his cigarette before lifting his eyes to look hard into Hippo's. 'Hippo,' he said, 'one of the prices of success is friendship. Your problem is you haven't offended anyone. Mine is counting the number of enemies I've made by being a huge success so young.'

'Well that doesn't get us very far, does it?' murmured Hippo. 'We know hardly any people in common, anyway. What do we have in common at all?'

Giles looked out of the window. Was Hippo being offensive, he asked himself. He could be pretty damned offensive when he wanted to, he was sure of that. All that talk about not having an enemy in the world. He had never heard so much crap.

'I've got it,' Hippo shouted. 'I know what it is. We have our neighbours in common. It's someone in the street. I'd stake my life on it.' Hippo was prepared to stake his life all over the place. Being a man of few convictions he considered his life a small price to pay for those he had.

Giles considered his position. He didn't much care for Hippo reaching the first sensible conclusion of the evening but on the other hand it would be churlish to deny that it looked good. 'Very good, Hippo,' he said. 'Well done. You're absolutely right. It must be someone who lives in Brain Street.'

'It's plain what we have to do,' Hippo said on a wave of inspiration. 'We will have to take it in turns to keep watch. If anyone is watching us, we will spot them. If anyone is going to strike again we can't afford not to be there when they do.'

'Eight hour shifts,' Giles suggested. 'That's what I propose. We will take eight hour shifts to stand guard. And we must not tell a soul. Secrecy is paramount.'

'That goes without saying,' Hippo agreed. They shook hands on it and as they turned to leave the loft extension they waved to Griselda, who had momentarily left off plucking her upper lip to stare out the window.

Chapter Twelve

There is nothing noble about being poor. Suffering does not enhance the spirit. Growing your own herbs isn't all it is cracked up to be. At the age of thirty-six, Beth Marsham discovered that as well as being in love with another woman's husband, she coveted that other woman's goods. She was suddenly tired of being hard up, making do and plodding through life like a well read peasant. She suddenly found it positively ridiculous.

There they were with the smallest mortgage in Brain Street, with nothing on Access, Visa, American Express or Diners, with no Peter Jones or Harrods accounts, without even the tiniest suggestion of an overdraft and they were living like paupers. They were actually better off than their neighbours, who appeared to have means but in fact knew only how to use credit. She decided to rebel. She decided to up the mortgage and knock a few walls down.

The knocking down of walls, as anyone who lives in a Victorian terrace will know, is a most popular pastime, increasing in popularity as opportunities for it decline. No one can resist the chance to convert a two-up-two-down to a one-up-one-down, or in the case of Brain Street, a six-roomed two-storey house into a five-roomed three-storey house. The Marshams were the only owner-occupiers with a loft extension who had every original wall intact. Any wonder Beth cracked.

It was with considerable passion that she announced to her husband, 'I want a knocked-through drawing-room with French windows leading out on to the garden. And I want to knock out the box room to make the bedroom larger because I also want a dressing table.' They were sitting in their pokey living-room listening to Orff's Carmina Burana and drinking elderberry wine. Rob blinked hard to pull his wife into focus. Fermented elderberries play havoc with the eyesight and, he thought for a minute, the hearing.

'What did you say?' he asked. She told him again and they sat together for a little while in silence, as words, concepts, theories, phrases, arguments and a cogent analysis warred with the alcohol that had seeped into Rob's brain. In the end his brain admitted defeat so when he spoke it was from his heart. He stood up and stumbled across the room towards his wife. He crouched at her feet. 'Beth, Beth,' he mumbled, trembling a little. 'What is wrong. Why are you unhappy?'

'Nothing is wrong,' Beth said, 'except this house and my life. I am sick of it. I am sick of being niggardly. We don't have to live meanly. I want to spread out and have more. Why must we scrimp and save when our mortgage is only £10,000 and we have money in the bank? Look at this room! Just look at it! No one has browns in their living-room anymore. No one has beaded cushions. This room has looked the same for fourteen years and I can't stand it. I want some space. I want some light. I want some curtains from Osgood and Little.'

'You can have anything you want, Beth,' Rob said. 'I love you and I will give you anything you want. But are you sure that that is what you want?'

'Of course I'm sure,' Beth said. 'Osgood and Little. They are in the King's Road. Or Designer's Guild. I don't really care which.'

'You know that's not what I meant.' Rob tried to take her hands in his but she pulled away. 'You know what we have always said about ownership and possessions for their own sake. You know what we think about acquisitiveness.' His brain hoped it would remember if she turned out to have forgotten.

'What is the point?' Beth said. 'I can't see anything wrong with making your home as nice as you can. I can't see anything wrong with spending money on creature comforts and that is what I want to do.'

'Oh Beth,' he gasped sadly. 'Don't think I haven't seen your misery. I know you are sad. I've watched your sadness but you won't let me help you. You must know how powerless I feel. I can't reach you anymore. I don't know how to reach you anymore. And I want to. I want to more than anything.' He was becoming maudlin.

'Oh really,' Beth said impatiently. 'You have reached me. You stood up, you crossed the room, and here you are, cutting off the circulation in my left thigh.'

Rob sank back on his heels, rebuked and rejected. He wondered if this was what it was like to lose a wife in a gardening accident; without warning, in unsuspicious circumstances. His whole body was awash with grief and elderberry wine. His sadness was beyond expression. In any case, he had no one to express it to, since Beth had been the receptacle of his every important thought and emotion from the very day he met her.

'You know money means nothing to me,' he said. 'You must do as you like.' He stood up, sadly fingered the turquoise cushion they had chosen together so long ago in Portobello Road, ran his hand along the dirt brown walls and left the room to spend the night in a sleeping-bag on the box room floor. He had been torn asunder.

Beth sat where he had left her and allowed an enormous gasp of relief to escape from her body, which collapsed with triumph. She had done it. She had said it. There would be no argument. She would raise the mortgage and buy a pastel drawing room with some doors to the garden and she would move the rubbish bins. She had taken a gigantic step forward.

Once she might have run after her husband and thrown her arms about his shoulders and cried that of course they stood as one against the rampant tide of materialism in Battersea. But now, she didn't. She had had enough articulate love scenes to last a life time, enough analysing of the intricacies of their relationship and examination of their relationship as it flourished and grew in a changing world. All she longed for was a man with only a small notion of marital dynamics who would accept her without torment. She wanted a man whose generosity of spirit streched beyond mankind in general to touch her specifically, and materially, who saw no wrong in spending money on frivolities. She longed for Sebastian Anderson Jones.

Sebastian had no idea that he was the object of Beth's adoration and base desire and he would have been frightfully shocked had anyone suggested it to him. Rob had no idea that his wife craved Sebastian, though he was confident she no longer craved him. Had he known that his relentlessly honourable view of his place in the world was at the bottom of her alienation he might have searched his conscience for a decent compromise, but he didn't. He remained hurt and puzzled and bewildered by ideas that had never had any part in his view of survival. He had never heard of Osgood and Little. About the only thing he no longer gave a second thought to was his desecration of the Parkers' rear windscreen.

In this, as in most things, he was just about the only person in Brain Street not to. He was the only one who knew nothing of a stiff in Putney called Hermione, who in life had been a greedy woman and who in death was gobbling up Jill Parker's good name with the same vigour she might have applied to a *fillet mignon*. He knew nothing of the Environmental Health Officer called Mr Fender who had written to Jill on the very day she had declared to Bella that she seemed to have frightened everyone off. And he was also among the very few who didn't look anxiously at his watch in the middle of the morning appointed for Mr Fender's inspection and wonder what was going on.

The rest of the street was on the tenterest of hooks. Myra telephoned Celia to ask with delight whether he was an O. Fender or a D. Fender, and the minute he arrived in his small white van, Minnie was seen to hurry along to Beth's and Sarah to Griselda's. They were seen by Giles who was aloof from it all, on watch in his loft extension, vigilantly noting every coming and every going. 'Man from health department arrives at No. 9,' he wrote. 'M.A.J. to B.M. and S. to G. Parker, Petrie and Whittaker Volvos in situ.'

Miss Smith was the only obvious face at a window but there were others. No one, however, apart from Jill, could hear what it was that Mr Fender was saying as he stood on the doorstep. 'We have had a complaint from Putney,' he was saying, 'about a death which could be related to food which I understand was prepared on these premises though devoured elsewhere. *Pot-au-feu*, I understand.'

Jill smiled at him brilliantly, but regally. She had decided that, in a situation so delicate, everyone would be most comfortable if she adopted the persona of a war widow whose husband had been very close to the Queen. This was sad but dignified, vulnerable but with connections. She didn't spell it out of course. She simply indicated as much, with inflexions and vowel sounds. She showed Mr Fender the Aga.

'This was where I simmered the *pot-au-feu*'—she used her very best French accent on the 'feu', employing her top lip to its full effect—'for thirty-six hours. Here is my list of ingredients.' It was a modified list containing no reference to prawns' heads or rolled oats because Jill had persuaded herself that to bore the man with minute detail would be the very worst mistake she could make.

Mr Fender thanked her and took the list to check it against the ingredients found in the deceased's intestines. Then he took swabs from work surfaces, drains, pots and pans, cutlery, the larder and the extractor hood. He took swabs from every nook and cranny and every conceivably contaminated utensil and finally he walked in silence to the kitchen sink where he washed his hands. 'That is all,' he said. 'You will be hearing from us. Thank you for your co-operation.' He wiped his hands on a small white towel which he took from his attaché case. 'You can't be too careful,' he explained.

'Of course not,' Jill agreed, discreetly turning her head to use some Gold Spot. 'It has been my pleasure.' (Royal connections.) 'I have always done my very best.' (War widow.) The minute he had left she rushed to her bureau in the drawing-room to bang out a swift note before any further developments could divert her from the course of her outrage. She informed Mrs Henderson Smyth that she had just given the fullest co-operation to the Environmental Health Officer, a perfectly sweet and reassuring man, and that Mrs Henderson Smyth could expect to hear from her solicitor the minute Mr Fender's report cleared her name. She intended to sue Mrs Henderson Smyth for loss of trade and reputation and she would bring an action not only for defamation but for trade slander, all of which terms she had looked up in a book from the library and all of which she considered suitably terrifying.

'There,' she said when she had finished. She stamped and sealed the envelope and in order to share her sense of accomplishment she bawled, 'Giles! Giles!' to her husband, who heard her but remained faithfully at his watch, fascinated by the way Brain Street residents could on occasion move like ants from house to house lugging giant bits of information behind them. As Mr Fender had emerged, so had Minnie and Beth carrying swatches of material to camouflage their curiosity, and so had Myra who had hurried across the road, consulted with them briefly, then dived into the Mercedes to disappear with a jolly wave.

'Giles,' Jill declared as she staggered through his study door huffing and puffing, 'the wretched man has finally . . . did you see him?'

'Looked like a rat,' Giles said, not turning to her but continuing to gaze determinedly on to the small stretch of road beneath. 'What did he say?'

'He didn't say anything. He said there had been a complaint which he was investigating and that you couldn't be too careful. I thought I handled him rather well. What are you looking at?' She heaved herself out of the chair she had fallen into to recover her breath and she crossed the room to him and slid a fulsome arm around his neat little waist.

'I am not looking at anything,' he told her. 'I am thinking.'

'Oh good,' she enthused. 'Going well is it? Gosh look at that, Tony Matthews going into the Dysons. What on earth could he want? He looks very bad-tempered. Do you think he is going to have a go about the pink?'

'He will find Richard at home but Myra out,' Giles reported.

'Richard came home about an hour ago. Work must be a bit slow, don't you think, if he comes home in the middle of the day? He doesn't usually come home for lunch.'

'They might have to sell an *object*,' Jill giggled. 'Speaking of lunch, I have some rabbit in raspberry sauce I can easily reheat. Do you want some?'

Giles at last turned his hungry little face towards his wife and said, 'Yum. Actually I won't come down today if you don't mind. It's going on so well I'll stay up here and work on. You couldn't bring me some up on a tray could you?'

'Of course I could,' Jill said. 'I'll bring up a cosy little lunch for both of us.'

'That would be lovely,' Giles said with his eyes now firmly fixed back at the window. 'But I think I had better be by myself while I'm ruminating. I'm sure I'd find your presence distracting. You understand, don't you?' and Jill said she did. And she believed she did, sort of. She lolloped back down to the kitchen, joyful to think that Hunk Billet seemed finally to have chiselled his way out from under Giles' block but disappointed because she wanted someone to talk to after her ordeal with Mr Fender and she was uneasy that though Giles had said he was working, and she wanted to believe he was working, she somehow couldn't bring herself to imagine he was achieving a lot at the window. She decided to take some rabbit into Brigid's room and eat with her. Brigid, she knew, would be gripped and overawed by the letter she had just composed to Mrs Henderson Smyth.

Tony Matthews had marched into No. 5 by appointment, and Richard had come home especially to see him when he might well have had a good lunch somewhere with Bottomley or Cholmondeley from Chambers. He had come home, despite the Matthewses appalling clothesline, because he was a kind and caring man.

'What precisely can I do to help you?' he said when Tony was perched on the edge of the Chesterfield and they had asked after each other's wives.

'It's advice I want mainly,' Tony said. 'About my dog's death. I want to be compensated for it.'

'Right,' said Richard smoothly. 'It's a simple enough

procedure. All we need do is contact the Parkers' insurers. Car insurance covers this sort of thing. It's perfectly straightforward. How much did you pay for Putney?' The Harveys who had talked most freely of the accident and its aftermath to their neighbours genuinely believed the dog to be called Putney and so now everyone did, except the bereaved owners.

'Putney?' said Tony. 'Do you mean Tango?'

'I don't know,' said Richard. 'Do I mean Tango?'

'I am talking about my dog,' Tony said carefully. 'Are you talking about the place down from Wandsworth, or what?'

'We are both talking about your dog,' Richard smiled. He was used to complications of this sort. Who isn't, in the law? 'How much did you pay for him?'

'Sixty pounds, but that isn't the point, is it?' Tony said. 'What he was worth to me can't be valued just like that, can it? I want the Parkers to pay for what they did to him. I don't want my money back. I want justice.' His right foot, swathed in impeccably shiny leather because he had changed into a smart suit for the visit, waggled energetically at the end of his neatly crossed leg.

'I see,' said Richard. 'I quite understand of course. But we truly ought to be realistic about it. In civil matters the law isn't very good at revenge.'

'I didn't say revenge, Richard,' Tony interrupted politely. 'I said justice.'

'Quite,' said Richard. 'I am absolutely certain that Giles will admit liability and that his insurers will be only too happy to cough up. I do think they are our best bet. I will happily do the paper work for you. How does that sound?

Tony's foot sped up like a clockwork key tightly wound, revving him up to find words to describe exactly how it sounded to him. 'Thank you Richard. It sounds inadequate.' he said. 'Why should he get away with causing my dog pain and suffering and me pain and suffering? Tango might only have been a dog but he must have had some rights.'

Richard sighed, then he smiled. 'The fact is, Tony, it was an accident,' he said. 'Now if it hadn't been, if Giles had done it deliberately, we might have had grounds for bringing a public prosecution, but that can cost a thousand pounds and, at the end of it, all you would have would be the satisfaction of hearing that he was guilty, or the frustration of hearing he wasn't. There would be no compensation. You could of course bring a civil action for compensation but that can also cost a thousand pounds and there are no guarantees of what you would get. But if we deal with it through the insurers there are no risks.' It was perfectly simple as far as he was concerned.

'He hated that dog,' Tony said. 'Miss Smith upstairs told Valerie. She said Giles Parker hated the dog. Everyone knew he hated the dog. I'm sorry, Richard. Insurance is not good enough.' Richard scratched his forehead and regretted his generosity. He was a criminal lawyer. He should have said straight away that dead dogs weren't his pigeon.

'Hate is an awfully strong word,' he mused. 'It may be perfectly true that Giles isn't fond of animals but I'm certain he wouldn't deliberately go out of his way to kill one.'

'He didn't have to go out of his way. He just had to reverse quickly.'

'Precisely,' said Richard. 'It happened in the course of a recognizably everyday action. Now had he dragged Putney by the throat and tied him to the road and reversed over him, we might have had a case. But it's terribly tricky to prove intent. Even had he not stopped when he had the opportunity, and even had he in a split second formed the intent to kill the dog, to prove it beyond reasonable doubt would be impossible.'

'I don't know what you're talking about,' Tony said. 'But if I can take Parker to court to prove he killed my dog and that he meant to, I will.' He hopped up and strode to the door. Richard also hopped up. 'Thank you for your time,' Tony said. 'You have been more than helpful.'

'I haven't been at all helpful if you are going to act against my advice. I can't tell you how strongly I feel that the best course would be the one I suggested. You stand to lose a lot of money by taking the other.'

'I appreciate your concern,' Tony said. 'But I think the best course of action is my concern. I am more than grateful that you have explained the alternatives to me.'

Richard shrugged miserably. 'I don't suppose you'd consider

moving your clothesline to the other side of the garden, would you?'

'The clothesline is Valerie's affair,' Tony said. Then he shook Richard's hand and left, feeling that The System was conspiring to squash Tango's memory even as it had squashed his body.

He marched home with his eyes fastened on his shiny black feet, transfixed by the prospect of litigation. He didn't know whether Giles had intended to kill Tango but he had been wounded by the cold-blooded way in which he had done it. He had five thousand pounds in the Abbey National which he had intended for the down payment on a house, but he would now use it to buy justice for his beloved pet. He didn't see Minnie, let alone hear her enquire after his health. He almost leapt out of his shoes when she tapped him on the shoulder and chirped, 'If you want to buy another dog I know a wonderful bitch who will produce the most sensational King Charles puppies in a matter of weeks.'

'Do you?' he said. 'I can't imagine getting another dog for a very long time. Certainly not while poor Tango is before the courts.' He scarcely stopped to utter the words. He left Minnie standing, wondering whether the dog was to be buried at Wimbledon. 'Fancy burying a dog called Putney at Wimbledon,' she said to herself. She looked around for someone to giggle with, but there was no one. Giles in his loft extension had fallen to the floor so that she wouldn't see him.

Chapter Thirteen

Miss Smith was intrigued by the new development over the road. She was fascinated by the appearance of Hippo Harvey at his curtains for eight hours at a stretch, his disappearance for eight hours and then his punctual reappearance. Situated as she was a floor below the Parkers' loft extension and on the same side of the road, she was in no position to see that when Hippo disappeared, Giles appeared like a small misshapen cuckoo. Had she been able to, she might not have leapt to the conclusion she did, which was that Hippo was mounting guard in the loft extension to catch Rupert Fox whom she knew for a fact to be up to no good.

It was a reasonable conclusion for one with so little information at her fingertips but it only partially satisfied her. She couldn't fathom why Hippo watched for only eight hours at a time and why it was sometimes through the night, when she had rarely known Rupert to appear after midnight, or even disappear. Nor could she fathom why, to begin with, Hippo had made notes and now no longer did. She felt as if she had missed several vital episodes in the Brain Street saga and she couldn't stand it. Since she could not insist on a replay she would have to take to the streets in order to catch up. She decided to hang round the gate of No. 6 and get herself invited in.

Hippo knew that Miss Smith had him under surveillance. He couldn't fail to when she insisted on saluting him with her binoculars as he took up his position and waved to him constantly when something amused her. It was most disconcerting. But what could he do? There was nowhere else that offered a better view of the street than the window in the loft extension and there was no other room in the house to which he could retreat for such long hours without causing alarm.

By the third day he was sick to death of watching and being watched and he was totally exhausted. He could barely keep his eyes open when so little happened to startle them into wakefulness. Unlike Miss Smith, he failed to be agog at the number of houses the postman called at or the frank exchanges between mothers and nannies that sent her into convulsions. Occasionally his heart stopped if a Webbs' truck tried to pass a Volvo in a part of the street where cars were parked on either side. But the manoeuvring of cars was his only source of tension. He had abandoned the diary he started on his first watch because as far as he could see it served no other purpose than to have him retrieve it every ten minutes when it fell to the ground as he dozed off. The entries he made did nothing to reveal the phantom accuser: 'Marsham child comes home from school. Minnie waters tree. Anna hits curb when parking. Minnie talks to tree. Beth Marsham goes out on bike. Beth Marsham comes back on bike. Tyre flat. Minnie kicks honeysuckle. Must be mad.' Where did it get him?

It all sounded so paltry when he reported it to Giles. Their arrangement involved a phone call at the end of each shift which ensured that the new watch was being taken up and gave them a chance to discuss any possibilities raised by observations on the previous watch. But no possibilities had been raised. Everything from their loft extensions looked utterly harmless, peaceful and ordinary. No one did anything untoward at all.

Of all the comings and goings on Brain Street, Hippo enjoyed Miss Smith's best. For a start it meant that her beady eyes would be off him for a while at least. And it was quite something to see an aged amputee in action, especially one with the vigour and skill of Miss Smith. He liked the way she lashed out at the ambulanceman with her crutches and insisted on swinging herself up into the ambulance without their help.

He had been on watch for three hours into his fourth shift when she appeared at the door of No. 3 with a large canvas bag which she arranged more comfortably across her body before heading off down the street. He assumed she was going to the park to feed the ducks and he was touched. He watched in admiration as she scooted along with an easy, graceful rhythm and he decided to be kind to her next time he was unavoidably in her presence. He caught sight of Sarah turning into Brain Street in their little Citroen at about the same time Miss Smith did, and he was astonished at the speed with which the old lady turned to sail back down the road to accost her.

By the time Sarah had found somewhere to park in Dishwater Terrace, having driven into Brain Street and hastily out again, Miss Smith was stamping her crutch impatiently and calling down the street to her, 'Cooee, cooee. I've got something for the little one. What's her name again?'

There was no escape for Sarah. That Miss Smith was addressing her couldn't have been more obvious. Hippo grinned as panic gripped Sarah's sweetly regular features and a scream of protest formed on her cherry lips. She took a quick peek over her shoulder, toying, he knew, with the idea of running back into Dishwater Terrace, but the girl had a conscience and, he suspected, had probably not had any breakfast.

'Morning Miss Smith,' she said. 'You're looking very perky today.'

'What do you mean, perky?' Miss Smith bawled. 'I'm not dying if that's what you think. I'm not on my last leg.' She chortled squeakily. 'I've got something for that Flora,' she patted the large canvas bag. 'She's not home, is she?'

'What a shame,' Sarah sighed. 'Oh what a shame. No she's at school and won't be home all day I'm afraid. She's an awfully busy little girl. It's very hard to tell when she will be in, if ever. You know how it is.'

'No, I don't,' Miss Smith grumbled. 'No one asks me out.

Can I come in and leave these for her?' She produced a ghastly bag of sweets and a faded colouring book from her satchel.

Sarah said, 'Why don't you let me take them from you, now? That will save you the bother of coming in.'

'It's no bother,' Miss Smith insisted. 'I could do with a cup of tea if you're making one. No, I don't get asked out much anymore. I think it's because of this.' She pointed to where her stump must have been under her long grey skirt. 'I think it makes people sick.'

'Of course it doesn't,' Sarah said urgently. 'Of course it doesn't. Do come in and have a cup of tea. You can talk to me while I make a cake. You don't mind the noise of an electric mixer, do you?' Hippo heard every word of this conversation and was entranced by it. He was delighted to have Miss Smith sitting in his kitchen while he was locked away upstairs. He adored the way she had manipulated poor Sarah and his mouth watered a little at the pretty way in which she had capitulated.

Miss Smith wasted very little time in coming to the point. Once she had handed over the gifts and Sarah had thanked her and agreed that Flora would be mad about them even though she wasn't allowed sweets she said, 'What's Mr Thingummy up to upstairs? What's he doing, looking out of the window all day and all night?'

Sarah had been about to turn on the Magimix to drown the conversation but she hesitated. 'What do you mean?' she said. 'Mr Harvey is very busy at the moment, stock-taking.'

'Stock-taking my foot!' Miss Smith cried. 'He's looking out the window. I've been watching him. That's all he's done all week. Who's he looking for, eh? That dark fellow, is it? He hasn't been sniffing around here lately though, has he?'

Sarah was, by most people's standards, a little dim, yet even she had no trouble recognizing Miss Smith's allusion to Rupert Fox. 'If you mean Mr Fox,' she said, 'he is in Hamburg. He will be in Hamburg for a month on business. You can hardly call what he does around here sniffing, Miss Smith, because he is Mr Harvey's partner.'

This explanation made Miss Smith laugh heartily and Sarah flush. 'You know what I mean. What's he up to?' Miss Smith winked to encourage Sarah. 'Looking out of the window, then nodding off, going away then coming back. He's there for hours. What do you think it is?'

'I really don't know, Miss Smith,' Sarah said. 'It really isn't any of my business what he does up there.' This made Miss Smith laugh even more uproariously and Sarah colour even more deeply. It was too terrible. 'He's probably thinking. I know he has a lot on his mind at the moment.'

'Of course he has,' Miss Smith agreed. She tapped her crutch thoughtfully. 'This tea's cold,' she said. 'I'm going home.' She was a woman who knew when she was about to overstay her welcome and when a supply of information was exhausted. 'Say cheerio to the little one for me,' she called as she swung through the door.

Hippo saw her go and waved uncertainly in response to her breezy greeting from the pavement. Miss Smith ascended her stairs not any less puzzled but convinced that whatever Hippo was doing he was doing in secret and she rejoiced. She could stand the suspense of not knowing. She would revel in it.

Sarah, on the other hand, could not. The minute Miss Smith left, she raced up to the loft and entered the office without knocking to find Hippo staring sheepishly after the elderly disabled pensioner. He didn't even hear her come in and noticed her only when she tripped over the futon.

'For God's sake, Sarah,' he shouted. 'Knock before you come in. You frightened the life out of me.' They had barely spoken since she had refused to clean 'Adulterers!' from the car. Sarah had decided to stay on for the reasons which had nothing to do with him and was now pretending she never had had anything to do with him. It worked extremely well.

'I'm sorry,' she said. 'I thought you might like to know that Miss Smith called in to ask what you were doing watching out of the window all day. She think's you're looking for Rupert but I told her he was in Hamburg.

'Silly old thing,' Hippo laughed. 'She's a bit batty. Why on earth would I be watching for Rupert? I come over here and look out of the window to give myself a break from stock-taking. What did you tell her?'

'Nothing,' said Sarah. 'What is there to tell?'

'Quite,' said Hippo. Sarah looked at him and she looked at the shelves which offered to the naked eye not the barest suggestion of stock-taking. 'Anna home?' Hippo asked her.

'No,' she said crisply. 'I'll leave you to it then.' Hippo sighed at her departing back and remembered how pleasant it had been when they had been on closer terms but then he looked out of the window and reminded himself where it had got him: on eight hour shifts of unbearable tedium.

At the Parker house Giles' extraordinary new schedule had not gone unnoticed either. Jill explained it as inspiration to Mrs Butt and to the children and to Brigid, whose mind was still inclined to wander no matter how fully Jill tried to occupy it with small chores. 'The writer's muse is an astonishing thing,' Jill said. But everyone was struck by the amazing regularity with which inspiration struck. And it didn't really account for the phonecalls he made or received at the beginning or end of each burst. 'Who was that?' she asked him every so often.

'Who?' he repeatedly replied. 'Oh, that! The library.' She received the information without a murmur because although it insulted her intelligence, he was funny about anyone querying his word. Brigid, in a kind of delerium, asked what library was open at midnight and was informed shortly that if Giles said it was the library, it was the library.

The calls were not properly accounted for until Sarah and Griselda visited Brigid sometime during the fourth day of the vigil and were staggered to find her looking so exhausted. 'It's not so much the work,' Brigid explained as she picked up pieces of jig-saw Amanda had scattered around her room, 'it's these phonecalls in the night. I can't sleep for Giles' inspiration.' And she told Sarah and Griselda about the regular bouts of genius which were throwing the household into chaos and disturbing her rest.

'But I 'ave seen 'im,' Griselda said in amazement. 'All 'e 's doing is looking up and down the road. All day long 'e 's looking. For hours and hours. I go away and 'e 's there, I come back and there'e is still.'

'No,' Sarah cried. 'So is Hippo. Miss Smith has seen him. And come to think of it, he has been getting calls in the middle of the night as well.' The girls all hooted together in amazement until Brigid clutched her head.

'What on earth do you think they are up to?' she asked anxiously.

'I will ask Minnie,' Sarah promised and she did, that very afternoon.

Minnie was fascinated but dumbfounded. She couldn't think of a single sensible explanation, other than that they were waiting for someone. She asked Beth who had called by with the dearest little jumper, which Rose had worn as a baby. It was very nearly good as new. 'You can hardly see the stain, can you Sarah?' Minnie gushed. 'What do you think, Beth? Why do you think Giles and Hippo are watching the street day and night?'

Beth, who was wearing lipstick and a small amount of mascara, suggested they ask Sebastian whom she could hear limping about the kitchen. He was bound to know, she thought.

'Don't be silly,' Minnie shrieked. 'Sebastian never knows anything. Darling? Darling, come in here. We have a problem for you to solve.' She failed to notice the glow that rose on Beth's pale face or the eager expression that stole into her eyes. She didn't even notice that Beth tightened her stomach muscles, moistened her lips and regretted her stretch marks.

Sebastian looked devastating, Beth thought, in his cream cricketing sweater and clear headboy complexion. 'What?' he said divinely. 'Hullo, Beth. Hullo, Sarah.' He kissed Sarah and he smiled at Beth. For one heady moment she thought he might kiss her too, since his mouth was in line with hers and to do so would only have involved him lurching a little to the left. But a kiss is a kiss and there are those you kiss and those you don't and Beth was among those you don't, even if she wasn't a nanny. She unfolded her lips quickly in case a tiny pucker had given her away.

'Giles and Hippo,' Minnie announced, 'have been seen standing at the windows of their loft extensions for hours on end taking it in turns to watch the street. What do you make of that?'

'How do you know?' Sebastian said, plonking himself painfully onto the sofa next to Sarah. His leg was playing him up terribly and he had it tightly strapped. He was contemplating a calliper.

'Miss Smith has been watching Hippo and Griselda has seen Giles. They just stand there, staring down on to the road. And Sarah and Brigid say they have both been locking themselves upstairs and not coming down all day and sometimes all night.'

Sebastian twiddled with his ear. 'Who is Griselda?' he asked.

Minnie groaned. 'What did I tell you? Griselda is at the Whittakers. The au pair.' Beth's heart went out to him as he struggled to marshal an opinion. She wanted to hug him and soothe him. She wanted to kiss his eyes and his lips and to tell him not to fret.

'What do you make of it, Beth?' he asked suddenly. The shock of the appeal immediately drained her mouth of moisture and her tongue seemed to cling to her palate. She feared for a minute that it might remain there for ever, glued by panic, and that she might never be able to speak again. Yet she knew he needed her, that he didn't have a clue why Giles and Hippo should be behaving so oddly, and that Sarah and Minnie were waiting for him to pass judgement. She could see the sneer of impatience that curled up under Minnie's nose.

'Gathering evidence,' she finally managed to say. 'They must be, mustn't they. I can't imagine that either of them would be likely to sit back and have their cars vandalized and then do nothing about it, can you? I think they are gathering evidence and when they have enough, they will probably act.' She smiled. 'Don't you think?' But Sebastian had grown pale and his muscles taut and he was gazing at her in horror.

'I think you have it in one,' he said.

Minnie shrieked. 'You're right. Vigilantes. I bet you are right. God, it's a frightful cheek though, spying on us and not saying anything.'

'I don't suppose they are spying on us in particular,' Beth said quietly, appalled at the effect her surmise had had on her beloved and anxious to recover his approval. 'Not us. They are probably just watching movement in the street to see who goes where and when. It's a jolly good thing really, because it protects the rest of us.'

'Though not you, exactly dear,' Minnie said, 'because you don't have a car, do you?'

'It protects her bike, Min,' Sebastian cut in, aware as an estate agent that remarks like that could be hurtful and damaging. 'Someone could paint all over Rob's bike.'

'It isn't the same thing, though,' Minnie persisted, cross with her husband for taking sides against her. 'I mean we are shortly to have two cars so it is going to affect us more. You can't argue with that.' Her eyes hardened as a notion formed in them. 'I think you should start watching too. You should go and see Giles and Hippo, well, forget Giles, and tell him that as it affects all of us we all ought to watch. They will appreciate it. It will make things easier for them.'

'I'm sure that's right,' Sarah said. 'Hippo is awfully tired because he is up all day and all night. He isn't making any headway with the stock-taking at all.' Sebastian looked to Beth.

'What do you think?' It was plain to him that she was the only woman in the room he could trust.

'It's up to you,' she said gently. 'They may not want any help. It may be one of those matters best handled by as few people as possible.' He smiled with relief.

'That's right,' he said. 'The more people you have watching, Minnie, the fewer people there are to watch.'

'Don't be so wet,' Minnie squeaked. 'You ought to be involved. Why should Hippo and Giles take over a matter that is important to the whole street?'

'Because Hippo and Giles are the only residents whose cars have been vandalized,' Beth said patiently. Minnie could be so obtuse.

'You only say that because you don't drive anything of any value. This is the honeysuckle all over again. Sebastian just can't stand to get involved in anything awkward or dangerous.' She urged herself to her feet and tottered angrily from the room, leaving Sarah to make her excuses and Sebastian and Beth to stare dolefully into each other's eyes. Sebastian was startled by what he saw, startled and frightened. It was so unfamiliar. He looked away immediately.

'It's the pregnancy,' Beth remarked kindly. 'It can make a woman tense and nervous.'

'It can make a husband tense and nervous as well,' he murmured. 'I have had a stiff neck for the last three months and with this damn leg. I feel like a . . . a . . . I don't know what I feel like. Actually, I feel like an R.S.J.'

Beth tutted sympathetically. 'Would you like me to massage your neck?' she asked, blushing profoundly. She had never been so foward. 'I did a course once. It does help you know.' Sebastian cleared his throat at the prospect. Innocent though it sounded, and would certainly be in his own drawing-room with his wife only a step away in her boudoir sulking, he sensed danger. He couldn't understand it. Beth had never felt dangerous before.

'I'm sure it does,' he said. 'But no thanks. I don't really like that sort of thing much. I'd better go and apologize to Minnie.' So Beth went home covered in confusion and Giles, spotting her, wondered if she was choking on something.

Chapter Fourteen

In view of his intransigence over the matter of the clothesline Richard Dyson felt no compunction to treat Tony Matthews' intention to sue the Parkers as a matter of confidence. Not at all. Seeing Giles staring zombie-like from his loft extension, towards the end of his fifth shift, he decided he must not let the matter slip.

'Hullo,' he called up. 'Hullo.' Giles, however, uneasy about conversing with anyone from his watching position, gave only a curt wave back, then he looked away in order to appear distracted. Richard turned into the gateway at No. 9 anyway and, despite the fumes of pickling strawberries which seeped from under the door, he rang the bell.

'Just passing, Jill,' he said, wiping at his eyes which were suddenly streaming. 'and I saw Giles at the window. There's a matter I rather want to discuss with him, oh heavens, excuse me!' He sneezed repulsively and Jill took a step back.

'Richard,' she cried. 'How lovely, come in.' He was the only blackish man she knew to speak to and though she had often remarked both to Bella and Anna that you didn't notice his colour, did you, when he was so, well, English, she frankly couldn't help it. It always made her overenthusiastic. And she was especially keen today because she was feeling desperate and rejected. She had no work, no obvious nanny, she was being investigated for manslaughter and her husband had fled to his loft.

'Come in, come in. I'll get some tea,' she cried. 'Giles,' she bawled up the stairs. 'Giles.' Brigid rushed out onto the landing, fluttering nervously.

'Do you want me, Jill? I was just having a sleep. I'll get on with the ironing. Sorry.'

Jill grinned at Richard. 'Go back to sleep, Brigid. I'm not calling you every time I raise my voice. Truly! What will Mr Dyson think? Come on up, Richard. Giles is obviously engrossed in his typewriter.'

Giles heard them coming and cursed. He didn't know what to do. To insist on staying at the window while he spoke to them would look ridiculous. To sit at his desk would mean deserting his post and to desert it even briefly would make a nonsense of the whole operation. To tell them to go away would not only be rude, it would make them suspicious and suspicion was something he and Hippo were determined to avoid. It was bad enough having to put up with Griselda's funny looks without the whole street wondering what on earth he was up to.

As he listened to Jill rumbling up the stairs his eyes darted frantically around his study, then with less than a second to spare, he was saved by a burst of quite genuine inspiration. He took from his filing cabinet an old shaving mirror which he placed strategically on his desk so that a reasonable view of Brain Street was possible if he sat at his typewriter. With the judicious use of restless pacing, he decided, he could get away with it, provided they didn't stay long.

'Knock knock,' Jill piped as she swanned in. 'I've brought you up a visitor. Now who is for tea?'

'Not for me,' Giles said abruptly. 'I'm rather involved at the moment. Nice to see you Richard. Anything I can do for you?' Richard recognised the brush-off immediately and wondered why he had bothered. He owed nothing to the Parkers.

'I just thought you would like to know . . . no, no tea for me either, thank you Jill . . . Tony Matthews intends to sue you for killing his dog.'

'What?' said Giles. 'What do you mean, sue? We've told him to claim through our insurers.'

'So have I,' Richard said. 'I've advised him most strongly. But he doesn't seem to think that will serve justice. He wants to go to court. I don't think he knows what he wants to achieve, but it's something dire, I'm afraid.'

'The turd,' Jill cried passionately. 'I'm sorry, but the turd. When I think how patient we have been. We didn't lift a finger when he painted all over our car, causing us considerable distress I may say. And look at the money we lavished on his animal. It had the very best vet money could buy. I simply don't believe it.'

'Quite,' said Richard. 'Actually I don't think he did paint on your car Jill. He isn't the type. But I take your point.'

Giles jumped up and strode up and down by his window in agitation, shooting dark looks at the pavement. The coast looked relatively clear apart from a Marsham or two listlessly kicking a ball outside No. 2.

'Unfortunately,' Richard continued, 'he has this extraordinary idea that Giles ran the dog down deliberately. At least I think he does. It is hard to tell. He stands no chance of proving it so you have nothing really to worry about, but I thought you should be warned. Things like this can become so unpleasant.' This speech had taken some time to enunciate with Richard's customary precision and Giles realized he couldn't take too many more of them, whatever Loony Matthews was up to.

'Good. Well thank you very much for letting us know. Jill will show you out, won't you Jill?' He began running his fingers over the typewriter keys although he was staring impatiently into the shaving mirror.

'Of course I will,' Jill agreed. She was startled by her husband's rudeness. He had never been rude to the Dysons before. He seemed to like black people. She wondered what was up with him and sighed and felt unhappy because whatever it was seemed also to be driving him from her. 'Are you sure you wouldn't like some tea?' she asked Richard as they went back down the stairs. 'What about a jar of pickled strawberries?'

Richard laughed. 'No thanks Jill. I only wanted to put you in the picture. I'm sorry for the man, myself. Litigation of this kind is never worth the trouble from a financial point of view. I wouldn't recommend it to anyone. It costs a fortune.' As he headed back down the path Jill stomped into the playroom and kicked down the Lego castle she had painstakingly helped Benjy to build. Then she threw her arms around the neck of the rocking horse and moaned gently to herself. What else could go wrong? Every area of her life was blighted, contaminated it seemed by the *pot-au-feu*. Mrs Butt hadn't pulled out the beds this morning after promising she would. And Benjy hadn't said why he kicked her at school even though she had spent ages probing over the Lego. And so on and so forth.

After a while she stopped moaning. The horse couldn't have taken much more. She said to herself, 'Pull yourself together. Now you have hit the bottom there is nowhere else for you to go but up.' And oddly, she was right. Short of Mummie arriving or there being a hideous accident with the children, her life couldn't have plummeted further. What it began to do was bounce about on rock bottom, causing additional bruising but suggesting hope.

In the very next morning's post she received a letter from Mrs Henderson Smyth, who declared herself to be wild with anticipation and more than eager to hear from Haute Food's solicitor. But she begged Jill not to bank on a lawsuit since the evidence was so heavily stacked against her. Everyone was talking about it, Mrs Henderson Smyth wrote. And it hurt. It really did hurt. Jill wished she had poisoned Mrs Henderson Smyth while she had been about it. She was certain the wretched Hermione would never have been so brutal.

'Bella,' she lowed down the phone. 'Bella. You had better come over. I've had the most terrible letter from Putney.'

'Oh Lord,' said Bella. 'I'm sorry, Jill, but I'm in a ghastly mess. Griselda has spilt a whole saucepan of beeswax over the kitchen floor and Mrs Butt says she can't possibly be expected to clean it all up. I am frankly up to my tits in gunge.'

'For goodness sake, Bella,' Jill said, brought to her senses by a phrase so unworthy of anyone resembling the Princess of

Wales. 'Make Griselda clean it up. She put it there, she ought to get it off. What was she doing with beeswax, anyway?'

'Getting hair off,' Bella said vaguely. 'And she can't clean it up because she has gone to her class.'

'You will have to sack her,' Jill ordered.

'You can't sack someone for an accident,' Bella pointed out.

'Griselda is a walking accident,' Jill snapped. 'She's never been any use to you. She's always up in her room, titivating. You should have given her up as a lost cause months ago.'

'Don't,' said Bella meekly. 'I know.' She did too. But Bella could rarely work up enough fury to give vent to about anything. A small amount could smoulder away and occasionally erupt when she was overtired or unwell but on the whole she allowed others to do more or less what they pleased in her life and she hoped it was all right by them.

Griselda, although she was twenty-one, had the mind of a fourteen-year-old and the body of a well-used thirty-six-year-old, from growing up in the sun, Marcus said, which addled the brain and wrinkled the body. There was almost nothing she could do and what she could do she tried not to, but she never sulked or threw tantrums and this, Bella pointed out to Marcus, was a major plus. Of course they could pay double for an English-speaking girl who had no difficulty understanding the word 'ironing', but since he was so concerned with tightening their belts and sticking to a budget there was no more to be said. She could tolerate Griselda because Poppy loved the way she put on so much make-up, and Griselda could keep Poppy amused for hours at a stretch with the ends of lipsticks. The beeswax, however, she was forced to agree, was stretching matters a bit. 'I've run out of scourers,' she said to Jill.

'I'm coming over,' said Jill.

Giles, wide awake in bed, unable to sleep in the pattern prescribed by the rota, heard the front door slam and heard Anna call to his wife, 'Brigid back on her feet again? Sarah says she is looking better.'

'She seems to be pulling herself together,' Jill replied. 'I have had to be firm with her, though. You can't let yourself go under at the first hint of stress in your life, can you?' Giles finally nodded off, soothed by his wife's resolute braying, and didn't hear her turn the conversation to her own worries or Anna try to escape them. 'I've had a threatening letter,' Jill cried, 'on top of everything else, over the business of that fat woman dying.'

'Really,' said Anna, pulling sunglasses from her bag.

'I wrote and told them that if they repeated their slander, you know about the slander, I gather, I would sue them and they have written back saying, sue away.'

'Ghastly,' said Anna, shielding her eyes from the glare of No.5.

'It's a bit much, don't you think? Especially when we are being sued ourselves. Tony Matthews wants to go to court over his dog.'

'He doesn't' said Anna. 'I thought the dog had died.'

'That's why he wants to court. He intends accusing Giles . . .'

'That house is outrageous,' Anna interrupted. 'I will never get used to it.' She climbed into her car. 'It sounds to me as if you'll soon be spending as much time in court as I do. It's rather fun.' She smiled as she drove off because she liked to remind her neighbours that she was a magistrate when they were not, and as she drove over Albert Bridge the significance of what Jill had been saying dawned on her. Of course! She must sue the Dysons. She would sue them for mental and physical anguish.

Jill had taken a new scourer over to Bella as well as the letter from Putney, so Bella was able to scrub around her as she poured out her heart while keeping her feet off the floor. 'What can we do? We can't afford to sue, but if we don't we will never get our reputation back. I hate that Henderson Smyth. I am going to make her pay.'

'Forget her,' Bella panted. The stuff was so sticky and revolting. 'It may take time but you'll just have to start again with new contacts. Word will get round fast enough with a new set of clients.'

'Time is what I haven't got,' Jill argued. 'You don't seem to appreciate how difficult things are for us at the moment. Of course it doesn't make much difference to you but to be quite blunt, we need the money. I haven't paid the last two terms' school fees.'

Bella stopped scrubbing and staggered to her feet. 'Gosh,'

she said. 'Haven't you? Do they mind?'

'Of course they mind,' Jill said. 'Wouldn't you? The grisly facts are that funds have been tight for the last two years and Haute Food has kept us going. Haute Food is for the money, Bella, not for the fun of it. I'd always hoped we could built it up to a point where I could let someone else do the dirty work and I could run the business and expand it into something really worthwhile. All this is a terrible strain on Giles, poor man. He can't stand lack of funds.'

'Who can?' gasped Bella, her face white with exhaustion and sympathy. She knew, as everyone else in Brain Street knew, that Giles never gave a second thought to funds. He had never had to. Somconc had always had enough. If it wasn't him then it was his parents or his wife's parents or his wife. He had always been content to let Jill handle the sordid bits which covered anything even moderately worrying. He certainly never troubled himself with bank statements or school fees. Yet Bella knew, as everyone else in Brain Street knew, that Jill would never hear a word against him. She idolized him. Everyone assumed it was because she was overweight and he was a writer.

Bella sat beside Jill on the pretty cane sofa in the bay window of the kitchen and wiped perspiration from her top lip. 'I bet Anna has friends who could drum up some business,' she said. 'And what about the Petries? They would be even better because they have film contacts. You know what Trudie Fanshaw says, film crews are the best way to make money: bacon sandwiches for breakfast, shepherds' pie for lunch and banana sandwiches for tea. You just need an introduction.'

Jill blinked a couple of times to absorb the proposition and she smiled. 'I could manage it easily, couldn't I? And Putney need never know. Do you think Tom and Celia would help?'

'We can only ask. I will ask. I'll go and see them tonight,' Bella declared. So heartened was Jill by the faint prospect of salvation that she dashed home, found a couple of bottles of nettle vinegar and removed all the beeswax from the kitchen floor in a trice.

Bella, as good as her word, called on the Petries after supper, having first telephoned to make sure they were not entertaining or watching a blue film which everyone said they did, all the time. Tom poured her a tiny gin and treated her to one of those looks that men who consider themselves touched by fame like to give; hard, bang between the eyeballs without the smallest trace of sexual interest.

'And what is this important thing, Mrs Whittaker,' he yawned, 'that brings you out so late and alone in your condition?'

He made her uneasy. She hadn't been happy about him ever since he had refused to come to dinner with the stockbrokers. Because he hadn't even made a decent excuse she and Marcus had inferred that they were not witty enough. Celia had said that they couldn't come because he was so awfully tired and honestly wasn't going out much these days, but they were seen poncing off in their Volvo at least four nights a week.

'It's about Jill, actually,' Bella said, smiling at Celia who was curled up on a heart-shaped chair in an astonishing black track suit. It was a track suit, Bella was quick to ascertain that. But it was the sort of track suit she imagined a stripper might wear, with zips in strange places and bits of leather. 'She's in an awful state about her business.'

'She killed someone, didn't she?' Tom remembered in amusement. 'The pongs have always been fairly deadly, haven't they?'

'How many did she kill?' Celia asked, knowing full well how many. 'Salmonella is fantastic for killing.'

'She didn't kill anyone, actually. Someone died. Hermione something, you wouldn't have known her, a fat woman. She could have died of anything but everyone is saying it's Jill's fault.'

'Who is saying?' Celia asked sternly. She loved being a television researcher. She wanted to be an on-camera reporter.

'A woman called Henderson Smyth. The woman who booked us in the first place.'

'But she hasn't been charged with anything by anyone, has she?'

'No,' Bella said, unnerved, but determined to carry on. 'That's just it. She hasn't. But everyone's cancelling all over the place and she is terrified that the business will go completely broke and then they will have no income. So what I wanted to ask you was if you could help out with a few contacts? I know you know lots of film people and really, that's exactly what she needs, some regular work catering for film crews. I'm sure she would make marvellous banana sandwiches and they don't smell a bit, do they?'

Tom yawned again. 'I've never much liked Giles,' he said. And then he started talking about the Harveys' adultery and the stupidity of misbehaving in one's own nest. By the time Bella stood up to leave because neither of them had addressed her for at least twenty minutes, he seemed to have forgotten all about the Parkers.

Celia hadn't. 'Give Jill my love,' she purred as she showed Bella out. But Bella vowed to herself furiously that she wouldn't. The Petries had no intention of offering their help. As she tried to formulate words of comfort for Jill a small cranky worm of disgust needled away at her serenity. The Petries had made her very cross indeed.

Chapter Fifteen

Tom and Celia, with only a little encouragement from Anna, decided to ignore Bella's visit. They had nothing against Jill personally, no one apart from dead Hermione's avengers and possibly Brigid had anything against Jill personally, but on the other hand, no one was demented about her cooking. 'Imagine if she killed off a film crew,' Celia snorted to Tom. 'Our names would be mud.'

Tom couldn't have agreed more and as he said, he didn't care much for Giles. There was something pretentious about the way he wrote, or didn't write, something snotty about the way he refused to get out and work like anyone else with artistic aspirations, something gruesome about the way he had been to Eton. They agreed to treat Bella's request as if it had never been made.

They probably would have been more than happy to do so even if Celia hadn't run into Anna at the Body Shop in the King's Road, but Anna's seal of approval reassured them.

'I'm very fond of them both,' Anna said. 'But what can you do? I'd love to be able to help but honestly, I couldn't recommend those prune things to anyone. My friends would die rather than eat them.'

'Mine would die if they did,' Celia murmured.

'I know they are skint,' Anna declared sniffing at a bottle of pearled pink lotion, 'but who isn't? None of us is as well off as we expected to be. Jill should do some typing. I'm sure she can type. She looks as if she might type, doesn't she? I wonder if I know anyone who wants any typing done.'

'That is a wonderful idea,' Celia enthused, holding a wrist smeared with simulated body odour to her nose. 'She can't do any damage typing. Giles could do some typing too. He's bound to know writers who want typing done.'

Anna chuckled. 'You are mean. As a matter of fact Hippo says Giles is working jolly hard at the moment, helping sort out his car fiasco. They have both thrown themselves into it.'

'Truly,' said Celia. 'How rivetting. Are they getting anywhere?'

'I haven't a clue,' said Anna. 'I don't suppose so. I'm sure I would have heard.'

'Heavens, how wonderful.' Celia's narrow eyes sparkled. 'I wonder if they want any help.'

'Oh I shouldn't think so,' Anna glinted back. 'It's top secret. No one's supposed to know anything about it.'

'Well, tell Hippo if he wants an extra hand I'd be only too happy to help. I love sleuthing.'

'You're sweet,' cooed Anna, knowing full well that Celia was as sweet as a tarantula and that her help would be as welcome as a tarantula on a lavatory seat. 'But why don't you and Tom come and have a drink with us tomorrow? We have to go out to dinner but drop round at seven. We'd love to see you.' She said this, even though she was at that very moment looking at Celia without much love, because she felt obliged to. As she hurried away to have her eyelashes dyed, leaving Celia in a haze of Aloe Vera and delight, she told herself that if Celia was going to get within an inch of Hippo it would be before her very eyes.

What delighted Celia was the glorious notion of a tiny vigilante cell operating outside her very front door. What thrilled her was the prospect of a documentary featuring herself as an undercover reporter helping to expose the skeleton in the neighbourhood closet. Already she could imagine the shadowy figures creeping about in a half light and she could hear the footsteps pounding into Dishwater Terrace in pursuit of a suspect. Above everything she imagined her own droll but pungent commentary and then, ultimately, the acclaim and the awards. It was wonderful and it was just as well she took pleasure from it while she could because the very next morning the fantasy was to explode in her face. In the dead of night, someone was to sneak across the road and paint across the rear window of the family Volvo: 'Stinking Hypocrites'.

It was the 'Stinking' that would hurt her most, because no one else had been subjected to an adjective, but it was the adjective that Bella rather liked. She wrote it as an afterthought because 'Hypocrites' on its own looked so puny and there was so much paint left in the can.

She did it to strike a blow for her beleaguered friend and colleague and because the Petries had refused to come to dinner with the stockbrokers. She did it because of the beeswax for which Jill had sacrified a good bottle of nettle vinegar and she did it because she wanted to, not with any great sense of mission, but because the Petries bugged her and she thought she could get away with it. Pregnancy often induces bewildering flights of delusion. She also thought it was pretty funny at the time.

She crept out of bed just before four when it was still quite dark and when she assumed everyone would be asleep. She decided to chance the Petrie alarm, imagining that if she stood well clear and fired the aerosol spray from a distance she wouldn't trigger it. Even if she did, she would say that on hearing the alarm she had rushed from the house, being downstairs and unable to sleep on account of her morning sickness, and that she had found the can in the road and seen a figure darting around the corner.

But the car alarm didn't go off, and her plan wouldn't have been believed if it had, because she was seen, not only by Miss Smith who was keeping a round the clock check on Hippo, but by Hippo himself who almost fell through his open loft-extension window into his honeysuckle at the sight of her. Had his camera been a gun she would have been riddled with bullets even before she had the top off the can, so frayed were his nerves from fatigue and boredom. Tears of joy and relief that the long waiting had paid off hindered his attempt to photograph her artistically but his foolproof camera recorded her every action, despite them.

Bella, unaware of her audience and perfectly happy at the wheeze, chortled quietly to herself as she finished her handiwork. She admired it and crept back inside to bed just as the first despondent rays of light dabbed at the leaden sky to reach Brain Street. Hippo fell back into the futon, shaking and sweating, unable to believe it was all over, and that there had indeed been a culprit and that he had caught her. It didn't strike him in any way as peculiar that it was Bella because he had been prepared for anything. He saw no need to tackle her immediately. A citizen's arrest in nightclothes would be undignified and could serve no useful purpose when he had everything on film. He wanted sleep, gallons of it, and when he was refreshed he would decide what to for the best. He forgot all about Giles. He stumbled down to the bathroom and crawled in beside Anna who gave only a faint groan and a small kick of recognition at his presence.

Miss Smith took to her bed full to bursting with simple pleasure. She had, as she had known she would, revelled in the suspense but to have had it broken in such a manner was sublime.

Because Hippo didn't phone him, Giles slept through the early hours of his shift and didn't wake until Jill shrieked through the bedroom door at him. 'You'll never believe it. Someone's attacked the Petries. Guess what they are?' She could hardly contain herself. 'You won't believe it. Hypocrites. "Stinking Hypocrites". Isn't it a hoot? I'd love to know who's doing it. Someone must have inside knowledge. I love "Hypocrites".'

She was slightly hysterical and not without reason. As well as the fun over the Petries, the post had brought her the news she had longed for. Mr Fender had written to inform her that as there was no conclusive evidence to suggest that her kitchen had bred the bug that caused the death in Putney, no further action would be taken against her. She could have laughed at anything, that morning.

'Oh no,' croaked Giles, scrambling from his bed in a panic.

'Oh my God. What time is it? When did it happen? Has anyone phoned?'

'No one's phoned,' Jill cried, leaping onto her husband as he was struggling with his socks. 'But I am a free woman. Mr Fender has found me blamless. Isn't it wonderful.' She lowered her voice to a sultry crow. 'Help me to celebrate.'

Giles fought her off, pushing and shoving and ultimately pinching. 'Not now, sweetheart. I can't breathe. Get off. What time is it? When did it happen?'

'The letter came in the post,' said Jill, ready for anything and pinning him beneath her. 'I told you. What's wrong? What's up?'

'Nothing is up,' screamed Giles. 'I have to go out. Will you let me out of here. It's very important. Why didn't anyone wake me?'

Jill was used to lack of rapture when she offered her body to her husband but she was not used to bad manners. She was wounded. She was piqued because he didn't seem to care that jail had vanished from the horizon outside the kitchen. 'Come back here,' she roared. 'Don't you dare run away from me when I am talking to you.' She lunged at the door and planted herself between it and her husband who tried to brush her aside.

'Don't be silly,' he wheedled. 'I'm not running away. And I'm very pleased about your letter. But I have slept through something and someone is going to be very put out unless I go somewhere and explain myself straight away. You understand these things. Now be a love. Don't make a fuss. I'll be back in a minute.'

He kissed her cheek and she obediently stood aside because he was a thriller writer and it stood to a kind of reason that he would be involved in plots that didn't concern her in the course of his research. 'It is good news about Mr Fender, isn't it, though?' she said sadly.

'Great. Must run.' He ran all the way down the stairs, out the door and over the road to No. 6 where Hippo was still almost dead with sleep and Anna was grinning to herself over the 'Stinking' in 'Stinking Hypocrites'. News of the inscription had flashed through every household within minutes of its discovery by Marcus Whittaker who cried when he saw it, 'Oh no!' Not for a second did he suspect his wife had done it. He dreaded having to break the news. He looked feverishly for Rob Marsham who was carefully avoiding his gaze inside his enormous motor-cycling helmet.

He sprinted down the road, with one trouser leg clipped up and the other trouser leg down like a boy in a nursery rhyme, calling, 'I say, I say Rob, have you got a minute?' Under normal circumstances the last thing he might have sought was a minute with Rob Marsham to whom he considered himself opposed from every conceivable angle. 'Look I wonder if you could come here for a tic. We seem to have a recurrence of the old problem.'

Rob, anxious not to appear stand-offish, struggled to free himself from his helmet and for several breathtakingly awkward seconds seemed to have permanently encased himself in it. 'Sorry,' he cried helpfully on his emergence. 'These things can be a bit tricky. What did you say?'

'Come and have a look,' Marcus suggested. They hurried together to stand in front of the Petries' car.

'Oh Lord,' said Rob, stifling a terrible need to collapse with laughter. 'Oh Lord. "Stinking Hypocrites". It's a bit much, isn't it.'

'The trouble is,' Marcus admitted nervously, 'I'm in a teeming hurry and someone's got to tell them. I wonder if you could just let them know? It won't take a minute. I would myself but I'm terribly rushed this morning.' As he spoke he was fastening his wayward trouser leg into place, mounting his bicycle and pushing himself off towards the City and out of embarrassment's range. To be the harbinger of one lot of bad news is all very well but to be on the spot for a third time looked bad, too bad for the comfort of a man who might one day try to secure a place on a list of prospective candidates.

So Rob broke the news and bore the brunt of Celia's fury at the use of the word 'Stinking'. 'Stinking,' she had screamed so that everyone in the street except Hippo, Giles and Jill, who was reading her letter, had been drawn to their windows. '"Stinking"! Of all the nerve.' She had turned at this impressive juncture to stare at No. 9.

'We all know who stinks around here and it certainly isn't

anyone at No. 7.' The suspicion had scudded into her rapidly calculating brain immediately that the one person who might wish her ill and who might find reference to the word stink at her fingertips in view of what Tom had said to her partner was Jill Parker. Celia was no mean communicator, the simple gesture of turning towards No. 9 had instantly telegraphed her opinion to the rest of the street, except Hippo, Giles and Jill, so that within a very short space of time the view was pretty well entrenched in common wisdom.

'Hippo's asleep,' Anna said to Giles, taken aback by his dishevelled appearance and faintly animal demeanour at so early an hour. She herself was only out of bed because of the fuss in the street and she drew Hppo's bathrobe around her modestly. She didn't like the disturbing sensation Giles caused in the back of her neck. There was something, she had always considered, humiliating about an attraction to short men, something less than totally feminine and red-blooded. This was a crazy view for a marriage guidance counsellor but she couldn't help herself.

'It's extremely urgent, Anna,' he said to her briskly, 'so if you don't mind I think I had better come in and that you had better wake him.' She was almost but not completely floored by the command he seemed to have taken of the situation. Napoleon she remembered had been a short man.

'But he's terribly, terribly tired, Giles,' she said. 'He didn't get to bed this morning until after dawn.'

'We have all been working extremely hard lately, Anna,' Giles said, and she detected a disconcerting note of menace. Was this menace, she asked herself? It couldn't be. Not from a man who wore tight white trousers. 'What time did he go to bed?' he asked.

'I don't know precisely,' she replied. 'But it was around dawn. It hardly matters Giles, because the man is whacked and should not be woken up.'

'It matters,' Giles insisted. 'Not to you at this very minute but to me, now, and others including you eventually.' Giles deduced that if Hippo had gone to bed at dawn he couldn't have waited for the end of his shift so he must have witnessed the attack halfway through it and therefore he, Giles, had nothing to apologize for. He could claim to have woken up at eight as he should have only to find that the street was in uproar.

'Look Giles,' said Anna. 'I'm only guessing, but if what you want to see Hippo about is the Petries' car then I can only advise you to forget it. If Celia is going to accuse Jill it isn't him you want, it's a good lawyer. What about Richard? I know it's grim but honestly I do think that is the best thing.'

'What on earth are you talking about?' Giles asked. He was by now in the Harvey hall but the door was still wide open as if he was expected to leave any minute, which indeed he was. 'Jill is not being prosecuted by the Health people so there is no question of anyone accusing her anymore. And Celia never came into it to my knowledge.' It occurred to him that he must have missed a lot during his long days and nights in the loft extension.

'Never mind,' Anna said, recognizing the corner they were both now in. 'It doesn't matter. I misunderstood you. Just wait down here for a minute and I will run up and see if I can wake him.' She shook Hippo because she was sick of arguing with Giles and confused by it. 'Wake up Hippo,' she yelled. 'You have to wake up. Giles is in the kitchen and he won't go away until he speaks to you. He doesn't care how sleepy you are.'

Hippo flicked open a dozy lid. His stomach rumbled at him angrily, the only stomach he knew to have a voice which roared in agony for no reason at all. 'What?' he said.

'For heavens' sake, get up. I'm not going back down to him. You will have to.' Hippo sat up. Surely it wasn't another day again. He began working his way back through the hours in bed to what had gone before. When he reached 4 a.m. he smiled at his wife and cried, 'Right. I'll see him. Fantastic. Where's my dressing gown?' He made her take it off because pleased though he would be to explain everything to Giles he had no wish to be nude when he did so.

'Well,' he said, robed, decent and eventually in the kitchen, 'it paid off. We caught her.'

'Her?' said Giles. 'Who?'

'Bella Whittaker.' Hippo announced triumphantly. 'I saw her with my own eyes. It was Bella.'

Giles sat down, stunned, open-mouthed, unable to accept

what he had been told. 'Bella! It can't have been. She is pregnant. Why would she do it? What could she possibly have against you and me and the Petries?'

'That is what you and I must work out,' Hippo declared, confident they could do anything now they had overcome the first obstacle. And, in a blaze of euphoria they did, in remarkably few minutes, because there is nothing easier than to ascribe motives to people you don't know very well. Giles reached most of the conclusions because motives were his business and he was determined not to let Hippo take credit for everything.

She had written 'Killer' on his car, he deduced, because she was terrified by the Putney death and wanted to make sure Jill was held responsible for it and not her. Tango's death had been a lucky break because it diverted the street from the *pot-au-feu* completely. As for the adultery, Giles had to choose his words carefully.

It was obvious to him that Bella had been referring to Anna and Rupert on the window of Hippo's volvo. She disapproved of Rupert, a close friend of her husband's, behaving in an untoward manner towards the man who was his partner. She thought it was dishonourable as did everyone. But since Hippo didn't know about Anna and Rupert, and Giles could not bring himself to tell him, he allowed Hippo to say, 'She probably wanted to protect Sarah. She is a very kind woman, Bella. Maternal and that sort of thing.' This was guilt operating on Hippo's judgement. He was beginning to feel terrible about having corrupted anyone as young and silly as Sarah: not to regret that he had, but to wish that he hadn't. This is a concept familiar to adulterers everywhere.

With her motives established Hippo and Giles had then to decide what to do about Bella and it was far more perplexing a problem. They liked Bella. She was sweet, good-natured, pretty and delicate.

'We must think of the unborn baby,' Hippo said.

'And Marcus,' said Giles. 'He's a big chap.'

'But we must also take into account our duty to the rest of the street. She might be working her way along it.'

'She's not likely to do her own car, though, is she? Then

there's only the Dysons, the Anderson-Joneses, the Matthewses and the Marshams. The Marshams don't have a car so that leaves only three.'

'They will have to be warned.'

'She will have to be stopped.' They sat together yawning, longing for a decent solution. Neither of them specially cared what happened to anyone else's Volvo now they knew what had happened to their own. They were intrigued by the idea that sane, sensible Bella was loopy at night and crept around performing weird acts with a can of spray paint.

'Do you know,' Hippo said eventually, 'I think the best thing we can do is nothing. Not yet. Let's just wait. I will get the film developed and we will wait and see. After all, she's not really doing any harm, is she?'

Giles thought about it. He considered Marcus' size. He told himself that now Jill was not to be prosecuted the word 'Killer' was null and void. 'You're right,' he said. 'Let's leave it for the time being. At least now we can get some sleep.'

Chapter Sixteen

Tom Petrie had no trouble removing the word 'Hypocrites' from his car with some stuff he had in the cellar. But he had a great deal of trouble expunging it from his wife's lips to which it clung in disbelief. 'It's so unfair,' she said over and over again. 'If anyone is intellectually honest in this ridiculous street it is us. It can only have been Jill Parker. Who else could it have been?'

It was hard to know, Tom agreed. It could have been Jill Parker, certainly, but he could think of no very good reason why it should be her and not anyone else. He didn't know that Marcus was mortally slighted by the night of the stockbrokers and nor did he know that Minnie thought Celia common. They did nothing to suggest it in public, anymore than Jill did. To his knowledge they had done nothing to offend Jill any more than they had done anything to offend anyone else.

'It isn't what we did,' Celia pointed out. 'It was what we didn't do.' They were having a quiet gin before preparing to join the Harveys for a drink before dinner. 'We didn't put her in touch with anyone in the film business who needed caterers.'

'Of course we didn't,' Tom said. 'But how was she to know we didn't? We didn't tell her we wouldn't and as far as I can remember we didn't tell Bella we wouldn't.'

'We didn't tell Bella we would, either, and I told Anna we wouldn't.'

'What on earth for?' Tom asked.

'Because she said she wouldn't either.'

'I didn't know Anna had film contacts,' Tom said. 'Surely she wouldn't have told Jill you weren't going to when she wasn't going to herself.'

'Don't you believe it,' said Celia. She had the measure of Anna to exactly the same degree that Anna had the measure of her. This naturally did nothing to impinge upon friendly relations or even upon their sincere affection for each other as the sort of neighbours they liked to have.

'Well sod them then,' Tom said.

'You can't just say sod them. The woman has insulted us. She has called us "Stinking Hypocrites". We have to do something about it.'

Tom took a few thoughtful sips. 'I don't know,' he said. 'The Harveys did nothing about being called adulterers. If they can tolerate "adulterers" I think I can stand "Stinking Hypocrites".'

'But they were adulterers,' Celia cried out. 'And they didn't know who did it. That's why they haven't done anything. But they will when they discover who it was, I'm sure of it. Hippo's no wimp.'

'He's mad, though,' Tom said. 'They're both mad.' This had always been his opinion. He took a dim view of their public indiscretion.

Hippo, who was rarely notified of his social obligations until the very last minute, was disconcerted to find the Petries coming to drinks so soon after he had witnessed the assault on their car. But he decided he could survive it by looking sleepy and aggrieved which wasn't too difficult since his stomach had been in chaos all day and he'd had no decent rest.

'Bad luck about your car,' he sympathized. 'Anyone see the boy at it this time? Someone will have to do something.'

'Boy?' said Tom, accepting a whisky. 'What boy?'

'The paper boy,' said Hippo, causing Celia to emit a careful carillon of unamused laughter.

'Oh, Hippo, you are funny. Of course it wasn't the paper boy. It never was and never has been the paper boy. Stop pretending. We're all in this together.'

Hippo smiled at her blankly. Celia made him nervous. She seemed to squint through him in a distressingly intimate way, as if to imply that she knew him better than he knew himself when she couldn't possibly.

'Wasn't it the paper boy?' he asked.

'Is it my imagination,' interrupted Anna diplomatically, 'or do we all agree that the Dysons' house isn't so much pink as violet? If it's violet then I do think we can get an injunction of some sort against them.' She spoke louder than was necessary in order to warn Celia to back away from the subject she had told her quite specifically was a secret.

'Puce,' said Tom. 'I would call it puce.'

'So would I,' said Anna quickly. 'You're absolutely right. They have painted their house puce. I can't understand how they have been allowed to get away with it when we all find it so repulsive.' Everyone sighed. She had become a complete bore on a subject that had long since lost its charm for anyone else. She had been told over and over again that the Dysons' house was their own, to do with it as they would, and they would paint it puce so that's all there was to it.

'You can't take out an injunction,' Celia said with only a small effort to conceal her impatience. 'There is nothing anyone can do.'

'I'm sure there must be something,' Anna insisted, appealing to Tom with, Celia told herself, a disgusting display of clammy femininty. But he shook his head.

'There isn't,' Celia said. 'I know for a fact because I've researched it.' This may have been a lie but a conclusive argument was required and Anna was in no position to dispute what Celia had or had not researched.

'Oh,' she murmured. 'Oh.'

'On the other hand,' Celia continued craftily, 'there is something we can do about our car. We're going to sue Jill for costs, not just to cover the car but our reputations as well.'

'Are you?' said Tom fascinated, though distracted by Hippo's spluttering on the whisky which he had been in the process of swallowing when the muscles in his throat froze with shock, not to mention horror.

'Jill?' Hippo gasped as he searched frantically for a handkerchief to stem the tide streaming from his eyes, nose and mouth. 'Jill, did you say?'

Celia was not only revolted, she was intrigued. 'Yes, I said Jill. Jill wrote "Stinking Hypocrites" on our car and I don't intend to let the matter rest. I'm sure you wouldn't if you knew who wrote "Adulterers" on your car.'

'I do know,' sniffed Hippo. 'And I am. I can't see any point in dragging things like this out forever and ever. I would much rather let the matter drop. No real harm has been done.'

'I don't know about that,' Tom said.

'Nor do I,' said Anna, giving a small toss of her gold and mud hair. 'If I knew who had written on our car I would want to do something about it.'

'And don't you know?' Celia enquired, smirking, Anna observed angrily. She looked furiously to Hippo for the information or explanation which would spare her further humiliation. She was outraged that he had said he knew, ill that whoever he knew it was might also have known about Rupert, beside herself that their front should be seen to be less than united by Celia Petrie, of all people.

'I have only just discovered who it was and I haven't had time to discuss it with Anna yet,' Hippo snuffled through the mound of tissues he had found in his pocket. 'To be frank Celia, I would much rather not discuss it at all at the moment.'

'With the greatest respect, Hippo,' Celia said, 'I think you must. Whoever did your car almost certainly did our car and whoever did our car almost certainly did yours, so we must pool our information. If Jill did yours that would be the final proof that she also did ours.'

'I don't think it would actually, Celia,' said her husband. 'You can't make illogical connections like that in matters as serious as this.' Celia, however, could see no reason not to, since they did in television all the time.

'Quite,' said Hippo, nodding gratefully at Tom. 'I hope I haven't misled you, Celia,' he added, hoping a backtrack would sound convincing, 'but what I should have said is not that I know for certain who did it, but that I have a fairly shrewd idea. That is not enough for a firm accusation though, is it?'

'She didn't mind accusing us of hypocrisy on less, did she?' Celia said petulantly. The atmosphere thickened and darkened and might have finished them all off had there not been the most fearful grinding and crashing noise outside at that very moment which caused them all to rush to the window to see what was happening.

All they saw was a monstrous growth of honeysuckle, but behind it the street seemed to be full of shouting and swearing and fist-shaking, though much of this was an illusion created by the fading light and the echoes a small road can produce when it has loft extensions on either side. At the heart of the uproar was the Marshams' skip which had been delivered partly onto the Dysons' Mercedes. Most of the noise was coming from Myra who was abusing not only the skip deliverer but also Rob, for calling 'Back back' once too often, and Sebastian Anderson Jones for refusing to be cut and dried about what he had seen.

'You were right here. How can you say you aren't sure?' she was screaming, but he didn't want to get involved.

'I don't want to sound wise after the event, Myra,' Rob said with some animation, 'but had you moved your car as we asked . . .'

As the party from No. 6 tumbled out on to the street Myra whirled to confront him. 'I told you I would move it when another space in the street became free. As you can see the Harveys' car is outside my place. Look at my car,' she yelled at them. 'You are extremely lucky it isn't yours.' They came and looked. 'This lunatic dumped his skip on it. He just drove straight back and dropped it. My Mercedes, look at it!'

The skip was now dangling in mid-air like a hanged man from the back of its truck, which was parked diagonally out into the road, waiting for a decision to settle its fate. The Parker Volvo appeared at the corner by Webbs and seeing its access blocked, stopped.

'You had better pull this thing back into the curb,' Hippo said sensibly. 'No one can get in or out.'

'Certainly,' said the driver, only to happy to follow orders since he had no intention of taking responsibility.

'He can't,' said Myra. 'Not until the police come. I want everything to stay just as it is so that there is no question of whose fault it was.'

'You don't have to worry about that,' Tom said. 'A parked vehicle can't be blamed for any damage done to it. The best thing you can do Myra is pop in, get your keys and move the Mercedes around into Dishwater Terrace. That way the driver can deliver the skip and leave. Rob can sort it out with the firm, can't you Rob?'

'Naturally,' said Rob. 'There's no space down here Jill,' he called walking a few paces towards her. 'You'll have to park back there.'

Myra glared at him. 'I don't know what Richard is going to say. He can't stand stupidity. He has no time at all for recklessness.'

'I asked her to move,' Rob explained as she strode across the road. 'But she wouldn't. She said we would have to manage as best we could.'

'It wasn't a very good best, was it?' Celia observed before joining the others who were wandering back into No. 6 for a last drink as Jill came bustling around the corner.

'It makes a change from red paint,' she chortled as she hurried by. She was still in high spirits because no one had told her that everyone knew that Celia believed she was the last user of it. It was just as well she didn't stop. Sebastian caught Beth's eye and was again shaken by what he saw. What could it mean? It certainly had nothing to do with the suspicion Jill was under or the skip the car had been under.

'Better push off,' he said to her. 'Good luck.' He limped home to Minnie who was asleep in a banana chair in the garden. He took an apple from the fruit bowl and a glass of milk from the fridge and he hobbled upstairs to his loft extension to contemplate the mysteries of his life. He liked the loft extension.It was solid and new and represented everything that was solid and new in his life which wasn't a great deal but would be soon with the birth of his heir. He could see the Marshams trying to sort out their small local difficulty and he sighed because it was so much smaller than his, unless of course it ended in another paint job.

The copycat graffitti had astonished him. It had never occurred to him that his own private frustration might lead to an explosion of resentment that would splatter across cars left, right and centre which had nothing to do with him. It made him feel proud. It was a great relief to him to know that he wasn't the only insignificant, impotent creep unable to give vent to anger in any way other than maliciously and anonymously. It was flattering to know that someone else considered his wheeze to be a good one. What's more it protected him. The more he was copied, the less he would be suspected.

On the other hand he was deeply troubled by the turn of events. It seemed to him that he had unleashed something bad into Brain Street, that he had pulled the plug on a reservoir of anger and cruelty which was now flooding slowly along it, leaving its mark in characters of sticky and incriminating red on the cars in its wake. What he had done as a kind of empty gesture, others were doing with more serious intent and he was frightened of what the outcome might be.

Sebastian was not a philosophical man but he wondered at the character of a neighbourhood which could give the appearance of harmony and well-being while it nurtured such a capacity for revenge. What, after all, had anyone done to deserve it? The Parkers had written off a dog and apparently a greedy woman in Putney had overdosed on *pot-au-feu*, but did this make them killers? The Petries, as far as he could see, kept up appearances in the same way that everyone else did, but they were no more hypocrites than anyone else and probably stunk less than most. What the Parkers and the Petries were guilty of, he guessed, was not what they were accused of, but of injuring feelings to a point where acceptance could not be endured, just as Hippo had done by being so superior and unapproachable over the honeysuckle.

In giving vent to his own unhappiness he seemed to have dropped a flag which signalled to everyone else that retaliation was all right. This struck him, as he sat on a window-ledge in his loft extension, as off. But what could he do? He couldn't confess. He couldn't do anything. He would have to put it to the back of his mind and join the Petries in stinking hypocrisy.

Why not? He asked himself. Everyone else did.

In the street he could see the skip being finally dropped safely into place. Myra was nowhere to be seen. Rob spoke to the driver and then went inside, leaving Beth to watch the truck disappear safely down the street. She stood looking at the skip for a little while, then she patted it gently and smiled to herself. Suddenly she looked up and saw him and when he saw the joy in her gaze, his stomach turned over delightfully. He lifted his hand and waved to her slowly, but encouragingly, he hoped.

'Sebastian,' Minnie called from the stairway. 'Sebastian, what on earth are you doing? I could be having a breach birth for all you care.'

Chapter Seventeen

Although news of Hippo's and Giles' secret vigil had taken time to filter into every household, the third daubing made it common knowledge. The whole street waited for them to break their silence and announce the culprit. But it waited in vain. Giles and Hippo were saying nothing. They were keeping their heads down. It was mystifying.

'If they know, why aren't they saying?' Marcus asked his wife thirty-six hours after the discovery. 'They have a duty to the Petries.' It was a clear, sunny evening and he was inspecting his roses, which seemed to be dead, and communicating with his wife through the open kitchen window. 'Unless they have already told the Petries. Do you think they have?'

She was sitting by the sink on the tiled work-surface, staring into space which she frequently did now nausea had given way to pregnant pauses. 'Are you listening, Bella? I must say I feel very left out. How long had they been watching the street? You'd have thought they would have mentioned it to me. I mean, I have a Volvo and it's a later model than either of theirs.'

'They didn't mention it to anyone,' Bella said cautiously.

'But everyone knew. It was very rude of them not to involve me, especially when I am chairman of the Brain Street

Residents' Association.' He began removing dead heads sulkily.

'I didn't know,' Bella said. 'No one told me they were watching the street until Sarah told Minnie who told me. Griselda had known for ages though apparently. And I didn't know they had seen who wrote "Stinking Hypocrites" until Anna told Sarah who told Griselda who told me.'

'I just can't understand their silence,' Marcus said.

'Celia thinks Jill did it. Maybe they're saying nothing to protect her and to avoid a scandal.'

Marcus laughed and threw a large chunk of rose bush into his compost bin. 'Why would Jill want to attack the Petries? It's a ludicrous idea.'

'Because the Petries refused to help her make new contacts in the film business. That's what Celia thinks, according to Anna.'

'Oh,' said Marcus, surveying his handiwork. 'There.'

'You have destroyed all the roses,' Bella remarked. The news that she had been seen had shaken her considerably. It had taken all the fun out of it. She wondered if she could now confide in her husband since he would have to know sooner or later but somehow, she couldn't bring herself to. While there was silence there was hope and so far, all that was coming from Hippo and Giles was silence. She couldn't understand why they hadn't tackled her. Surely if they had seen anyone they had seen her. She hadn't tried to look like anyone else though she had slung Marcus' Barbour across her shoulders.

A less pregnant woman might have been frantic at the prospect of being soundly fingered on irrefutable evidence. But Bella's hormones, combined with her usual evenness of temper, led her only to be bemused by it all. She had acted honourably, after all.

Rob Marsham, not being pregnant, was a great deal more upset. He didn't know how long Giles and Hippo had been at their posts either but it was odds on they had watched him brand the Parker Volvo. It was inexplicable to him that, if Giles had done so, he hadn't rushed out and smashed his head in, but it was also inexplicable to him that neither of them had accosted the Petries' assailant whom they had seen in action. He didn't know what to think and this was distressing because knowing what to think had been his strength until such a short time ago.

He no longer had much faith in what he was used to regarding as his strengths. The simple artisan cottage he had taken such pride in was being battered into the sort of house he had always found most absurd. And Beth, who had always shared his contempt for his neighbours' pretensions, was happier than she had been since the days when she had taken her shirt off at concerts in Hyde Park. She had scarcely blinked at the incident over the Dysons' car, not in his direction anyway. 'You can see why she was cross,' was all she had said. 'It's last year's registration.'

'I know,' he had said. But how many allowances did you have to make for another human being because she was the colour of an oppressed minority? Myra had been so unreasonable with all that yelling and screaming. He didn't yell and he didn't know anyone else who did. Where did yelling get you? Perhaps if he yelled at Beth she would reconsider her need to keep up with the Anderson Joneses. She might look at him with less contempt. She might listen to him again. But it wasn't in him to yell. He had been brought up to swallow pain, anger, frustration and insult which he did, except when it was on someone else's behalf. Then he spoke up, or thought he did, as in the case of the Matthewses' dog against the Parkers.

As Bella sat on her kitchen tiles astonished at the disappearance of her rose bed, Rob prowled about the wreckage of his living-room and waited for the knock at the door that would decide his fate. Why were Hippo and Giles saying nothing? Their silence was agonizing. He hated silence above everything. Outside he could hear the carefree chatter of two people without a worry in the world. He couldn't hear what they were saying. He could only envy them their peace of mind.

'Poor Myra,' Anna was saying, looking at the crushed boot of the Mercedes. 'What an utter bore for you. It's not the cost, is it? It's the inconvenience.' This was the first time they had spoken since the painters had moved in.

'Exactly,' Myra said. 'But you try telling Rob Marsham how beastly it is that the garage can't take your car for a week. It's like talking to a Care Bear.'

Anna giggled. 'You are naughty, Myra. I see you've had your house painted.'

'Like it?' Myra asked. 'It isn't exactly the colour I asked for but then you never get exactly what you ask for, do you these days?' She asked in the certain knowledge that Anna would reply politely. She knew Anna could not confront the object of her anger any more than anyone else in the street could. Only she enjoyed that freedom because, she admitted it to herself now, she was the street's only artistic radical.

'It's jolly cheerful,' Anna said. Then they proceeded to discuss the Petries' car as if the house was brilliant white.

'Is it true Hippo saw Jill doing it?' Myra asked.

'I'm awfully sorry, Myra, but I've been sworn to secrecy.' Anna said lowering her voice and glancing anxiously over her shoulder. 'Of course Celia has made it plain it was Jill, but Hippo can't possibly get involved at this stage.'

'Why on earth not?' Myra asked. 'If he saw her.'

'I'm sorry Myra, but it's not for me to say,' Anna repeated. 'Oh Lord, look at the time,' she cried before retreating in some confusion into No. 6.

The truth was she didn't know anymore than anyone else why Hippo and Giles were keeping so quiet having watched and waited for so long and with such diligence. She had been unable to prise the truth from her husband. The minute she left Myra she stormed to the loft extension to have another try. Honestly, it was too humiliating not knowing.

'I told you,' said Hippo whom she had found snoozing on the futon, 'I don't want to say anything until I am absolutely sure.'

'But you are absolutely sure. You saw. If it was Jill you should say so. You owe it to us.'

'It wasn't Jill,' he said.

'Then who was it?'

'I've told you. I'm not completely sure. I have taken photographs which will make it all clear.'

'But you think it's someone you know.'

'I think it could be.'

'Well who?' They glared at each other. 'I've as much right to know as you have. The Volvo is as much mine as yours and whoever wrote "Adulterers" was plainly meaning both of us.'

This was a startling admission, Hippo thought. Was she saying she was an adulterer like him, or what? Anna's face never revealed anything and there was no point in asking.

'It's something I want to sort out with Giles,' Hippo said. 'As soon as we have sorted it out I will tell you. I promise. In the meantime I must do this stock-taking.' He stood up and began to busy himself among the shelves giving Anna no choice but to leave, none the wiser.

In many respects Hippo was none the wiser himself. He couldn't understand his reluctance to confront Bella and ask her to account for her actions. Justice clearly demanded it. But he felt it would be so unfair. She was such a splendid girl, so gracious and dignified, so similar to the Princess of Wales. He couldn't bear the thought of her crying. She might have hysterics. She might even have a miscarriage. Marcus might be furious. It would cause the most fearful ructions. But he could see he wouldn't be able to protect her much longer because Giles would soon be under considerable pressure to clear his wife's name.

He would do as he said. He would have the photographs developed and then he and Giles would take them to Marcus who would know best how to put them to Bella. It was obviously some terrible pregnant aberration. There was probably a gynaecological term for it. But it made him nervous,

He was right in imagining it would not be long before Celia decided to make her suspicion official. Even as he stared out of the loft extension window to which he was now irresistibly drawn even though he no longer had a reason to be, he saw Celia nip into No. 5 with the clear intention of seeking legal advice.

Richard allowed himself a small grunt of dismay when Celia outlined the nature of the help she wanted, even though he prided himself on his professionalism. He offered her a seat in his study and a cup of Lapsang Souchong with a dash of Earl Grey and a hint of Mango tea.

'As I said to Tony Matthews,' he told her, recovering quickly, 'you can only sue the Parkers if you have good evidence, and it is a costly business. How certain are you that it was Jill who painted on your car?'

'As certain as I can be, Richard,' Celia replied crisply. 'Hippo saw her.' She was so persuaded of her facts that she saw no harm in involving Hippo in her version of them.

'He saw her?' Richard was impressed. 'And is he prepared to say so in court?' This was clearly a step up from the case of Matthews v. Parker. In this case the knife was all but embedded in the Parker back.

'I think he will when the time comes,' Celia said, 'although of course I haven't yet asked him. I am only taking advice at this stage.'

'Quite,' said Richard. 'It is terrible to have someone wilfully damage your car. I know exactly how you feel. Have you seen the Mercedes?'

'Awful,' Celia agreed. 'I was so sorry. Imagine being married to the man. It must be dreadful. Poor Beth. But it isn't really the same, is it?'

'What isn't?'

'Having a skip crush your car. There's no slur on the reputation.'

'Not on one's own, no,' Richard agreed. He found Celia puzzling. He decided not to digress because it was tricky digressing with Celia. 'Do you know what I would do if I were you?' he asked, pouring a little more tea. 'I would have a chat with Hippo and see if he is prepared to go to court for you because if he isn't, then frankly I think to sue would be a waste of time. It will cause a lot of ill-feeling and cost you and the Parkers a lot of money. You may not be aware that money is in rather short supply at No. 9 at the moment.'

'I can't see that that has anything to do with me, Richard,' Celia murmured blandly. 'If Jill had wanted to avoid ill-feeling she should have thought twice about accusing me of stinking hypocrisy. I'm sure you appreciate how hurt I feel. The last thing I consider myself to be is a hypocrite. And as for stinking . . .'

'I know, I know,' Richard said. 'It's rotten. And I have never ever heard of anyone talk of you in such terms. But I wonder if you might consider the position Jill is in at the moment. She has an awful lot to contend with, what with the whippet falling off the twig and that woman in Putney falling off the twig and the nanny going round the bend and I don't want to be indiscreet but I don't think Giles earns a great deal. They rely on her income which has of course dwindled to nothing . . . you've probably heard.' His face suddenly broke into a smile. 'Actually you could probably help her there. Don't you have any contacts in your business who use private caterers? She would really appreciate your help.'

Celia's grey eyes almost disappeared behind her enormous cheekbones as she cried out in disbelief. 'Help Jill! Are you mad? What sort of a lawyer are you? I wouldn't lift a finger to help anyone who has wounded me as she has and I am astonished that you have the nerve to suggest I should.' Richard's smile, slow in coming was dynamite at finishing.

'I am sorry,' he said. 'It is none of my business. I was speaking out of turn as a Christian and a friend to you both. I beg your pardon.'

But Celia wasn't fooled for a minute. She saw immediately which way the cookie was crumbling. She had no intention of wasting any more of her time being lectured to about Christian duty and social obligations. It was absurd. She was a sophisticated committed atheist as he might have taken the trouble to find out. God alone knew what he was. She smiled at him and stood up.

'Well thank you for your time and the tea. You've been terribly sweet. Of course I can see now how difficult it all is.'

Richard saw her to the door and stood looking after her, perplexed. This was all getting very messy. He absent-mindedly strolled out to the road to have another look at his poor car, and while he stood there, stroking it, he thought, 'Poor Jill. She will have to be warned.' The idea of going to see her again appalled him. Being an honest man he knew he could not face it. But he was also a kind and caring man and not prepared to allow undue suffering where it could be avoided. On the spur of the moment he crossed the road to consult Marcus. Marcus would know better than anyone the state of play in the Parker household. He would get Marcus to warn Giles to warn Jill before anything nasty came through the letter-box.

As Richard had hoped, Marcus was genuinely horrified and

he immediately summoned Bella from the kitchen tiles to come and be horrified too. The Whittakers were a couple who were unified in horror. 'You will have to warn her,' Marcus said to his wife. 'She will have to prepare her defence. Bella? Bella?'

Bella, having settled comfortably into the sofa to hear the terrible news, now found herself transfixed by a point on the drawing-room wall where the marbling was especially pretty and the whorls of coffee-and-cream paint disappeared into each other forever and ever. She was asking herself if she should now, in the presence of a lawyer, confess all, and she was persuading herself that no useful purpose could be served by her doing such a thing. She had no intention of admitting anything until she absolutely had to and now she could see no absolutes, not anywhere, not even in the immaculately rag-rolled wall.

'Definitely,' she said. 'She must be told. I will tell her that Celia is going to sue her. I will go first thing in the morning.' She told herself that Jill would laugh it off because it was so silly. She told herself Jill was on top of the world now and she was no longer accused of murder. Even if she was still being sued by Tony Matthews, no one was taking that seriously. She said to herself that Jill wouldn't attack her physically because she was pregnant. And she was right. Jill didn't. Not physically.

Chapter Eighteen

Jill greeted Bella with a smile. She was feeling as bouyant as a woman can feel who is bouncing about in the pits. Life, she felt, would be manageable if only it turned a couple of pleasant corners, if Giles, for instance, finished his book and earnt some money, if she successfully sued Mrs Henderson Smyth and restored the good name of Haute Food, if Brigid could only pull herself together. She wasn't hopeful about Brigid who had taken to loud, tuneless, passionate singing. It was doubtful that Brigid would ever be fit for anything but the briefest of school runs ever again.

But the smile she gave Bella was one of hope. Bella, she knew, had been working on her behalf with the Petries, whom she expected to hear at any minute had a wealth of contacts to put her way once they had sorted out their wretched car business. She felt a little guilty that she hadn't been around to offer her sympathy but she had been so busy. It was a daft accusation anyway. She herself was partial to hypocrisy. It saved so much bother sometimes.

Bella, she noticed, as they sat down together in the kitchen, was looking less than buoyant. She was looking frayed, Jill thought, which she put down to having a baby on the National Health. It was such an unnecessary sacrifice, too. 'Unbelievable about the Petries car, isn't it?' she said, clearing a space among the hundreds of onions she had bought from a French onionseller in Clapham. She was extremely pleased with the distinctive cordon/disque bleu air they gave the kitchen.

'Don't,' murmured Bella. 'Celia has gone right off the deep end. Have you heard who she thinks did it?'

'Tell me,' said Jill. 'Beth Marsham? Minnie?' She laughed loudly at the prospect. It was such a delicious idea.

'You,' said Bella. The laughing stopped.

'Me what?'

'She thinks you did it. She thinks you wanted revenge because she didn't suggest any film contacts.'

'I never discussed film contacts with her,' Jill protested.

'But I did. I said you could do with a few.'

'And what did she say?'

'Nothing. She said neither one thing nor the other.'

'Then how could she think I would take offence?'

'She just does. She is being ridiculous.' Bella looked vacantly at the onions. She imagined the awful smells they would one day turn into and was astonished to note that her stomach remained where it was. The baby had passed the stage of heaving at the suggestion of a smell.

'I don't understand what you are trying to tell me Bella,' Jill said shrilly. 'Go back to the beginning. When you asked about the film contacts, what did she say?'

'I told you, nothing. She and Tom started talking about the Harveys as if I'd never mentioned it.' She didn't say that Tom had yawned and said he didn't like Giles. There was no point in inflicting that upon her, Bella told herself. It was bad enough without that. It was bad enough for both of them. She wasn't enjoying herself. She loathed other people's torment. The only reason she was able to sit, as she was, brazenly telling another woman she was being accused of an act of vandalism she herself had committed was that she no longer associated herself with it. She knew she had done it, of course, but she had decided to stop recognizing the fact. Besides, she told herself, Jill wouldn't suffer in the long run. Celia's anger only made everyone feel even more sorry for her.

'Well, what did you say? You must have said something to make her think I would be upset.'

'I didn't. It must have been her conscience. Her conscience made her leap to the conclusion it was you.'

'But that's not fair.'

'I know it's not fair,' Bella said. 'But there you are. You don't have to worry about it because everyone thinks that Celia is nuts. Richard says if she sues she is crazy.'

'Sues?' Jill shrieked. 'She isn't going to sue me? Oh no. That's not fair. It's not true. She can't sue me for something I haven't done. We're already being sued. We'll have to leave the country.' She began to pound the table and the onions rolled hither and thither in a woeful nervous frenzy.

'You won't,' said Bella. 'Don't be silly. She can't sue without proof and she has no proof. You've got nothing to worry about. The only reason I'm telling you is to warn you about what she is saying. I thought you would prefer to know.' The enormity of her deception escaped Bella because her detachment was complete. It can be in a pregnancy. Jill was now on her feet and the floor was awash with onions which Bella considered could lead any minute to a tragic accident. 'You don't have to worry about it,' she said lamely. 'It'll sort itself out, wait and see.' It sounded lame, even to her.

Jill didn't want to wait and see. She wanted to have it out with Celia there and then like civilized human beings. 'It won't help,' Bella advised. 'It will make matters worse. Just leave it. If we all pretend it isn't happening it will go away.' She knew this from her own experience. 'What you need is something else to think about and I have the very thing. Marcus needs some cocktail food for an office party tomorrow and one of the reasons I came over was to ask if you could do some of those nice prune things and a few curried pineapple vol-au-vents. Could you manage it?' This was a stroke of genius. She knew Jill would be unable to resist it.

'I can't afford not to, can I?' she said wearily. She sat down again and took up her notepad and pencil. 'How many does he want and where does he want them? Do we need to serve them or will he arrange that? Do you think he would like some pickled strawberry toasts?'

'He'd love them,' Bella said and she went home to telephone Marcus at work to tell him that he must. He didn't, however. He not only didn't love them, he rejected out of hand the idea of forking out for a bogus party in order to keep Jill distracted from the mess she was in.

'We can't afford to subsidise the Parkers,' he said angrily. 'If they are in hot water it is up to them to get themselves out of it.'

'You said you were sorry for Jill,' Bella argued.

'Of course I am sorry for her. But I didn't say we would give her a couple of hundred pounds for food you couldn't even foist on to a hospital. You will have to go back and cancel the order.'

'I won't,' said Bella. 'I couldn't possibly. It would make you look so mean and foolish.'

'It will make me look neither,' Marcus said coldly. 'Only a fool would give away £200.' It struck Bella that this was her come-uppance for involving herself in someone else's affairs. She was being punished for scrawling on the Petries' car when she had only done it to avenge Jill in the first place. She wished she had let Jill do her own scrawling.

'You must pay for the cocktail food,' she declared, breaking a hectic silence. 'We owe it to Jill. She didn't write on the Petries' car. I did.' She said it without really intending to, to penetrate the thick layer of stinginess that coated her husband and rendered him unreachable.

'You did what?' His horror was plain down the phone. His voice was sticking to its box and coming out in lumps.

'I wrote "Stinking Hypocrites",' said Bella, giggling at the recollection. It was the first time she had done anything as underhand and bad since she had skipped a Classics lesson at the age of twelve. It was terribly, terribly funny. You had to laugh. Marcus, however, did not.

'That was a very stupid thing to do,' he said. 'Stupid, mindless and selfish. What about the Harveys' and the Parkers' cars? Did you do those too? Stop laughing, Bella, for God's sake.'

'Of course I didn't. Why would I? I did the Petries' because they were mean and pompous. They are mean and pompous. Remember how they wouldn't come to dinner the night you asked all the stockbrokers?'

'Of course I remember. Tom was too tired. I don't know how you could have done it.'

'It was easy,' Bella said. 'I went to a car place, bought some spray, and I crept out when you were asleep and did it.'

'But you were seen,' Marcus remembered. 'Hippo and Giles saw you. There's going to be the most awful stink when it gets out.'

'It isn't getting out though, is it?' Bella pointed out. 'They haven't said a word.'

'They will,' snarled Marcus, crosser than she had ever remembered him sounding. 'They will. And then how is it going to look? Did you think of that? How it will look to have a wife with a conviction for wilful damage? I am coming home immediately and I want you to stay put until I arrive. Don't answer the phone or the doorbell. Don't talk to anyone. Are you listening Bella?'

Marcus was right, of course. It had to come out eventually. It seemed astonishing to him as he cycled frantically along the Embankment that Giles had not told Jill already. Bella seemed not to understand just how lucky she had been.

Perhaps there might have been circumstances under which Giles would have held on to the secret but those in which he revealed it were desperate. A few hours after Marcus scurried furtively into Brain Street and double bolted the door, he strolled up to his house, whistling. He had had a very good lunch in Covent Garden with a young journalist who was sure his father had read *Hunk Billet*. It was plain to him as soon as he entered his house that all was not well.

Drawn to his kitchen by a high-pitched wailing, he found the table strewn with hundreds of tiny little bits of nonsense which some women used to decorate hats and others might serve with cocktails, and there was his wife, standing amid them with his nanny, their arms about each other singing for all they were worth 'Jerusalem' with the children smiling in wonderment at their feet because it was better than television.

It was an eye-opener. Giles had never been called upon to give his wife a helping hand ever in the whole of his marriage to her. In fact he had not contributed a huge amount to the arrangement because he had never been expected to. What he had taken from it, on the other hand, was everything, and he had all but drained his wife. Though the shell that was left was generously proportioned it was, nonetheless, a shell, and now it was singing 'Jerusalem' as a shell can do when it is finally cast adrift from everything it understands.

The temptation was to run. He wanted to leave Brain Street and his marriage as fast as he could because he had never liked children, his wife was fat and he couldn't write anymore. He wanted to run as far as he could from the loft extension with its 546 blank pages and its 22 typed ones and he decided briefly on a new career as a private ingestigator. But he looked at the carnage in his kitchen and the wreckage of poor Jill's life and he decided not to run but to stay and save her. He loved her.

'Would you mind shutting up,' he said. 'I don't think I can function with that noise. Brigid, go back to bed. Children, go and watch television. Jill, come into the drawing-room.' It was a pretty impressive performance and everyone was so taken with it that they immediately did as they were bid.

The minute Jill hit the drawing-room she came to her senses and apologized. 'Sorry,' she said. 'It was an awful racket, I know, but you have to do something to keep your spirits up.' At this her bottom lip trembled. She pulled it into line with her immaculate white teeth. Jill might have been overweight but one thing she had in her favour was teeth, really very good teeth. They came from her father's side.

'Now,' he said, hands on hips, taking control, he felt, by placing his hands on his hips and standing sort of akimbo. He supposed he was standing akimbo. He would look akimbo up. He was fairly sure akimbo was how he was standing. 'What's up?'

'Everything,' she said without hesitation. 'Absolutely

everything.' Then she told him between small hiccoughing sobs the lot: the whippet, greedy Hermione, trade falling off, the beeswax, Brigid, Tony Matthews suing them, then Celia. Nothing but nothing had gone right for her since she chopped the onions for the blasted *pot-au-feu*.

'What about Celia?' Giles asked softly.

'She says I painted on her car and she is going to take me to court. But I didn't and it isn't fair.' She put her head in her hands and wept quite openly and Giles, shocked at the extent to which it had all affected his big strong wife, went across to where she was sitting and patted her head. 'Poor old Jillie,' he said. 'If only I hadn't been so busy.'

'It's all right,' she replied sadly. 'You have your book to do. I know you'll help when you have finished.'

'I'll help immediately,' Giles said. 'To begin with you can stop worrying about the Petries. I know exactly who wrote on their car. It's time everyone else did too.'

'Who?' cried Jill, gazing up at her small husband in admiration and wonder.

'It was Bella,' he announced. 'Bella did it. She was seen.'

'It can't be true,' Jill gasped. 'She's such a weed. Why would she do it? She was here only this morning telling me that Celia thought I did it and she didn't utter a squeak. The little liar. After all I've done for her. The stinking hypocrite.'

'We will fix her,' Giles said and Jill agreed. She was all for fixing her, all for rushing across the road and screaming at her and possibly hitting her and her stupid child, Poppy. That was how angry she was. But she knew jolly well it wasn't what she would do because people didn't.

It crossed neither of their minds that a few weeks ago they would have said exactly the same of 'fixing' anyone. They would have snorted that it wasn't something one did. One rose above things. But ever since the Harveys' adultery had been brought to the world's attention, the word 'fix' had become somehow dignified. To fix was something that was now available to anyone in Brain Street who had access to a can of red spray paint.

Jill was keen to try strawberry pickle instead of paint but

Giles said that this was the very thing, in his experience, to give the game away. 'Think about it, Jill,' he insisted. 'Who else would have so much strawberry pickle at their disposal?'

So instead they agreed to buy some paint and they spent the rest of the day preparing a meal for the family and dreaming up all sorts of combinations of adjectives and nouns with which to assault the Whittakers. They decided to include Marcus in the insult because although they rather liked him, he was fastidiously mean and it would look better plural.

Chapter Nineteen

Bella woke with the weight of three hundred and twenty cocktail pieces on her conscience as well as the worry of how to save Jill from Celia's wrath which she felt honour bound to do in view of the fact that it should have been directed at her. Marcus also woke with the weight of the cocktail pieces bearing down on him. The thought of them rotting had driven him crazy through the night. He had dreamt about a very large mouth chewing £200 in crisp notes and the mouth, he had known, was Jill's. He could tell from the teeth.

When he saw Bella still in the bed beside him and not vanished mysteriously in the night as she might have done had she any real consideration, he remembered that he was married to a woman who had selfishly put an end to any political aspirations he might have had by committing a stupid criminal act. Who would vote for a man whose wife sprayed insults on used cars? It was plain to him that the secret that Hippo and Giles were keeping would soon be out and the world would know him for what he was, an upright man married to a criminal, even if she did look royal.

'We'll have to do something,' he declared. 'We can't let matters stand.'

'All right,' she agreed. Matters, as far as she could see so early in the morning, were so far out of her control that someone else might just as well make a grab for them and it might just as well be Marcus. Then he would be responsible for anything further that went wrong.

'The important thing,' he said, 'is to come out of it with honour. I suppose we can explain what you did simply enough. You have gone made in your pregnancy. And I'm sure we will be able to persuade everyone that you should be spared any sort of . . . punishment. We are, after all, a civilized nation. But this won't be enough. We will have to atone. We will have to do something so astonishingly kind that everyone will forget the astonishingly mean thing you did and we will be back where we started. Do you follow?' He was calming down as a plan took shape.

Bella tried to follow. It made her very tired. It was doing astonishingly good things that had brought the whole ghastly business to pass and she pointed this out to her husband as tactfully as she could because she knew he did not like to have arguments with flaws in them.

'I know, Bella, I know,' he said patiently because he had the flaw covered. 'But you were acting without thinking. Now there will be some brainpower behind our efforts.' He almost smiled at his wife. He was fond of her, after all. She had borne him one perfectly acceptable child and was shortly to present him with another. He liked her. She wasn't usually stupid. She was usually quite intelligent and she was nice to look at. Not flashy like Anna or Celia, but sweet. And he still considered her eyes beautiful even though they had closed on the pillow next to his for more than eight years. 'We will sort it out,' he said.

The very good act he chose to perform was to remove a major worry from the Parkers' life with a quiet assurance that must win praise all round. He would get the Matthews off the Parkers' backs by persuading them to drop their litigation. He was perfectly confident he could talk to Tony man to man. He was used to dealing with men, man to man, and he had a pretty good success rate as captain of the bank's cricket team. He intended to call on him that very evening, provided of course nothing unpleasant hit the fan in the meantime. To avoid this possibility he warned Bella not to communicate with Jill or anyone else during the course of the day. His parting shot to her as he wheeled his bike through the front door half an hour early was, 'Hide.'

This Bella knew would be impossible. She had somehow to dispose of the cocktail pieces. She struggled with the problem all morning and was still struggling when the telephone rang just before ten. 'It will be Jill,' she told herself. 'I won't answer it.' But Griselda did because Griselda believed all calls to the house would be for her and when they were not she assumed an injured air. 'Bella, for you,' she called down the stairs.

'Is it Jill?' Bella hissed back.

'I didn't ask,' Griselda replied. But it wasn't. It was Jasmine Henderson Smyth from Putney.

'I know this might strike you as rather an odd call,' she cooed down the phone before Bella could register a chill, 'but I really would like your help. Of course we are all delighted to hear that Jill is not going to be prosecuted after all—as a matter of fact it now seems that Hermione choked on an eclair—but the fact is we have this awful defamation business hanging over our heads and I really would like to find a way round it. You must appreciate there was no malice whatsoever in our earlier concern. We were all simply so worried that there may have been a tiny little bug somewhere in the kitchen over there and you know how it is when one is bereaved. We were all desperately fond of Hermione, glutton though she was. Surely we don't need to drag it all before the courts. It will be so tiresome and so expensive and if you don't mind me saying, people will say there is no smoke without fire.'

'Oh yes?' said Bella coldly. She remembered Jasmine Henderson Smyth. She was a tall, steely-haired woman with protruding lips and slim chins that hung in delicate folds towards a bossy bosom. To help her would be treacherous. Jill would never forgive her.

'I mean these things can go on and on and frankly I don't have the time and I'm quite sure Jill doesn't either.' Bella could see no reason to help her. On the other hand, she had a point. Pursuing a costly law suit wouldn't do Jill or the business an ounce of good and the woman was right. It probably wouldn't do anything for her reputation either.

'It occurred to me that I could make some sort of gesture of good will. I've talked to the other ladies and we are all agreed that the best thing all round would be for us to order a buffet from Haute Food for our next little event and that way everyone would know that we had complete faith in you. What do you say?'

'I'm not the one to convince, Mrs Henderson Smyth,' Bella said. 'It is Mrs Parker who is suing you.'

'Of course it is,' said Jasmine. 'But you are so close to Mrs Parker and so sensible. I thought when we met how sensible you were and so, I'm sure everyone says, so like the Princess of Wales. You're not related are you?'

'No,' said Bella.

'No,' agreed Jasmine. 'Now this is what I thought. We meet again for Africa in six months but this struck me as perhaps being a wee bit far away for our purposes. However we do meet for literature in the Autumn.'

'I don't think that will be any help at all,' Bella said, 'Mrs Parker's reputation cannot hang on till then.'

'Oh,' said Jasmine. 'Yes, I see. But the trouble is we've nothing any earlier. I'm not sure what to do.'

'You could order for a cocktail party tonight,' Bella said. 'That's the only thing I can think of that might be any use at all.'

'But I'm not giving a cocktail party,' Jasmine protested.

'Bad luck!' said Bella. 'I can't suggest anything else. I happen to know that Haute Food has 320 cocktail pieces spare at this very minute. If you don't want them . . . what can I say?'

'How much are they?' asked Jasmine Henderson Smyth.

'With V.A.T. and delivery, £200 cash,' Bella said. Jasmine shuddered noisily. She sensed blackmail. But she had to concede it was cheaper than an hour with her lawyer so she agreed and Bella told her to expect delivery before lunch. Then Bella sat down and smiled to herself for a full five minutes. All that remained was the minor obligation to persuade Jill that Jasmine Henderson Smyth was a good sort after all, but if she failed, it hardly mattered. She would simply tell Mrs Henderson Smyth that 320 cocktail pieces had not done the trick. It wasn't dishonest, Bella told herself. It was great good fortune, at last.

Just before lunch Bella bowled across the road to collect her order and to cheer Jill up. It was plain to her immediately that she needed cheering. She barely spoke to her as she led her into the kitchen. She didn't respond when Bella said, 'They look delicious. I wonder if I should have ordered more. You know how greedy they are in the City.' She wondered what it was. She wondered if Jasmine Henderson Smyth had also telephoned Jill and Jill was waiting for her to admit it. But she had no intention of abandoning the pretence of the office party, not without a challenge. It would spell certain trouble.

'You're not still fretting about the Petries, are you?' she enquired.

'No I'm not,' said Jill. 'Could you ask Marcus to pay up quickly? I need the money.'

'I'll try and get it for you today,' Bella replied. She was puzzled. It was unlike Jill to be surly. If she was cross she was more likely to be noisy. She wondered what had been said. Surely if anything had been said, about the snacks or about the car, Jill would have been the first to repeat it. 'You'll never guess who's just been on the phone,' she ventured. 'That Henderson Smyth woman. Wanting to know how to win you round. She's terrified.'

This was very difficult for Jill to resist and she did try quite hard. But she never could maintain sulkiness for more than one or two exchanges. 'Truly?' she enquired flatly. 'What a scream. What did you say?'

'I said it was a bit more complicated than winning you round. I said to slander somebody's reputation and ruin their business was a dreadful thing and you couldn't expect to get away with it in a quick grovelling phone call.'

'Quite right,' said Jill. 'Well done.' She could feel herself warming to Bella as one often does when the object of one's hate behaves in a perfectly normal, even decent manner.

'Guess what she told me.'

'What?' said Jill. 'Want some coffee?'

'No thanks,' said Bella. 'I'll have to fly with these in a second. She said Hermione didn't die of food poisoning. She choked on an eclair.' And at this they both screamed with cruel laughter for whatever else had happened between them, this was surely something to celebrate.

Giles, in his office, heard Jill and Bella laughing together and rose swiftly to intervene. He would not tolerate fraternizing with the enemy at this stage. It was foolhardy. They had yet to buy the paint. It would be disastrous to befriend the very foe you were about to annihilate. He hurtled down the stairs and into the kitchen to warn Jill to be more circumspect and she, catching sight of his grave expression and his nodding and pointing behind Bella's back, got the message.

'Bella's just picking up her order,' she explained as frigidly as she could. 'She's going now.'

'Hello Giles,' Bella said. 'You and Jill must pop over for a drink. I'll give you a ring.' She extended the invitation automatically, forgetting Marcus as she was sometimes prone to do.

'Lovely,' Giles murmured.

'I hope the traffic isn't too terrible,' Bella sighed as she carted the trays to the door. 'Wandsworth's atrocious at lunchtime.'

'Wandsworth?' Jill said quickly. 'Where are you going? I thought they were for Marcus in the City.'

'Of course they are,' said Bella, dropping but saving a tray or two in her confusion. 'Talking about Mrs Henderson Smyth has unsettled me.' She laughed without conviction and slammed her Volvo door.

'That's odd,' Jill remarked to Giles under her beath.

'I wouldn't trust Bella Whittaker as far as I could kick her,' he replied. 'Or her husband.'

This was extremely hard, considering the trouble Marcus was going to on his account. With great difficulty he had put the cocktail food to the back of his head while he addressed the problem of Tony Matthews whom he duly called on at seven o'clock.

'Oh,' said Val when she opened the door to him. 'Hullo.' She smiled at him so winningly that he thought she had mistaken him for someone else. 'Tony's out. Did you want something?' Val Matthews was almost as beautiful as Anna Harvey. There were probably a few people in Tulse Hill who might have considered her more beautiful. Only the expression in her eyes left anything to be desired. Desire was that something, men realized on reflection, and they usually reflected a long time after a spell in her presence.

'I do actually,' Marcus said awkwardly. 'Um, when will he be back?'

'Tommorrow,' Val said. 'He's got a job in Coventry so he's staying over. What is it?'

Marcus looked up and down the street, knowing how odd it must look, him hovering on the doorstep of No. 3. 'Could I come in for a minute?'

'Of course,' said Val. She stood aside and smiled again and pointed with her head towards the orange lounge. The flat still smelt of dog, Marcus noticed.

'I'm sorry to crash in on you like this but it's fairly important. Actually I don't think I've seen you since the terrible accident with . . .' he paused for the shortest of moments to choose between Putney and Chutney . . · 'Chutney. It was very sad. We were all most terribly sorry.'

'What Chutney?' Val said.

'Putney,' Marcus corrected himself. 'Sorry.'

'I'm not with you,' Val smiled. She had always regarded Marcus as an odd man. He looked ridiculous with his trousers rolled up, on his bike with his pale sharp features heading east and his briefcase stashed on behind.

'Your dog. It was rotten about the dog.'

'Poor Tango,' Val agreed. 'Yes it was rotten. Tony was very cut up about it.'

'Exactly,' said Marcus. 'That's why I'm here. I know you'll think it's none of my business but we are all—that is, some of us along the street—a little concerned about Tony taking the Parkers to court. I mean it does seem a bit excessive. It was a shocking accident, of course, but to go to court isn't just expensive, it can be very messy, for everyone.'

He was watching her anxiously as he spoke because he hadn't the remotest idea of how she might react. He half expected her to clam up and order him out of the house, saying he was as bad as the rest of them and a dog hater to boot, at which he intended to produce with a flourish photographs of Jessie, their own little spaniel. But she didn't.

'Don't talk to me about it,' she sighed. 'He's gone mad over this suing business, Marcus. I've told him. I said it will take all our savings and we'll never get into our own house. But he's set on it. He says the principle is more important than a house. He won't budge. He's a very stubborn man.'

'Does he know he can never win?' Marcus asked.

'Richard Dyson told him but it didn't make a scrap of difference. He thinks you're all in it together. I only wish we'd found a house and put the money on it before all this came up. That way it could have been avoided because he's not a man to go into debt. But it's happened and that's all there is to it.'

'So it's no house,' Marcus said sympathetically.

'No. No house.' He longed to be able to help her. She deserved a house, he told himself. All women deserved houses. She smiled at him wanly and he smiled back and as he smiled he saw quite clearly a way in which he could get her one and save the situation. It was Sebastian Anderson Jones, forcing himself to go through his front gate to greet his wife.

'It's not too late, you know,' he declared without excitement. He never showed excitement. 'You could find the house you want tomorrow, pay the deposit and settle it before he puts it into the hands of a solicitor.'

'I could,' said Val. 'I could also win Miss World.'

'Really,' said Marcus. 'No, I mean it. I know the very man to help.' And he took out his cheque book and wrote on the back of it Val's requirements for the perfect house and told her to leave it to him which she did. She thought he was half-witted.

Marcus set the wheels in motion that very night with a short, masterful phonecall to Sebastian who agreed that he could probably come up with something suitable in Balham or Norwood or somewhere and that he might be able to knock a pound or two off the fee. 'Good fellow,' Marcus grunted, then he settled down to supper a satisfied and contented man. He kissed Bella heartily when she told him she had managed to off-load the cocktail order and together they congratulated themselves on a fine day's work on the Parkers' behalf.

When they woke next morning the customary crowd was gathered around their Volvo. ' "Cheap Sneaks",' Rainbow Petrie was yelling across to her sister, ' "Cheap Sneaks". Do you think that's better or worse than "Adulterers"?'

Chapter Twenty

Marcus and Bella were under no illusions at all about who was to blame. In a way, they had been expecting it. In a way, it was a relief. This, however, did not prevent Marcus from embarking on a shocking decline because, above everything, he respected his property. 'I'm going over there,' he stormed at his wife. 'And I'm going to tell them exactly what I think of them.' They both knew he wouldn't.

'How dare they call us "Cheap" when we have just raised £200 for them. And "Sneaks"! When I think of everything we have done for them behind their backs. Well that's it! I can't go into work today. I'm finished for working now. And bang goes the Porsche. They're not going to give a Porsche to a man who takes time off work to deal with his criminal wife and Mafia neighbours.' He was white and trembling and unable to prevent himself from pacing around the drawing room, terrifying his child and his dog who were cowering under the piano.

'Get out of there Poppy,' he yelled. 'Go to school or something. Oh my God! She can't go to school. What will everyone say? What will they say to a child whose parents have been branded "Cheap Sneaks" by their business partners? Those bastards.'

'Marcus, stop it at once. Come on Poppy. Beth's taking you today. Look here she is now.'

As Poppy was urged tearfully through the gate Beth said, 'It's terrible. Surely Giles and Hippo can do something about it. They were supposed to be keeping watch. They must know who's doing it.'

'I suppose you've heard the gossip,' Bella replied blithely. 'You know how things are at No. 9.' Beth nodded.

'She's under a great deal of strain, poor thing. But why on earth write on her own car?' Like most people in Brain Street, apart from the five who knew for a fact there were more, Beth assumed there was only one vandal and as Jill almost certainly did the Petries and the Whittakers, she was it.

'Who can say?' Bella said, carefully avoiding an out and out lie. 'Who can say? Now stop blubbing, for heavens sake, darling. You can kiss Daddy's bike tomorrow.' She waved the unhappy child good bye, pulled her cardigan about her against a biting wind and then with a brief heroic backward glance at the stricken car, hurried inside. It moved Celia Petrie who had been watching her from her bedroom window thoughtfully.

A few minutes later she dropped in the remains of the paint remover Tom had used on their car. 'It comes off as easily as anything,' she assured Marcus. 'Honestly. It's nothing to get worked up about.' She could see he was seriously distressed.

'I'm not worked up,' Marcus said, appreciating immediately that this was the Celia Petrie who had yet to learn that her own car had been attacked by his wife. 'Of course I'm not. It's a laugh really.' He tried to laugh. It was ugly.

'It isn't easy to forgive the insult though, is it?' Celia said. 'I can't forgive that. We are suing the Parkers and I suggest you do the same. In fact we could probably sue together. I'm sure I could do a deal with our solicitor, two for the price of one-and-a-half or something. We'll talk about it later.'

'Right,' said Marcus. 'Thanks.' The horror was breath-taking. When she had gone he slumped on to the piano stool. 'This is completely out of hand,' he declared. 'Someone is going to have to do something. I am going to see Hippo.'

'If you think you must,' Bella said serenely. 'You must.' But when he called on him half an hour later he was out.

'I think he's at the Parkers,' Sarah informed him. 'I heard him say he needed to see Giles urgently. Do you want to wait?' He didn't wait. He hurried home to sit and wonder what on earth they were talking about.

'What the hell is going on?' Hippo was demanding of Giles. 'You've seen the Whittakers' car. You can't tell me that was Bella's work. We've got more than Bella on our hands. Thank heavens we waited.' They were back in the loft extension, sitting as they had sat before, watching Griselda preen. She was apparently plucking hairs from her breast. Unpleasant though this spectacle was, they had too much on their minds to be concerned by it.

Giles smiled at Hippo patiently. 'Come on, Hippo,' he said. 'Work it out.'

'Work what out?' Hippo snarled. 'There we were on the brink of accusing Bella of being the neighbourhood canker when she herself is attacked. And badly libelled into the bargain.'

'We did it,' Giles said. 'Jill and I did it. We were getting our own back.' Hippo sat in silence while he digested the declaration. He found it as acceptable as a cucumber and capsicum scone. It offended all decency. The woman was with child.

'You what?' he cried. 'How could you? How could you? What did you hope to achieve?'

'I hope we achieved what we set out to achieve,' Giles informed him, no longer as cheery as he had been. 'It wasn't much, after all. We just wanted to get even.'

'But you don't know that Bella wrote "Killer" on your car. And even if the photographs do turn out to be of her, it wasn't your car she wrote "Stinking Hypocrites" on. It was the Petries'.' Giles wriggled a bit then stood up to inspect Griselda more closely. He sensed a growing need to talk about something else.

'She saw to it that we were blamed for the Petries' car. And there were other things,' he said defensively. 'She's told a great many lies to Jill and me that I won't burden you with, Hippo. It's all too sordid. But believe me when I say she had it coming.'

Hippo felt suddenly unwell. He would take no more. He

headed for the door pausing only to say, 'I'm sorry you feel like that, I truly am. I am going to see if there is anything I can do for her.' He went directly, chivalry churning in his breast, along with the image of a leaden savoury scone.

Marcus very nearly kissed Hippo when he heard his voice in the hall. 'You are the very man I wanted to see,' he said warmly, shaking him by the hand. 'I went over to your house to find you.'

'No work today?' Hippo said. He had imagined that Bella would be alone, abandoned, lost, in the kitchen or in the garden while the lazy au pair was indulging in her toilette upstairs.

'Work!' said Marcus. 'I couldn't go to work and leave Bella to clean up this terrible mess. You can see for yourself how things are. You will have seen the car.'

'Terrible,' Hippo agreed. 'Where is Bella?'

'Here,' she said, tripping into the room, gently smiling, delicately burgeoning. 'How nice to see you, Hippo. Coffee?' She made the suggestion with all modesty, from beneath her sweetly lowered lids.

'That would be lovely,' he said. 'She looks marvellous,' he remarked softly when she had gone.

'Thank you,' said Marcus coming up very close to Hippo who took an anxious pace away. 'You know she did the Petries' car?'

'She told you?' Hippo whispered.

Marcus nodded. 'And the Parkers did ours. "Cheap Sneaks". I will never forgive them. Did you see them do it?'

Hippo shook his head.

'But you saw Bella? Well, everyone knows you saw her.'

'Who knows? How do they know? I only told Giles. And Anna.'

Marcus cackled. 'How many people do you think you need to tell? Everyone knows.'

'They know I saw someone,' Hippo corrected him. 'Only Giles knows it was Bella.'

Marcus sighed. 'Giles was enough. It was only a matter of time before it became public knowledge.'

'But surely Bella didn't write "Killers" on his car or that thing on mine?'

'Oh Hippo,' giggled Bella, carrying a tray with cups and saucers and cream and sugar and a coffee jug back into the room. 'As if I would.' Hippo leapt to his feet to take the tray from her.

'No, of course you wouldn't,' he gushed. 'But someone did, God alone knows who. No cream, two sugars, please. Not that I suppose it matters. What is passed is passed. Let sleeping dogs lie, really, don't you think?'

'Poor Chutney,' Bella agreed.

'That's all very well,' Marcus said, 'that's all very fine. But the Petries are threatening to sue and when they find out that Jill can't be sued they will sue us. It's completely wretched. And when I think of all the trouble I took yesterday to help the Parkers I could spit. Sebastian is at this very minute trying to find a nice little cottage in Balham for the Matthewses.'

Hippo gazed at him blankly. He was beginning to feel as he had felt constantly over the past week or so, that he had taken on a problem which was far greater than himself, that events had not only overtaken him, they had encircled him at least twice and he could no longer distinguish a beginning or an end. He invited Marcus to explain himself and when he had done so, Hippo believed he understood but truthfully wasn't sure.

Indeed Sebastian, who was at that very moment tearing about South London looking at possible properties, wasn't too clear why he was either. But he had taken on board the urgency of Marcus' request and the writing on the car that morning had reinforced it. As luck would have it, he didn't need to tear very long. He was alerted to the existence of a small gem in the late morning and telephoned Marcus to delight him just as Hippo was declaring his intention of seeing the Petries to see what could be sorted out.

'Marcus,' Bella called from the downstairs phone. 'Sebastian says he has found something.'

'Humph,' Marcus snorted. 'It hardly matters now.' But Bella persuaded him that it did, to Val if not to anyone else, so Marcus told Sebastian how he could contact her and asked that she be taken to see the snip in her dinner hour.

When Sebastian called his wife to impress her with his kindness and efficiency she said, 'I don't know why you are bothering.' Like everyone she met that day, she believed the Parkers deserved to be taken to court because the attack they had made on the Whittakers was savage and unprovoked, as had been the attack on the Petries.

Life, however, had to go on. Everyone pretended, especially to the Parkers, that no one they knew had painted anything on anyone's Volvo. Children were taken to and from school, Volvos and Citroens came and went as usual, and those who met, waved and chatted as they usually did. 'Heavenly smell,' Minnie called to Jill from behind her robinia.

'Grilled watermelon,' Jill called back.

Minnie hoped the compliment would distract Jill from noticing that she had yet to put on make-up and, rather than risk being seen again, she scurried upstairs to dress.

She spent considerable time over the selection of her favourite drop-waisted flying suit and on the colours which flanked her eyes. She wiped here, spat there, shaded around and about, and made the sort of subtle adjustments she prided herself on. Then she stood in front of the enormous mirror to gauge the effect *in toto*, and burst into tears. She looked fat and pregnant, no longer youthful, vibrant and alluring; just gross and boring and hideously mature. She threw herself onto the bed and had hysterics until she heard Mrs Butt's key in the door, then she went angrily downstairs to say that she wanted the skirting boards scrubbed today, thank you very much.

To avoid the look on Mrs Butt's face she took a banana and vitamin milk shake out to the honeysuckle where she was spotted by slim, youthful Anna on her way out to lunch somewhere over the river. 'Hello Minnie,' she purred. 'How are you keeping? Will you look at this honeysuckle?'

Minnie beamed, thrilled at the way opportunity could sometimes present itself. 'This honeysuckle,' she laughed, 'is about to destroy my beautiful tree and my climbing rose. It will have to be cut back.'

Anna giggled too. 'The poor Whittakers. "Cheap Sneaks"! Hippo is trying to sort something out but frankly things are going from bad to worse. You begin to ask yourself what the street is coming to.'

'Tell you what,' Minnie persisted, not about to let the chance slide away, 'if I give you a cutting from my rose, will you prune the honeysuckle?'

Anna climbed into the Citroen. 'Minnie, it's no use at all giving me cuttings of anything. Plants and I are allergic to each other.' Then she tooted and sped away.

Without caring what Mrs Butt thought, Minnie tore inside, upstairs and back onto the bed where she wept for a solid hour or so and came down only when Mrs Butt screeched, 'I'm off now. Can I have my money? Lord,' she added on seeing Minnie, 'you look awful. You need company, that's your trouble. Why don't you have lunch with someone. It would cheer you up. I'd stay myself but I'm off to the Parkers.'

'Goodbye Mrs Butt,' Minnie replied, handing over the money. 'See you next week.' She didn't feel like lunch. She felt like tipping a tin of red paint all over Anna, the honeysuckle and the Harveys' two cars. But when she saw Beth passing on her way home from school she ran to the door and called to her, 'Pop in for a minute. I haven't seen you in ages.'

Beth looked at her watch. 'Actually Minnie,' she said. 'I'm incredibly busy. I have to see the builders and then I have to deliver some material to the lady who's making my curtains. I don't really have a minute to spare. How are you, anyway? How is Sebastian?'

'Sebastian is the same as he usually is,' Minnie said crossly. 'Why?' Beth's enquiry struck her as less than innocent though she couldn't say why. She had felt funny about Beth ever since Beth had announced she was having walls knocked down. Today she was wearing a dress Minnie was sure had been bought in South Molton Street. She looked carefully and noted also to her extreme vexation that there had been a dramatic change to Beth's hair. It was no longer a shapeless blob of dark brown waves. 'What have you done to your hair?' she said.

Beth coloured a little, rather prettily, and said, 'Just a few highlights, a few streaks of red and amber. Do you like them?'

'No green?' Minnie said without mirth. 'Quite nice. Who cut it?'

'A horrible man over in Knightsbridge. He does Anna's.'

'Oh,' said Minnie. She could feel tears welling again in her throat, nose and behind her eyes. Beth was supposed to be plain but here she was looking unplain, making an obvious effort to add points of interest. She gave the honeysuckle a vicious tug. 'That's funny,' she said. 'I'm off there this afternoon.'

'Are you?' Beth said. 'What are you having done? My heavens, the time. Let's have coffee soon. Bye.'

So Minnie booked an urgent appointment over in Knightsbridge to have her hair coloured and cut and she spent the afternoon having her confidence restored. She was pleased with the effect, a faded leopard look, with black and yellow stripes and a shape which provided the air of a bewildered faun. It was her, she decided; past her prime and vulnerable.

She saw Anna again, as she drove home, climbing out of her car outside a motor-accessory shop in Pimlico. But Anna didn't see her so she kept going and didn't think of her till next morning, when, by the time she came downstairs, the entire street was buzzing with the events of the night before. Whoever it was had struck again, this time against the poor battered Mercedes. "Phillistines," the ravager had written, without the decency to get the spelling right.

This time there were lots of theories. Myra believed it was Rob Marsham, the Petries were anxious to blame the Parkers, who told each other it was Bella, because she had always resented Poppy Dyson being Poppy. Bella wondered if it was the Matthewses because of the clothesline. Only Hippo, who said nothing, knew who it was for certain. He could spot Anna's spelling a mile off.

Chapter Twenty One

Miss Smith could take no more. She had watched and laughed and guessed and puzzled for long enough and now there were too many gaps spoiling her pleasure. She was unused to so much happening so quickly. She had lost track of who was doing what to whom and she had never known why. The only answer was to get in amongst it, picking up what she could from where she could and adding to it where spice was lacking. Life had never been so gripping, not even when she had had two legs.

She prepared carefully, as she always did for excursions of this nature, fishing from the bottom of her linen cupboard an old pink bonnet which she knew everyone would feel obliged to say was very fetching. Strategy was crucial. She needed to glean little bits of information from one, which she could use to prise further details from another. It would be no use, no use at all for instance, going directly to the Parkers where Jill might offer her lukewarm coffee, ask her about her health then bore her stiff with chatter about her amazing children. That would be a complete waste of time. Mrs No. 9 needed to be shocked into saying more than she intended.

Her first call was to the Dysons who were in the throes of

fresh anger and outrage because of that morning's attack on their car. 'I wonder if I could use your phone,' Miss Smith said to Myra, smiling at her pitifully and bobbing her head a bit to draw attention to the bonnet.

No one minded letting her use the phone. They positively liked it. They felt good about not letting her pay as well because they were so much better off than she was and when she thanked them and said, 'You're very very kind,' they simpered and felt assured of their place in heaven. It was a small price to pay, 10p.

'What?' Myra said. 'Oh yes. Come in. It's in there.' Without so much as a glance at the hat she opened the door into the sitting-room and left Miss Smith to it. This was not a good start, Miss Smith felt. She dialled a few random numbers then waited a while before making her way to the kitchen where she said to Myra, 'They're talking to someone else. I don't know who. You won't mind if I wait a minute will you?' She allowed herself to drop on to a chair, without waiting for Myra to reply. 'I see you've got trouble with your car. It's a nice car too, isn't it, a big one. Ford is it?'

Myra's need to give vent to her fury bubbled inside her and spewed from her mouth even though her teeth were clenched. She had already railed at her husband for an hour and Jill for fifteen minutes, holding up the school run, but it was not enough. 'It is a Mercedes, Miss Smith,' she said, putting down her pen. She had been composing a letter to the skip firm. 'And it was a nice car. It is no longer possible to keep a car nice in Brain Street. If it hasn't been crushed it is being sprayed with the worst sorts of insults. Have you seen what is on ours?'

'I couldn't read it,' Miss Smith said.

'It says "Phillistines". "Phillistines" with two ls,' Myra said, a small spray of spit betraying her hurt.

'And you don't come from there, do you?' Miss Smith observed ruefully. 'What is it, Phillistinia?' Myra stared at her. She could see from the mad pink hat and the dotty expression that the silly old woman had no idea. 'Who wrote it?' she was asking. 'Who called you that, dear?'

'I don't know,' said Myra. 'Do you want to try your number again?'

‘They won’t be finished yet. I suppose it was that woman from over the road, the one at No. 8?’

‘Mrs Whittaker? Good Lord no. Why would Bella want to do anything like that? Of course it wasn’t Bella. We are the best of friends and always have been.’

‘What is a friend, eh? What is a friend? That’s what you need to know. Who doesn’t like me? It’s a funny old world, isn’t it, when you have to ask yourself questions like that?’ Miss Smith was bouncing her crutch up and down on the floor encouragingly, which Myra dismissed as yet another irritatingly elderly habit.

‘You can say that again. But I think I know who my friends are and who they are not.’

‘You’re luckier than most then,’ Miss Smith said with a wide brown smile.

‘It isn’t hard,’ Myra said crossly, ‘when your enemies dump skips on your car with as little consideration as was shown me. It isn’t hard at all. There is only one man in the world who would write something like that on my car, Miss Smith, and he lives at No. 2. Now what about your call?’

Miss Smith jumped to her foot. ‘I won’t bother now, thank you. I’ll try later next door,’ she cried. She swung herself out of the house and crossed the road to bang on the door of No. 2, puzzling and unsettling Myra who told herself, ‘She is barmy. Everyone knows she is.’

‘Can I use your telephone?’ Miss Smith asked Beth politely. ‘You’ve had your hair cut. What have they done to it?’

‘Just changed the colour a little,’ Beth said. ‘It’s a bit of a mess in here, I’m afraid but come in. Would you like a cup of tea?’ Miss Smith cast her eye up and down Beth’s strangely elegant figure and grinned to herself.

‘That would be very nice. New dress, is it?’

‘No,’ Beth called. ‘Just an old thing I found in the back of the wardrobc. Thc phonc is in thc coat cupboard. It’s the only safe place for it with all these walls coming down. Can you manage?’

Miss Smith negotiated the dustsheets and the debris and followed Beth to the kettle. ‘Just as well you don’t have a car,’ she shouted over the din of the hammering. ‘Cars are a damn nuisance in this street these days, aren't they? Have a car and you're asking for trouble.'

'I know,' said Beth. 'It's awful, isn't it. Let's go out into the garden to get away from the noise. I love your hat. It's a gorgeous colour.'

When they were seated uncomfortably on the cracked stone bench under the white lilac tree, Miss Smith took no time in mentioning that the black girl over the road was very upset about being called a Philistine when she had been born in England. 'And she says your husband did it, dear. That can't be right, can it?'

'She what?' Beth said. 'She says what?'

Miss Smith pretended not to notice the green shadow which crept across Beth's face to cast a film of blank horror over her blue powdered eyes. 'Funny isn't it?' she said. 'Because you fell out over that truck thing. She says your husband is her only enemy.'

'She's mad,' Beth cried. 'It's Anna Harvey's spelling. I must tell Rob. I must warn him. I had better telephone him at the college. You will be all right here for a minute or two on your own, won't you?'

'I won't wait, if you don't mind,' Miss Smith said, getting up with Beth. 'I can see you're busy. I'll be on my way.' Beth didn't even ask about the call she had wanted to make. She saw Miss Smith to the door then grabbed the phone, incensed at the slur on her husband's literacy, drawn to him suddenly when he was threatened with an attack from a tricky and powerful quarter, if you could call Myra a quarter.

Miss Smith didn't go directly to the Harveys'. Spotting Celia Petrie at an upstairs window in No. 7, she headed there instead, waving her crutch at the window and calling to her so determinedly that there was no way Celia could pretend she was out.

Celia Petrie prided herself on knowing exactly how to speak to old people without patronising them. You spoke to them rudely so they knew you respected their clarity of thought. They hated the cloying baby talk she knew most people resorted to. 'Hullo,' she said when she opened the door.

'I need to make a phonecall. Can I borrow your phone?' Miss Smith said.

'It's not good timing, I'm afraid, Miss Smith. I'm on my way to work.'

'Oh, work,' said Miss Smith. 'Funny time to go to work, in the middle of the day. It won't take a minute.' She put her crutch through the door and bowled into the hall before any protest could be lodged. 'In here, is it?'

'In the kitchen,' Celia said. 'You won't take long, will you. I'm running awfully late.' She stood by the front door to make her impatience as clear as possible while Miss Smith dialled a number.

'It's engaged,' she said. 'Oh dear. What will I do? I have to get through. It's very urgent.' She leant on her crutches waiting for Celia to tell her she could stay a minute and try again but Celia didn't. She tried harder. 'My leg's playing me up something shocking today, too. I think it's stress. Know anything about stress, do you?' This was a bold stroke and it paid off. Celia was that very day researching yet another programme on stress, which was dull in the extreme. She came in from the hall, her eyes ablaze with a new light. The effect of stress on an elderly amputee had to be an original angle.

'Why don't you sit down for a minute,' she said. 'Work can wait. I'm very sorry about your leg. What sort of stress are you under. Isolation is it, the approach of death?'

Miss Smith longed to snigger but she composed herself. 'Not so much that dear, no. I think it's the stress of this neighbourhood. I can sense it. Even where I am up in No. 3 I can feel the tension. They say lost limbs are phantoms, don't they? Well my lost leg is wandering up and down the road, suffering. Can you understand that? Am I mad?'

It was raving bonkers, Celia thought, but vivid, amazingly vivid. 'Of course it's not mad. There is a lot of tension in the street with all this vandalism. No one is safe. Our own car was painted on. I don't know if you saw it?'

'Shocking,' said Miss Smith eagerly. 'What did it say?' Celia studied her nails.

'"Stinking Hypocrites". Can you believe it?'

'"Stinking" what?'

'"Hypocrites". You have to know who did it to appreciate it. But it was hurtful. You can't help being hurt. I pride myself on being straightforward even if I don't pride myself on much else.' She gave Miss Smith an award-winning grin, a grin that could close a programme on an up-note and win the critics' hearts if it could only make its way before the camera.

'She probably couldn't help herself, being in the family way,' Miss Smith said thoughtfully. 'You know how some women are. The stress. Morning sickness stress.' She had seen Bella's ghastly dashes from the Parker kitchen when smells were at their peak.

'Jill isn't pregnant,' Celia said. 'Why would you think that? She's had her tubes done, I know. I interviewed her for a programme on sterilisation. I am in television,' she explained. 'No, Jill can't be pregnant though I'll admit she could be under stress.

'Which one is Jill? The fat one, do you mean?'

'No. 9. Yes. The fat one. The one whose husband killed the dog.'

'Oh it wasn't her,' Miss Smith protested. 'I saw who it was and it wasn't her. It was the pregnant one. Not the silly little one. The nice one from No. 8.'

'It can't have been,' Celia said. 'You must have mistaken her. It wouldn't have been Bella. Bella would never do such a thing.'

'She did. I saw her. And so did Mr Thingummy in No. 6. You ask him. We both saw her, plain as day.' She prepared to leave. 'I'll be off now, thank you very much. Talking to you has done my leg a power of good.'

'What about the phonecall,' Celia asked, bewildered. 'Don't you want to try again?'

'I won't bother thanks all the same,' Miss Smith said and she adjusted her bonnet and left. As Celia climbed into her Citroen a few minutes later, she was fascinated to see the old lady banging on the Harveys' door. 'She's up to something,' she thought. But even she couldn't imagine what.

Sarah's heart sank to find Miss Smith on the doorstep again. 'No one's home,' she said.

'I only want to use the phone,' Miss Smith whined. 'My leg's bad. I won't stay long. They wouldn't mind.' She was disappointed with the failure of the bonnet.

'All right,' said Sarah. 'Come in.'

'Still no sign of that dark fellow,' Miss Smith observed slyly.

'No,' Sarah agreed. 'Mr Fox is still in Hamburg.' But she blushed and Miss Smith knew she was lying. She had spotted Rupert Fox at least three times in the last two weeks as she had been driven to the day centre. He was always slumped in the back of a taxi, trying to avoid being recognized.

She followed Sarah out into the garden where little Flora was sitting in her sandpit. 'The phone's not out here,' Sarah said rudely.

'Just let me get my breath back,' Miss Smith puffed indignantly. 'Hullo darling.' Flora didn't reply. Like all the other children in Brain Street she had learned to be frightened of the old lady. 'Let's hope she grows up to be a better speller than her mother,' Miss Smith chuckled.

'Sorry?' said Sarah.

'Philistines has only one 'l'. Didn't you learn that at school?'

'No,' said Sarah. 'Why?'

'"Philistines" is written on the back of No. 5's car with two. The little one's mother wrote it wrong.' She cackled away merrily.

'Mrs Harvey didn't write on the Dysons' car,' Sarah squealed, outraged. 'That's a terrible thing to say.'

'Of course she did. Everyone knows she did. Because of the house. She didn't take to the pink, did she?' Miss Smith continued to laugh and spit a bit and Sarah moved away, astonished. She was outraged. She had no great love for Anna but you had to be loyal to your own and this was the limit.

'I think you had better use the phone,' she said. 'Come on, it's in here.'

While Miss Smith was performing her charade in the drawing-room Anna hurried through the front door and would have dived upstairs without so much as a nod to anyone, let alone her daughter or Miss Smith, had Sarah not grabbed her arm and whispered horribly, 'There's awful trouble. Everyone is saying you did the Dysons' car.'

Anna shook her arm free and gave her head one of her defiant tosses. 'Let them say it. Hullo Miss Smith, lovely day.'

'Lovely,' Miss Smith agreed. She gave a gleeful wave of her crutch and sped through the open door to make a final call on the Parkers.

Mad Brigid opened the door and allowed her in without asking who or what it was she wanted. Brigid had given up asking questions. Hers was not to reason why, and even if it had been she had nothing left to reason with.

'Anyone in?' Miss Smith demanded.

'Mr Parker. He's upstairs,' said the poor vacant nanny.

'Call him, will you? I can't hop up there.' Brigid obediently went to the first floor landing and bellowed until Giles screamed back.

'What the hell is that noise?'

'Miss Smith wants you,' Brigid screeched. 'She's here with her crutches and her hat on.' She was confident this would bring him running and it did.

'I'm an old nuisance, I know,' Miss Smith simpered in her best vamp-like manner, 'but could you take a look at this for me? It's giving me a load of bother.' She held out her left crutch to him and swayed uncertainly without its support.

'Sit down, Miss Smith, do,' Giles urged her. 'I'm not too good at crutches but I'll see what I can do for you.' He stared dumbly at the lump of wood in his grasp. He knew nothing of wood, let alone bits of wood stuck together.

'What are you going to do about that Marsham writing "Killer" on your car?' Miss Smith said, out of the blue.

'That Marsham writing "Killer" on my car?' Giles said, still examining the wood. 'I don't know what you are talking about Miss Smith.'

'Yes you do,' Miss Smith insisted. 'Someone painted the word "Killer" on your car, didn't they? I saw that man Marsham from No. 2 do it. While Mrs Blackie was running around with her signatures.' Giles finally looked up and was staggered by the cunning in her ancient blue eyes.

'He didn't,' he gasped.

'He did,' Miss Smith assured him firmly. 'You've all been at it, haven't you? Any wonder my crutch has gone.' She removed it from his hands and stood up. 'Ah, that's better,' she said. 'Thank you very, very much. I can go home now.' Giles saw her to the door in silence. He didn't know whether to believe her or not and until Jill came home he had no one to ask.

Miss Smith was too tired to go much further. She was pleased with what she had accomplished although she still didn't know who had written "Adulterers" on the Harveys' car. As she tottered home she congratulated herself. All she had to do now was wait.

Chapter Twenty Two

It was the Petries who demanded an extraordinary meeting of the Brain Street Residents. They wanted the whole shoddy business brought out into the open and dealt with once and for all. They telephoned Marcus at 7 a.m. the morning after Miss Smith's grand tour. 'Tonight, if you don't mind Marcus,' Tom said. 'We're booked up for the rest of the week.' Marcus gathered from his tone that he had certain information at his disposal regarding his car and Bella so he chose not to haggle, even though he personally had hoped to watch something rather good on television.

As chairman of the association he notified all of its members in a curt communication by phone or by a note shoved through their letter boxes shortly after breakfast and all agreed to do their best to attend. 'We'll have it here,' he said to Bella. 'Damn the expense. I'd rather be on home ground when all this goes up.'

'I suppose no one will like me much afterwards,' Bella said sadly and with some surprise, as if she had just realized there might be an aftermath to her bit of fun.

'Don't worry,' Marcus consoled her. 'The Parkers will have a lot to answer for as well.'

'And Anna. Do you think she will own up? Sarah told Minnie that Miss Smith says everyone knows Anna did it but I know Myra thinks Rob did.'

'If you own up she jolly well ought to,' Marcus said, 'though how it's going to be afterwards, I don't know.'

No one knew how it would be afterwards. It was the question that lurked about the loft extensions and hung in the folds of the interlined curtains. How would they be able to pretend that none of it had ever happened? How could they apologize enough? And who would have to apologize most, the sinners or the sinned against? Who would admit to being the sinners, those who had caused offence in the first place or those who had taken it and caused it in the second? Nerves were wracked to the point of snapping as finer details were contemplated.

'Oh Anna,' Hippo said to his wife when he finally met her in the bathroom on the first floor of No. 6 a good eighteen hours after she had misspelt Philistines. 'Why did you do it? Couldn't you have looked it up in the dictionary? It puts me in such a rotten position. Surely you could have thought of that.'

'I didn't, as a matter of fact. And when you proposed to me I don't remember spelling being a qualification. You didn't say "Marry me, Anna, but before you do please spell the following." ' She was in the bath and he was sitting on the edge, frowning down at her. 'I wrote Philistines on the Dysons' car because they are. They have painted their house a perfectly beastly colour and no one seems prepared to do a thing about it except me.'

'There was nothing anyone could do, that's why,' Hippo said. 'Everyone has told you. I told you. Dyson could have told you. If they want to paint their house in stripes there is nothing anyone can do. I'm surprised at you, Anna, behaving so recklessly. It's not the sort of thing I would have expected of you.'

Anna splashed her prettily pedicured left foot and sprayed her husband with small drifts of foam. 'It's not the sort of thing I would have expected of myself, either,' she agreed, because she truly did want to stay married to him and the life they had together. 'But it seemed such a good opportunity to make a point, when insults were flying all over the place.'

Hippo sighed. 'Well I don't know how you can apologize for it. There's no pretending you didn't do it when everyone knows you did. And there's no pretending Philistines wasn't what you meant. You know how sensitive Myra is about culture.'

'Oh God,' Anna said. She gave a small laugh but it was no laughing matter, she knew. 'Do we have to go to the meeting?' she asked. 'Why can't we just all forget about it? We forgot about our car. Why can't everyone else forget about theirs? Why don't we all pick up where we left off and never talk about it again?'

'Because we wouldn't be talking about anything else ever again, either,' Hippo said. 'And the Petries are hell-bent on suing the Parkers, so I suppose the Parkers will sue the Whittakers and I daresay Myra will sue us. Funny thing though, I don't think she's holding it against me. She was perfectly friendly when I ran in to her a few minutes ago.'

'Oh Lord,' Anna said, now totally miserable. 'Divide to rule. She's going to be sweet to you so you can't be rude to her and that will leave me alone with everyone against me.'

'That is paranoid,' Hippo said fondly, but he couldn't help dwelling on the difficulty. What Anna had done was indefensible. Everyone would say so and even he, if called upon, would have to say so. He would have felt no easier knowing that Myra believed Rob Marsham had committed the atrocity on the car, because his conscience would never allow him to let another man take the blame for something his wife had done.

Rob Marsham, on the other hand, could see no other course of action to take. 'I can't very well say it wasn't me, it was her,' he said to Beth as they sat together on the floor in their drawing-room enjoying their longest conversation since the wall had come tumbling down. There were dustsheets all over the furniture and there was a hole where the wall onto the garden used to be, but these are the sacrifices you must make in order to have what everyone else has in a Victorian terrace. Part of the ceiling had also started to give way but it was a minor detail. Ceilings in Battersea very often are. 'I am going to have to take the blame,' he announced. He felt rather good about it.

Beth, toying with a piece of plaster, resisted the urge to slap him. She hated him playing the martyr. She hadn't telephoned him at the college on a matter of extreme urgency concerning a serious miscarriage of justice just to have him say, 'So be it.'

'You are mad,' she said. 'You are crazy. You will be branded a racist and you will be branded illliterate. Do you want the whole street to think that a college lecturer doesn't even know how to spell Philistines?' This horrible point had escaped Rob. It was a major point, he had to admit. Racist was one thing. He trusted his reputation as an all-round humanitarian to come to his rescue there. But illliterate. No one would believe he wasn't. The fact remained, however, that to point the finger at Anna would be cowardly and dishonourable. He couldn't. He wouldn't.

'You don't have to say Anna did it,' Beth said shirtily. 'All you need say is that you didn't.' She saw her husband's eyes fill with grateful tears and she wanted to scream.

'Thank you,' he said. 'Thank you for your support. You are right, of course. That is what I will do.' Then he crossed the room and put on a record to drown his emotion which he feared any minute might spill forth and make a mess of the rubble. There were weeks of emotion stored in there; frustration, fear, anguish, anger, humiliation, you name it, he was storing it. And the very worst part, he knew, was that if he allowed any of it to escape matters would become much worse. He dreaded the meeting. He was terrified of losing control; it would appear on the minutes.

The Matthewses were not looking forward to the meeting either. Tony Matthews had no wish to appear in public with those he intended suing without being represented by a lawyer and Valerie was overcome by shyness at the thought of all the trouble that had been taken over a house she was not being allowed to have. She was going all out to improve matters before it was too late. 'It's a beautiful house,' she argued. 'Truly it is. You will love it. And Sebastian can fix up the finance. He's been really kind.'

'What do you mean, Sebastian?' Tony asked huffily. 'Do you mean the chinless wonder?'

'You know who I mean. He may not have a chin but he has been very helpful. Oh Tony, please come and look at it. We can move right away from here and memories of Tango. We won't have to worry about the Parkers or anyone else. Going to court will only hurt you more. We will lose everything and you promised me a house. We've worked so hard for one.'

'You don't care about the dog, do you?' Tony said. 'He's dead now and good riddance. That's what you think, don't you?'

'Don't be like that, Tony. Please don't. If we settle through the insurance company we can buy him a nice headstone. You can get another dog. But can't you think of me as well? I've been saving as well you know. Let's get out of here. It's not a nice street. They're a bunch of thugs, spraying each other's cars. They're pathetic.'

'They're pathetic, all right,' Tony said. He put his head in his hands, a man torn between loyalty to his dead dog and concern for his beautiful wife who wanted the house he owed to her. It was a tough one, all right. He could see Tango now in the dark of his cupped hands, his deep doggy eyes peering up at him, challenging him, Tony thought, to forget him. But he could feel his wife, sense her body, tingle to the closeness of her flesh which quivered with desire for this house in Balham and the finance arranged by the man across the road with no chin. He couldn't bear to hurt either of them but he was doomed to, he knew. He had to choose between trampling across the memory of the pet who was gone forever, or the wife who was here now, massaging his shoulders gently, dropping little kisses onto the back of his neck, murmuring please, Tony, please. The dog didn't stand a chance.

Had Giles known what was going on a few doors along he would have taken off his hat, had he had a hat, to Val, whose charms he had always admired. And he felt grateful, because although he knew Tony's charges against him were groundless and any action futile, he dreaded having to devote time and energy to defending himself from it. He was forty-two and he could feel his time and energy ebbing away with still no sign of a permanent place in literary history or even money in the bank.

When Giles looked about him he could see Hippo, a substantial man from a substantial family, barely having to lift a finger to keep his cash flowing. He could see Marcus, on his way to the top of some City tree, not only making money but hanging on to it. He could see Sebastian, even Sebastian, better placed than he was because he was so damned young, and he could see Tom, soaring above him, waving his creativity at him like a flag of colonisation. Just about the only person he couldn't see was Rob Marsham who had been no more than a shadow until Miss Smith's declaration had brought him sharply into focus.

They would have to deal with him most sternly at the meeting. They would have to get him to account for his ludicrous gesture. As Jill prepared peach in pasta packets to hand around to ease the strain, they asked each other in amazement, why them, why "Killer"?

'He couldn't have known about the poisoned *pot-au-feu* for Africa,' Jill said, slurping a piece of squashed fruit from her fingers. 'He must have been incensed that you killed Mango.'

'But he knew we had done our best for the blinking animal. The bill ran into thousands. Why spray it onto a perfectly innocent Volvo?'

They didn't know. They intended to find out. Every house in Brain Street waited, intending to find out something or other. Had Sebastian realized the extent to which he had brought this state of affairs to pass he would have been extremely pleased. Not many men his age could claim to be so astonishingly cataclysmic. Of course he couldn't take credit for Valerie Matthews' sensuality but he had given it a peg to hang on, as it were. The house in Balham, Balham South East actually, wasn't a dream exactly but it seemed to be exactly what she wanted. If she could persuade Tony to snap it up, he would indirectly have saved the Matthewses from a hideous expense, the Parkers from a great deal of aggravation and he would have done Marcus Whittaker a pretty big favour. As well as that he would have made some money.

As he waited for the meeting he couldn't be sure he had brought this all about but he hoped that he might, and he would have been pleased with himself and proud had he not been so distracted by the awful problem of Minnie's hair which was falling out in chunks, all over the house. 'Do something, do something,' she was wailing at him. 'For God's sake help me.' But there was nothing he could do, as usual, for Minnie, so he didn't feel so proud after all. And he began to worry a lot about the dastardly act he had committed which had set the vandal train in motion.

He followed his wife around picking up clumps, trying to grab at her to console her and to tell her that she had so much hair that no one would notice a few missing wheelbarrowfulls. 'You are useless,' she screamed at him. 'Utterly, utterly useless. Whenever I am in trouble I know I cannot rely on you. You are a worm.' And those were her last words to him before the meeting.

All he had to console himself was the thought that Beth Marsham would have never talked to him like that. She would have respected him and stuck her hair back on again, or something.

Chapter Twenty Three

Miss Smith was the first to arrive at the appointed place bang on the appointed hour because she didn't want to miss a single minute and everyone else wanted to miss as much as possible. Bella was relieved to greet someone so neutral and she kissed her in an awkward moment of effusion.

'Come in, come in,' she cried. 'Come in and make yourself at home. Can I take your fur?' Miss Smith had dressed as for a film premiere in furs and marquisite. 'Would you like me to take your crutches and put them somewhere safe?'

'No thank you,' said Miss Smith. 'I will keep them by me if you don't mind.' She placed them in front of her as she took up her position on a small hard chair by the window that let on to the street, gauging this to be the centre of the circle of seventeen chairs Bella had placed around the drawing-room. It was the centre, she told herself, if you counted the door from the hall as being the beginning. Marcus who had been uncorking bottles of Tesco's dry white said, 'Hullo Miss Smith. How good of you to come when you don't have a car. Can I offer you a drink?'

'I only had to hop over the road,' Miss Smith said sweetly. 'A port and lemon please.'

'No, I meant it was good of you to come when what we are discussing is the wave of spray painting . . . actually I can only offer white wine, I'm afraid.'

'Or Ribena,' said Bella hastily, trying to indicate to Marcus that he should offer her a sherry which was hidden with everything else to drink in a saucepan cupboard in the kitchen. But Marcus ignored her because he believed that to make one exception would start an avalanche of alternative orders and he had no intention of producing the gin or the whisky when he had bought the Tesco's white especially.

Although the meeting had been timed for nine sharp no one else knocked on the door until 9.11, when the Petries, who like everyone else had been watching from their windows and waiting for a few more to arrive, decided that unless they appeared no one else would, and the night would be spent with everyone watching from windows and the Whittakers conducting a meeting with Miss Smith. 'Honestly,' said Celia out of the corner of her mouth as they closed their front door, 'they are feeble.'

Marcus had decided to survive the evening by treating it as a small, friendly political gathering. He would adopt a no nonsense approach to all participants whom he would shake warmly by the hand just as a prospective candidate might. But Celia from force of habit put her cheek out to be kissed and he kissed it, which caused Bella, who had been hovering, to welcome her like a long lost friend, even though Celia was the woman she had so brutally libelled only a few days before.

And so everyone was treated. Everyone kissed everyone else and said how well, lovely, thin, brown and gorgeous they looked and no one for a single minute suggested to Miss Smith that, beneath all the shrill squeals of surprise and delight that everyone looked so wonderful, was bitter acrimony and God knows how many cans of aerosol paint. Even the Matthewses were talked to with a warmth they found bewildering. But this is how it was in Brain Street. The hypocrisy was not only blinding, it was deafening.

Finally, when everyone was seated clutching a glass of wine or Ribena or water or, or as in the case of Miss Smith, all three for that was the compromise that had been reached, and when everyone had sampled a peach in pasta packet and the room reeked of Diorissima, Charlie, Au Sauvage and lavender, Marcus licked his fingers and opened the meeting. 'Well, I think we ought to thank Jill for her sensational nibbles.' Everyone applauded loudly and longer than was necessary because of the sensitive nature of Jill's food.

'So,' he continued, 'welcome, everyone, to this extraordinary meeting of the BSRA. We will not be dealing with Webbs' reports tonight for reasons which I am only too sorry to say, are distressingly obvious to each and every one of us here.' He looked at his notes because he was no great orator and the occasion was bigger than he could manage, ad lib. Also he had nowhere else to look. There wasn't an eye in the room he could bear to catch.

'A week or so ago we all woke to find to our very great dismay that during the night someone had taken a can of red spray paint and daubed the rear window of the Harveys' Volvo with the word "Adulterers". Not many days later, in the broad daylight of a spring evening, someone took a similar can of paint and wrote the word "Killers" on the same window of the Parkers' Volvo. You will recall that some days after that, during the night, the words "Stinking Hypocrites" were sprayed on to the Petries' Volvo and the very next day but one we woke to find letters in the same red paint on our own Volvo which read . . . ah . . . "Cheap Sneaks". Finally, only yesterday, the Dysons discovered the back window of their Mercedes to have the single word "Philistines", two ls though, I'm afraid, splattered across it.

'Now I don't think any purpose would be served here tonight by a general discussion about the accuracy or otherwise of the insults which have been made so astonishingly, and may I say unsportingly, public. But we all know that allegations have been made concerning the perpetrators of these, well, messages, which do seem to require some clearing up. The fact is that with one notable exception everyone seems to think they know who did it and it is my unfortunate duty as chairman of the Brain Street Residents' Association to have to report that all the allegations concern our own members.'

Miss Smith gave a loud joyous laugh, quite impervious to the embarrassed shuffling around her. Only Jill felt able to smile at her and she raised her index finger to her lips because Jill believed her consicence to be the clearest in the room.

'I suppose we should start at the beginning,' Marcus said. He coughed. Then he cleared his throat and coughed again. 'Excuse me,' he said. He knew it was going to be awful. 'In the case of the Harveys' car I'm right I think in saying, aren't I Hippo, that no one has even the foggiest idea who did it. We believed for a little while, I think, that it was the paper boy but that turns out not to be so.'

'That's right,' Hippo said, half rising from his chair. Rob Marsham put up his hand.

'Can I ask whether the paper boy has been compensated for wrongful punishment?' A loud sigh swished around the circle, a gust of boredom and derision.

'I wonder if we could take that up later, Rob,' Marcus said politely.

'Of course,' Rob said, nodding energetically.

'Does anyone want to own up?' Marcus enquired, peering around at everyone, like an auctioneer confronted with a job lot of false teeth. No one spoke.

'Could we open a window?' Minnie said. 'It's awfully stuffy in here.' It wasn't her nerves oppressing her, it was her enormous head scarf which, wrapped carefully around every inch of her head, somehow interfered with the intake of breath.

'There are windows open Minnie,' Bella said. 'Would you like to change places with Beth? There might be more air over here.' Beth was across the room and next to Sebastian before Minnie had time even to consider the benefits of such a swap.

'Thank you,' she was forced to whimper as she scampered across to Beth's chair. 'Sorry.'

'All right Minnie?' Marcus said. 'Right. No takers on "Adulterers" apparently, so on to "Killers". There was talk here that Tony Mtthews might have had good reason to spray the word "Killers" onto the Parker Volvo . . .'

'I certainly did not,' Tony interrupted. 'Who said I did? I was the person who discovered it.' He looked accusingly at Anna Harvey who looked away. She couldn't remember whether she had told anyone he had done it or not.

'I know, I know. Fortunately we have a witness who can bear testimony.' Miss Smith beamed at the room and gave a small wink to the Parkers. 'I wonder if I could call upon the person who did it to explain the position.'

Everyone looked at their feet. The tension was unbearable. A few people asked themselves if they had done it and lost their memory immediately afterwards as they all waited. Finally a chair fell over next to Minnie as Rob Marsham stood, awkward and pink, causing Beth to utter a small moan of astonishment. She wanted to yell at him to sit down and not be stupid but she didn't get the chance.

'I'm sorry Giles, but it was me. I did it because I felt, rightly or wrongly, that the Matthewses were getting a raw deal.'

'What raw deal?' Jill cried. 'That stupid vet cost us a fortune. The dog had the most expensive treatment in London and it still died. How can you say raw deal?'

Rob scanned the room for even the tiniest suggestion of sympathy but couldn't find it. Even his wife who might have stood by him, and the Matthewses on whose account he had acted, were eying him with irritation. They were irritated, he could see, because he had implicated them, one way or another.

'Well I do say it,' he said defiantly. 'We have all been extremely rude to the Matthewses and we have treated them shoddily. We have made it plain to them that this is now a middle-class street and they are not very welcome in it.' He was now scarlet, as was Beth.

'What's he talking about, Valerie?' Tony Matthews asked loudly. 'We are middle class. And we're as entitled as anyone else to live here. We pay our rent. What's he going on about?'

'I don't know,' Val murmured. 'But we are moving anyway.'

'You're being offensive,' Giles said to Rob. 'I think you should retract what you just said.' Beth held her breath. She could see Rob's brain formulating a long-winded social analysis and she prayed most fervently that he would not deliver it. 'Strike him dumb, oh God,' she prayed. 'Let his tongue drop off.'

'I can't retract the reason I sprayed the word "Killer" on your car. "Killer" was what I felt at the time. Killer of the rights of the individual. I'm sorry you don't like it. But I regret the spraying because it was silly and futile. It didn't have a great deal to do with the dog and nothing at all to do with the lady who died in Putney which I understood is what most people thought I meant. I'm sorry about that Jill. I have always rather liked your food, whatever anyone else said at the time.'

Celia Petrie laughed softly and Miss Smith guffawed loudly. Several leaping pulses appeared in Rob Marsham's face as he sat down. 'Thanks for nothing,' Jill said.

'Thank you, Rob,' Marcus said. 'I wonder if we could now move onto "Stinking Hypocrites".'

Celia Petrie was on her feet before he could utter another word. He had planned a small introduction to justify his wife's action and to draw attention to her pregnancy and good motives. 'Bella,' she declared warmly, 'I want to say something first. Tom and I were both terribly hurt . . .'

'I thought Jill did it,' someone was heard to whisper.

'Tom and I were both very hurt by what you called us because it was so unfair and because you said it on our car, publicly and without the courage to identify yourself. To begin with we were so outraged we only wanted revenge. As you know to begin with we didn't realize it was you.'

'Charming,' Jill muttered to Giles.

'But really, now, I don't see the point in dragging it all out. We accept your apology in advance and think it would be best if nothing more was said.' There was a ripple of clapping led by Miss Smith but Jill had seen through Celia's ruse. Celia, she knew, didn't want anyone to know what had prompted Bella to call her a "Stinking Hypocrite" because she was a stinking hypocrite.

'That isn't fair,' she cried. 'Bella should be allowed to say why she did it since everyone was pleased to assume it was me. Come on, Bella, why did you do it? It would never have occurred to me.'

Bella thought she could hear malice in Jill's goading. Her old dislike surged from her heart into her bloodstream and finally reached her brain, nudging her into action. She would speak out and she wouldn't try to protect anyone. Why should she? Where had protecting anyone ever got her in the past? She didn't bother to stand up. She spoke from her seat, looking lovely in a pink flowered smock of the sort Jill favoured to disguise lumps which could never be delivered no matter how many months passed. She looked at the floor as she spoke and she addressed the room shyly. Her resemblance to the Princess of Wales was uncanny.

'I know what I did was mad,' she said. 'But honestly, I was so frustrated. Jill was in a terrible state because of the Putney business . . .'

'What is this business at Putney?' Miss Smith roared. 'Will somebody kindly tell me.'

Bella smiled prettily at the old lady who was drinking her wine, Ribena and water very quickly and with great excitement. 'A greedy woman called Hermione who lived in Putney died after eating some of Jill's stew and everyone said Jill was to blame but she turned out to have choked on an eclair. So after the Putney business everyone said that Jill's food was contaminated and business fell away terribly. I don't know how many of you understand the sort of financial straits the Parkers are in but they are pretty dire.'

'Just a minute,' Giles yelled, but everyone told him to be quiet.

'Haute Food is pretty well the only income they have. Jill came over to see me hysterical about it one morning just after the dreaded Griselda had spilt steaming beeswax all over the kitchen floor. While I was scrubbing away I thought about what could be done and it occurred to me that if we asked the Petries, they could help because they have billions of contacts in the film world, or so we have always been lead to believe. Catering for film crews is a breeze and very well paid. So I told Jill I would go and see them and she got the beeswax off with some stuff from her larder.'

'Yuk!' Minnie gasped.

'I went to see the Petries that night and they made it plain they didn't want to help,' Bella concluded, 'so I thought it wouldn't do any harm if everyone knew how mean they had been.'

'If you don't mind my interrupting, Bella,' Tom said frostily, 'I don't recall saying that we wouldn't.'

'To be honest Tom, you didn't need to,' Bella said and she

appealed to the room. 'Do you know what I mean?' Everyone did.

'Surely you knew that Hippo and Giles would see you. We all knew they were watching. Even Griselda knew.' Minnie said.

'I didn't,' Bella admitted. 'Obviously. That's why I was caught. But it's all over now and I am very grateful to Tom and Celia for being so gracious about it. Thank you.'

Marcus beamed at his wife. He thought she had done terribly well and completely redeemed herself in the world's eyes. 'Thank you darling,' he said. 'OK "Cheap Sneaks".' He looked crossly at the Parkers.

'All right, all right,' Giles said. 'We shouldn't have done it but how were we to know that Bella had written on the Petries' car on our behalf? She was perfectly content to let Jill take the blame for it. You have been behaving very oddly, you know, Bella.'

'She's pregnant,' Anna and Myra said together.

'I know she's pregnant,' Giles said, smiling at them brilliantly to compensate for his money problems. 'But Rob isn't. Being pregnant isn't why you spray nasty things on other peoples' Volvos.'

'I have been feeling a bit peculiar lately, actually Giles,' Bella said. 'I've had terrible nausea with this baby. I suppose it's affected my judgement. I never meant to harm Jill, I only ever wished her well.'

'That's why she made up that story about my office cocktail party and organized a sale for you,' Marcus threw in.

'Didn't I say there was no party?' Jill said to Giles. 'Didn't I say? What happened to all that stuff then? I spent ages over it.'

'I told Mrs Henderson Smyth that she had to buy it if ever she wanted to get back into your books,' Bella giggled and Jill, who had wanted to scream "Traitor!", also laughed because in the end it was simpler. Miss Smith, who had wanted to frown because it was all petering out so stupidly, also laughed because there seemed to be a funny side to it.

'Who's Mrs Henderson Smyth?' she asked through her chuckles.

'The woman who accused me of the murder in Putney,' Jill explained, wiping her eyes and Miss Smith positively hooted and stamped her foot.

'Now,' said Marcus, 'enough of that, what about the Mercedes?' This only made Miss Smith noisier because nothing the whole night had amused her more than the sight of half the room looking to Anna and the other half to Rob. Hippo nudged his wife.

'I did it,' she mumbled.

Myra allowed a small scream of surprise and anger to escape before she said, 'Well! That doesn't surprise me at all. Not at all. I often suspected she was an ignoramus.'

'Just because I can't spell,' Anna replied coolly, 'you cannot assume I am ignorant. Some of the finest minds in the country can't spell.'

'Oh yes?' said Myra. 'Which?'

Anna didn't know which, but Rob Marsham, grateful that he wasn't being lumbered with a second charge, said, 'She's right, actually. It's a fact.' No one asked him which because they knew it would take too long.

'May I ask why, Anna?' Richard Dyson said. His voice shimmied around the room and caused a shiver to run down Miss Smith's spine.

'You may, Richard,' Anna said. 'I did it because I couldn't stand the colour of your house and there wasn't a thing I could do about it.'

'You never mentioned it,' he said.

'Oh yes she did,' Minnie screeched. Like Miss Smith she had been drinking quickly and as she had drunk almost nothing during the six months she had been pregnant, the effect was drastic.

'But not to us,' Richard said with a wry smile. 'I'm sorry we have caused you offence. I'm sure you appreciate that Myra is very much an individual and the pink is an expression of her individuality.'

'We are all individuals,' Anna said, scathingly. 'But none of us would dream of doing anything to our house that would not be to our neighbours' taste, that is why our houses all look the same.'

'I see,' Richard said. Myra squeezed his arm because of the trap he had laid but no one seemed to have noticed it. She sighed. She asked herself whether SW3 could be as moronic as this.

'Anyway, there was no harm done. In fact there was no real harm done by anyone,' Marcus declared, keen to end on a peaceful note. 'Was there? When you look at it?' No one agreed. There was no point in abandoning your claim to harm done if no one else was going to.

Miss Smith, by now faintly purple and obviously overwrought yelled, 'But who wrote "Adulterers"? Who wrote "Adulterers"?'

'Quite,' said Hippo. 'Who did write "Adulterers"?' Everyone, relaxed by the wine and the easy atmosphere after the purge, looked at each other enquiringly and urged each other to own up but no one did.

'I think we may safely say that no one has the faintest idea,' Marcus announced. 'It will be a mystery for ever and ever.'

But Celia, smarting from what had gone before and cheated, it seemed, of the chance to sue anyone, decided the time had come to draw upon the information she had kept to herself since the morning the car alarm had lured her from her bath. 'I have some idea,' she said lazily and throatily. She stared hard at Sebastian who grew pale and clammy so that Beth beside him, attuned as she was to his feelings, guessed exactly what the situation was. 'I did it,' she said. 'It was me.'

It was the sensation of the evening. 'I did it because I was jealous of Anna. I am deeply sorry,' she said. Sebastian's heart bobbed frantically. He was aghast at her confession, astonished at the boldness of this woman who loved him. If he was to be worthy of that love he knew what he had to do. He stood and with a voice creaking with emotion said, 'Thank you, Beth. Actually, I did it.' Miss Smith was beside herself with excitement.

'I don't know why Beth has offered to take the blame like this and I am mortified that she has, because this is the truth. I did it because of the Harveys' honeysuckle which they have allowed to run riot all over their trellis across into our place and all over our garden. Poor Minnie has been desperate about our robinia.

I wanted them to know they couldn't get away with it.'

At this there was pandemonium. No one knew who to believe. Both reasons were so utterly implausible compared to what had gone before. And why would they leap to each other's defence? What was going on? Minnie was dumbfounded and appalled. A lump of hair fell from beneath her giant scarf. What did it mean? Did it mean he loved her and wanted to save her beloved tree? Or did it mean he loved Beth and wanted to protect her? She didn't know what to believe. It was awful. And he looked so handsome tonight in his pale pink shirt and pale blue trousers. He looked so wonderful. She couldn't remember when he had last looked so wonderful. She began to weep. Her hair was falling out, her husband was in love with another woman and there was a baby on the way.

'You only had to mention the honeysuckle,' Hippo was saying. 'And of course I would have cut it back.'

'But I did mention it,' Minnie sobbed, 'lots and lots of times, only no one would listen.' Everyone was on the verge of rushing to comfort her when there was a shocking gurgle from Miss Smith's chair and she fell in extremis to the floor. Everyone gasped.

'Oh my God,' said Marcus. 'She has fallen on the floor.'

'Hypoglycaemia,' Celia said with some authority. 'I am researching it. And stress.'

'Who's done first aid?' Hippo cried. Almost everyone had but no one could remember it.

'Stand back everyone please,' ordered Rob Marsham, striding across to the body purposefully. 'Could we please have some space. Bella would you ring for an ambulance? Could everyone else move outside please.' It was astonishing. In a crisis, he was cooler and braver and more decisive than anyone had imagined a bumbling bearded socialist teacher could be. He dropped to the floor, checked for pulse and heart and then, with more gallantry than any of the others could muster between them, he gave the vile old lady mouth to mouth resuscitation and his wife, who had gone silently to his assistance, knelt beside him to massage the ancient heart.

'Dear heaven, how could he?' whispered Minnie from the rhododendron in the garden to which they had all retreated.

‘He is a brave and good man.’ She spoke for them all. His courage, his knowledge and his nerve in putting his mouth to anything so elderly and dirt-coloured overwhelmed them all. He was the hero of the hour.

Perhaps it was his own lack of self-interest that moved them. Maybe everyone decided on the spur of the moment that they could save themselves a lot of awkwardness. In the hour of crisis enemies were drawn together and wounds which were just beginning to fester were healed. Men and women who had vowed silently never to speak to each other again found themselves united in admiration for a man who, until such a short time ago, had seemed totally trying.

The ambulance arrived within the hour and Miss Smith, who had seemed devoid of life, was clinging on, breathing again it seemed, and functioning. ‘Let us hope she is not brain dead like poor Tango,’ Tony Matthews said, though he had never much liked the old woman.

‘Hear hear,’ they all agreed and when the ambulance was gone they hurried in to offer Rob their congratulations for saving them from a dead body on their hands. Marcus offered him a Scotch and Beth, Rob could see from the look in those expressive eyes, offered back her respect.

Brain Street staggered home eventually, a little shell-shocked but on the whole a good deal healthier and happier than it had been several hours before. Myra declared to her husband that the evening had been a work of art and that the residents had finally woken up.

Marcus said to Bella as he carried glasses into the kitchen, ‘I think it went rather smoothly, don’t you? The wine went down well.’

Chapter Twenty Four

Two weeks to the day after Anna had defiled the Mercedes, she banged on Minnie's door just as the lunchtime school run was disgorging its tiny passengers into the street. 'Sorry to wake you,' she said, as Jill yelled at the children to mind the dog's mess, 'but it's a bit of an emergency. Did you know Sarah was going to run off with Rupert Fox?'

'She hasn't,' Minnie squeaked. She hastily finished tying the scarf she had grabbed on her way to the door. Her hair, though stable, was still on the critical list.

'They have telephoned us from Hamburg.' Minnie took in Anna's pallor and unmade-up eyes and knew at once that she was suffering.

'Anna I'm so sorry. I truly am. It must be awful.'

'Of course it's awful,' Anna said sharply. 'I haven't got a nanny. What on earth am I going to do?'

Jill, steering Flora Harvey towards her mother and overhearing the last remark said, 'Join the club. You can't call Brigid a nanny nowadays. I'm completely stuck and Giles and I are going to be run off our feet for the next few months. We have been asked to do a book together.'

'What book?' said Anna absently. Manners decreed that she

showed an interest but frankly she couldn't have given a monkey's in the face of her own crisis.

'Jasmine Henderson Smyth has asked us to do a book called *A Bit of a Stew*. It's a scream, isn't it, but we're being terribly well paid. At least we will be if we find the time to do it. It won't come to much while the only help I have is a half-crazed Irish woman.'

'And Griselda's leaving too, isn't she?' Minnie yawned. 'So you're all stuck. Thank heavens my nurse was booked ages ago. Did Sarah take her clothes?'

'Not a stitch,' Anna said. 'She just upped and bolted in the night. I don't know what I can say to her mother.'

'She won't mind,' Minnie said. 'She died ages ago.' She smelt the neatly pruned honeysuckle and sighed with pleasure. Then they all waved to Bella who was on her way to the tennis, looking cool and dozy. 'Awful day,' she called.

'Ghastly,' said Jill and as Bella reached Minnie's gate added coarsely, 'Sarah has bolted with Rupert Fox.'

'Did you know she was going to?' Anna asked her suspiciously. 'Marcus sees quite a lot of Rupert, doesn't he?'

'Not nearly as much as you do,' Bella replied in all innocence, forcing Jill and Minnie to bite their cheeks.

'He's been abroad for the past six weeks,' Anna reminded her crossly. 'We have hardly heard from him at all.'

'Oh,' said Bella firmly, knowing that Rupert had had lunch with Marcus only two weeks before.

'So she's even more nannyless than I am,' Jill said. 'Did you hear that Jasmine wants Giles and me to do a book together?'

'No!' said Bella, 'That's fantastic. Is there money in it? Jasmine who?'

'How many Jasmines do we know? Henderson Smyth. But I'm totally stuck until I get rid of Brigid. She's completely impossible.' They stood there as a few thick clouds scudded over the park towards Wimbledon as they usually do at that time of year.

'Henderson Smyth,' Bella repeated. 'I don't believe it. What's she doing asking you to write a book?'

'Benjy, come back here,' Jill roared. 'I know. It's mad. She turns out to be a publisher. We went to dinner with her and she said what with Giles being a writer and me being a cook it would be a tragedy if we didn't work together.'

'What are you doing about replacing Griselda?' Anna asked, bored by Jill.

'I don't know. I'll have to do something with the baby due.'

'Have Brigid,' Jill laughed. 'No, seriously. Why don't you? I'm sure she could cope with your household far better than she can cope with mine. It's so much slower. And she loves babies.'

'I'll think about it,' Bella said, smiling. 'Funny, isn't it, having two For Sale boards in the street at once.'

The landlord of No. 3, hearing that Miss Smith was to move to Jersey to be with her niece and that the Matthews were buying elsewhere, had wasted no time in offering vacant possession to anyone interested in modernizing a Victorian terrace in one of the most desirable streets in South London. He had heard from Myra who had, after all, decided to abandon her scheme to create a community spirit that was non alcoholic. She now fancied W11 for her children which she understood was rife with culture and local colour.

'At least we might end up with two more loft extensions,' Anna said. 'And houses all the same colour.'

'Depends on who moves in, doesn't it?' Jill said. 'Look, there go Beth's french doors.'

'They're exactly like yours, aren't they, Anna?' Minnie said.

'I don't care who moves in,' Bella sighed. 'So long as they're nice.'

'They're bound to be nice,' Jill said cleverly. 'No one else could afford it.'

This is how it is now, south of the river, quite absurdly expensive but very nice. Brain Street is, in this respect, exactly like dozens of other Victorian terraces which attract similar people to each other so they can live in harmony. In Brain Street there is now perfect harmony. The honeysuckle, however, is growing alarmingly and every so often twitches at the robinia just for fun, for old times' sake.